Secrets, Lies & Homicide

Patricia Dusenbury

ISBN-13: 978-0692537404
ISBN-10: 0692537406

Cover Design: Saille Graphic Design for Books / www.sailletales.com
Photography: © Alex Postovsky/ Colourbox.com

Secrets, Lies & Homicide was initially e-published with a different cover by
Uncial Press
www.uncialpress.com
ISBN 13: 978-1-60174-192-9

DEDICATION

To New Orleans, where I've spent many happy hours, and particularly to the Jazz and Heritage Foundation, which every spring delights the world with Jazz Fest then uses the profits to keep the music alive. A portion of the proceeds from the sale of this book go to support their good work in education, economic development, and cultural enrichment.

ALSO BY PATRICIA DUSENBURY

A Perfect Victim

A House of Her Own

ACKNOWLEDGMENTS

I am grateful to George for his encouragement, to Alicia for her constructive criticism, and to the many other people, too numerous to name, who helped me along the way.

Patricia Dusenbury

1

January 11, 1994

Claire looked at the house then double-checked the address, 712 Terpsichore. That's what her notes said. Why, she wondered, would a wealthy celebrity want to restore this ordinary little house? She studied the façade.

Screening the front gallery had been a mistake, but it would be an easy fix. Remove the screens, restore the columns, and *voilà*, a fine-looking house. Fine-looking, yes, but still modest and still in a neighborhood that was far from exclusive. She climbed out of her car and went to take a closer look.

Several of the windows were old glass, wavy in the sunlight. Nice. The siding was the original cypress and in decent condition. Nice again, but still nothing special. She walked around back.

The front yard had been shabby but sunny and lively with birdsong. The back was a jungle. Weeds by the house gave way to a thicket of scraggly azaleas and towering camellias. Vines climbed a long dead pine. A faded path led through the overgrown shrubs toward the far corner. She followed the path to the edge of a small clearing. In its center was a small outbuilding.

It was the size and shape of a double garage but elevated on piers and boarded up. Weathered two-by-sixes crisscrossed the door, and warped plywood covered the windows. Black mold, so thick she could smell it, streaked cinderblock walls once painted white. More black covered the far corner. Soot? Perhaps there'd been a fire.

Later, when the secrets had been uncovered and the lies stripped away, Claire would remember how this derelict little building demanded her attention. She would wonder if she'd heard a dead man's call for justice—or revenge. She'd regret the damage caused by events she set in motion. On first sight, however, she felt only curiosity.

She stepped closer and saw the spiders, yellow and black striped with fat bodies and long legs, each one as big as a child's hand. There were dozens of them. Everywhere. Webs hung from the rotten eaves. Gray tatters of old webs glued dead leaves to the walls. People had abandoned this building long ago; the spiders owned it now. Something moved behind her, and she whirled around, a scream in her throat.

"Hey, I'm sorry. I didn't mean to scare you." He held out his hand. "Tony Burke."

"Claire Marshall." She cursed her startled reaction and the blush warming her cheeks. "I was early, so I took the opportunity to look around. I hope you don't mind."

"You found my dad's studio. He was an artist."

"This was your parent's house?"

"And mine, until I moved to Italy."

She should have guessed. She knew he'd grown up in New Orleans. She remembered a name, a local artist who'd died years ago. The timing was right.

"Was Jim Burke your father?"

"You've heard of him." Pleasure warmed Tony's voice.

"I'm a big fan of New Orleans' art as well as her architecture." Claire looked at the little building with new eyes. "Are you planning to restore your father's studio?"

"No." For a moment, Tony stood with his hands in his pockets, staring at the studio, his expression unreadable. "Let's go look at my house."

"Lead the way." She stepped back to let him pass, but he took her arm, and they walked side by side on the narrow path.

"How'd you get involved in the construction business?" he asked. Everyone asked.

"I like fixing up old houses. Jack Giordano and I met when his company did some work for me. He's a wonderful craftsman, he was looking for a business partner, and I wanted a new career."

It was her standard answer and, as far as it went, true. That she had foundered lost and alone after her husband died, that she'd quit a well-paying but boring job and invested not just her money but also herself in Jack's little construction company, that there were still nights when she lay awake wondering if she'd done the right thing, if the business would make it, if she would make it—none of that was Tony Burke's business. She looked up and caught him studying her.

"Are you and Jack partners outside the office?"

"No." She laughed. "Jack has a wife he adores and five kids who call me Aunt Claire."

Tony unlocked the front door, and they walked into a too-small foyer. The living room was visible through a wide arch on the left. He opened a door to the right.

"I don't know what this room is supposed to be—off by itself."

She pressed her hands against the doorframe. "There was an archway here, like on the other side. A double parlor extended across the front of the house, and a wide center hall ran all the way to a back door."

"How do you know?"

"That's how these houses—they're called villas—were built."

"Villas?" He looked incredulous. "I own a villa?"

"That's what people in New Orleans call a raised center hall cottage, which is what this is."

"Tell me more."

She pointed to the back of the foyer. "This wall was added, probably to create a space for a half bath." She had his full attention, so she backed off a bit. "If there's no half bath, there's a closet."

"Half bath. You had it right the first time." He shut the door. "On your left is the living room, previously known as the other half of the front parlor." He grinned. "I'm a quick study."

As he walked her through the rest of the house, Tony explained that he'd returned to New Orleans, intending to move into his boyhood home, but one look and he'd gone to a hotel. "The next day, I found a furnished apartment."

Their tour ended in the kitchen, a cavern with dark wood cabinets and a water-stained acoustic tile ceiling. His gesture encompassed it all. "Half kitchen, half dungeon. I'd forgotten how ugly this house is."

"Your house isn't ugly. It's just a bad renovation. The kitchen would be fine if you got rid of that back stoop, let in some light, and put the ceiling back to its original height."

"If we do that, I won't hit my head on the chandelier." He pointed a yellowed globe hanging from the ceiling.

Claire heard the "we." Things were going well. "We might get rid of that chandelier," she said. "Your house has good bones, Tony. I think you'll be pleasantly surprised by the difference a few changes can make."

"I'm already pleasantly surprised. I was expecting a woman, but not a beautiful redhead. Can you turn this dump into something special?"

"If you give me free access, I can have rough plans by the end of the week. Then, you can judge for yourself." She wasn't beautiful, but she'd be very happy to get this job.

"Four o'clock Friday. Here." He handed her a key. "Bring your plans and a contract. I'm in a hurry."

"I'll start this afternoon." She zipped his house key into her purse, and they walked outside together.

He nodded toward her car. "Is that yours?"

"Uh huh. Her name is Felicia, Felicia Miata." Claire loved her bright blue roadster. When she was feeling down, just sitting behind the wheel could brighten her mood.

"His name is Igor." Tony pointed toward a gleaming black Ferrari parked behind Felicia.

When Claire returned to the office, she found Jack pouring over a set of blueprints. She gave him a big smile and a thumbs up. "The Burke project looks like a go. We're meeting again Friday afternoon. Tony wants plans and a contract."

"In three days?"

"I volunteered. This is a real opportunity for us. Think about it. We could do a before and after spread in the Sunday paper. People are always interested in how celebrities live. Tony would have to agree, of course, but why wouldn't he?"

"Sloooow down," He raised his hand like a traffic cop. "You're counting your chickens when you might not even have eggs."

"What?"

"You wouldn't be the first woman to learn the hard way that Tony Burke didn't exactly say what she thought she'd heard."

"Jack, this is business. I'm not ..." She saw his grin and stopped.

"Gotcha," he said. She shook her head and he continued. "I'm just giving you a hard time. If we get the job, that's great."

"Did you know that Jim Burke was his father?"

"Never heard of Jim Burke."

"He was an artist—a pretty good one—who died in an automobile accident back during Hurricane Camille. And his son becomes a racecar driver? Those little cars that go two hundred miles an hour, right? That's an interesting career choice."

"Word is he's faster off the track than on."

"Tony flirts, but he's not pushy. I like him. He's funny, and I bet he's smart."

"You're smart too, and I wasn't kidding about his reputation. Did you read those articles I left on your desk?"

"Supermarket tabloids aren't the world's most reliable source of information."

"Yeah, but everyone says essentially the same thing. Where there's smoke…"

"You know, I thought a race car driver would be small, like a jockey, but Tony's big, tall with broad shoulders. I bet he's strong." Claire sighed. "Pictures don't capture his charisma. There's this energy field around him." Her sigh turned into laughter at Jack's alarmed expression. "Gotcha back. That's one for me." She licked her finger and painted a vertical line in the air.

"Okay, but I'm right about him."

"Tony's a good-looking man. So are lots of other guys. I don't understand the fuss."

"Other guys don't hang out on the Riviera drinking champagne with movie stars. What is Tony Burke doing with that house? I bet the neighbors are falling out of their windows."

"He grew up there."

"That doesn't mean he still belongs there."

"I like him. I like his house. I hope we get the job."

"We could use the work."

Friday afternoon, Claire walked Tony through her proposal, marking the suggested changes on a diagram of his house. He approved everything she'd roughed out, so she moved on to price, a crucial topic. Before she came on board, Jack's company had teetered on the edge of bankruptcy. He tended to price projects too low, and he'd misjudged a big project. She'd bailed him out, and the money side was her responsibility now.

"I usually spend more time with a client before we get to the contract stage," she said. "But we've been on a fast track, and there are expenses I can't estimate. For example, you can spend $15,000 on kitchen cabinets or you can spend $50,000. Appliance costs are all over the board. I don't know what your budget is." She'd called his office twice and left messages, which he'd either not gotten or ignored. "Given that, the only contract I can offer today is cost-plus, which protects us but leaves you a lot of uncertainty."

"I understand how cost plus works, sweetheart, and if you'll hand me that pen you're waving around, I'll sign on the dotted line."

"You don't want your lawyer to look it over first?"

"My lawyer wouldn't approve, but I've checked your references, and I'm ready to go." He winked. "Unless you want to run it by your manager."

She gave him a blank look.

"Sorry, Claire, a bit of car salesman humor. You know I bought a BMW dealership?"

She nodded. Jack had told her.

"I've been spending too much time with the sales force." He took the pen from her hand and signed his name with a flourish. "When can you start?"

"As soon as we get the permits. I'll start the application process Tuesday. Monday is the Martin Luther King holiday."

"This calls for a toast." He disappeared into the kitchen and returned with a wine bottle and two stemmed glasses. "Prosecco. I developed a taste for it in Italy." He opened and poured the wine with an expertise that suggested long practice.

She raised her glass. "To your house."

"To our project." He touched the rim of his glass to hers. "I've been too busy to return your calls, but that's going to change. I intend to be involved. I can give you pictures showing how I want the kitchen to look. Then we'll talk budget."

"Pictures would be great." She took a sip of the bubbly wine. "What about old photos? Do you have any that would show what the house looked like when you were a child?"

"It looked like this only in better shape. Come on, Claire, the house is over a hundred years old, and I'm thirty-four."

"Which leaves a few years unaccounted for," she agreed. "Does your mother still live in New Orleans?"

"She lives about an hour north, outside Greensburg on a farm she's turned into a refuge for abused horses." His lip curled. "Geneviève Burke, savior of the Tennessee Walking Horse."

"I'd like to talk to her about the house. If she agrees, I could drive up there."

"You don't have to. She fell off one of her precious horses last week, dislocated her shoulder and broke her hip. She's staying in town for rehab."

Tony's attitude suggested a poor relationship with his mother, which was none of her business unless... "Does she still have an interest in the house?"

"Neither financial nor otherwise. She gave it to me years ago, as a wedding present, and I kept it in the divorce. I'm your only client." He lifted the wine bottle. "Another glass?"

"Thank you but no. My workday isn't over yet. Where can I reach your mother?"

"I'm already sorry I mentioned her."

"You didn't. I asked, and I'm eager to talk to her."

"Why?"

"Your house was renovated back in the fifties. If your mother was responsible, she might remember details about what was there before or, better yet, have pictures. How can I reach her?"

"I don't see her being helpful, but who knows." He shrugged. "She's at Sunny Gardens, a new assisted living place over on Claiborne."

"Assisted living. Is this permanent?"

"No. They have a few apartments for people with short-term needs. The doctors expect a complete recovery."

"That has to be good news."

He drained his wine glass before speaking. "From everything I've seen and heard, you're a nice person. Geneviève is not. When you meet her, she'll be charming. She'll ask about you, your family and where you come from, play a couple rounds of who-do-you-know."

"Lots of people do that." Most of the people she'd met in New Orleans did.

"Lots of people are looking for a context to help them feel comfortable with you. My dear mother is looking for your weakness. She has an instinct for the jugular and enjoys what she calls stirring things up, which translates into causing pain for other people."

Tony's warning struck Claire as melodramatic. She wondered if he was letting her know that he was aware of her history. Last fall, she'd caused a man's death. It had been self-defense, but some people would never see her as totally innocent. Had the gossip reached his ears in Italy?

"I'll be discreet." She stood up to leave. "Thank you for the wine."

"I'll see you out." He took her arm. "Be careful where you step. This place is a mess."

"Tony, I'm used to walking around construction sites."

"Yeah, but this afternoon you've been drinking." She looked up, ready to protest, and saw his teasing grin.

Before she drove away, Tony delivered one more word of caution. "Don't forget her name is *Zhon*–vee–ev, the French pronunciation. If you call her Jen-ah-*veeve*, she'll come out from behind her walker and kick you across the room." He pantomimed drop kicking a football.

"*Zhon*-vee-ev." Claire enunciated each syllable.

"And she insists upon calling me Layton. She knows I prefer Tony, but she doesn't care."

"I'll call her next week."

2

It was Tuesday before Claire found time to call Sunny Gardens and Wednesday before she actually spoke to Tony's mother.

"Your message said this was business. Are you interested in a horse?" Geneviève Burke said.

"I'm the contractor your son has hired to restore his house." Claire said. She explained that her company specialized in the restoration of historic houses. "The more we know about a house's history, the better. Talking to previous owners is a good starting point."

"Historic? That house?" Geneviève laughed. "It's just old. I doubt I'll be much help, but if you want to come by, I'd welcome a visitor."

"How about tomorrow?"

"Late afternoon is best for me. I spend mornings in the gym and nap after lunch."

Thursday, Claire arrived a few minutes before the agreed upon four o'clock. She flipped through a brochure while she waited for the concierge to finish discussing an upcoming excursion with a group of older women. Sunny Gardens described itself as resort living for the discriminating senior. Smaller print offered a continuum of care, fees available upon request. The brochure's tone reminded her of the old saying about yachts. *If you have to ask the price, you can't afford it.*

The women finished their discussion, and she stepped forward. "Good afternoon. My name is Claire Marshall. I'm here to see Geneviève Burke."

"Mrs. Burke is expecting you." The concierge's welcoming smile held firm, but an edge of distaste crept into her voice. Claire remembered Tony's warning; she would be cautious. She signed her name on the visitor's log and followed directions to the west parlor.

A slender, dark-haired woman stood by French doors leading out to a garden. Despite the walker and the sling on one arm, she had better posture than most twenty-year-olds. Claire squared her shoulders and sucked in her stomach.

"Mrs. Burke?"

The woman turned. "You must be Claire. I'm Geneviève."

"I'd recognize you anywhere. Your son looks so much like you." She'd started to say Tony, remembered his mother called him Layton and didn't feel comfortable using either.

Geneviève grasped the back of a sofa with her good arm and lowered herself onto the seat. She patted the cushion. "Come sit by me, so we don't have to yell. Half the people here are going deaf, and the rest are already there. Everyone yells. It's enough to give you a headache."

"Thank you for agreeing to talk to me."

Up close, Geneviève showed her age. Time had etched lines onto her face and thinned her lips, but her eyes, the same blue-gray-green ocean color as Tony's, were clear, and her smile, like his, could melt stone.

"I apologize for meeting you in this hideous parlor," she said. "But my cell of an apartment is even worse."

Claire made sympathetic comments about this being a difficult time, and Geneviève responded with more grievances. The food was bland. The décor was a pastel hell of overblown floral prints and plastic plants. She saved her harshest criticism for the staff.

"They spew platitudes and don't have manners enough to look at you when they're speaking. The only one I can stand is Iris, who is an actress pretending to be a nurse."

"Have you met many of the other people living here?"

"I had the misfortune of knowing several of them, years ago." Geneviève tilted her head toward a woman sitting near the entrance. "For example: the fat woman in the ugly green blouse is Amanda Pierce. Her brother was crazy about me, but the family didn't approve of a divorcée." She took a mint from a bowl on the table and popped it into her mouth.

Claire murmured something innocuous about times changing, but Geneviève wasn't through with Amanda.

"She's been pretending to look at the same page of Vogue ever since

I came in, ten minutes before you arrived. She's really stalking Harry Durand over there, the one playing bridge, in the blue and white striped shirt. Harry is a wealthy widower with no children."

Apparently unaware that he was the object of anyone's attention, the man in question studied his cards and laid one down. Claire glanced around the parlor. Amanda caught her eye and glared, but no one else was reacting. Claire hoped they really were hard of hearing.

"Amanda, for all her airs, has very little money of her own. She never married. No man wanted her then, and Harry certainly doesn't—" Geneviève stopped in midsentence. "Forgive me. I'm being tiresome."

Tiresome? She was being horrible. Claire looked for a graceful exit. "I can come back another day when you're feeling better."

"I'm feeling fine. It's these people; they get under my skin. They have everything and appreciate nothing. I've had to do for myself. I don't weigh an ounce more than I did when I was twenty. I run a horse farm and keep the books. On a computer I taught myself to use." Geneviève tapped her mouth. "There I go again. I'll stop. Promise. You're here to talk about Layton's house. Why is a mystery to me, but go ahead." She sat back, a woman prepared to listen.

"You bought the house back in the fifties?"

"I didn't buy it. I was married to Roger Devereux. You've no doubt heard of the family."

Claire nodded. The name was familiar to anyone who did business in New Orleans.

"When we divorced, Roger kept our lovely house, and I was allowed to select one of his family's rental properties. That would have been 1956." Her expression said this still rankled.

"Did you have it renovated?"

"I never did a thing to it, and last I saw, Layton hadn't either. I'm not surprised it needs work. He's been renting it out since he moved to Italy, and tenants don't care. They leave a mess."

"Nothing like the mess we'll be making. We're gutting the kitchen back to the original walls, getting rid of the lowered ceiling, removing the hall bathroom and the back stoop."

Geneviève burst out laughing. "You're taking out all the modern improvements that led me to choose that house. Of course, after all these years, they're not so modern anymore." Her expression softened. "People used to call that little house Chez Geneviève. It was the gathering place for the avant-garde of New Orleans. Every night was a party with fascinating people and brilliant conversation. My second husband was an artist, but the people came to see me."

It was the perfect opening. Claire wanted to ask why Jim Burke's studio had been boarded up and left to rot, but she bit her tongue. Tony had warned her not to mention his father or the studio and, if either subject came up, to pretend ignorance. When she asked why, he'd offered no explanation beyond "trust me."

"Do you have pictures from those parties?" Claire said. "I'd especially like to see any that show the front of the house."

"There might be some snapshots in the old sideboard, which last I knew was in Layton's attic, but they weren't taken outside. Our parties began well after sundown and lasted until the wee small hours." She waved a dismissive hand. "Of course all of that ended when Layton came along."

"What about first day of school pictures, Layton standing on the front steps?" Her mother had taken one every year, from kindergarten until the September morning she left for college.

"I wasn't that kind of a mother." Geneviève picked up another mint. "I'm sorry, Claire, I can't help you. I live in the present, and I don't look back. That's why I hate it here. Old music, old movies, and a constant blah blah blah about the good old days, which we all know weren't nearly that good."

Faced with a dead end, Claire shifted into small-talk mode, planning to make polite conversation for a few minutes and then leave. "How long will you be here?"

"I'll be home by the end of the month or die trying. I miss my horses."

"I used to spend a lot of time around horses, but you're the first person I've met who rescues abused horses."

"Layton didn't tell me you were a horse person." It was an accusation. "He doesn't like horses; they're not fast enough for him." Another accusation.

"When I was a little girl, I preferred horses to people."

"I still do." Geneviève didn't appear to be kidding. "Soon as I'm better, you'll have to come visit. We can go for a ride."

"That's very kind of you, but I haven't ridden since college." Claire didn't take the invitation seriously. People in New Orleans said, "you all come see me" instead of good-bye.

"Riding a horse is like riding a bike, your body remembers. This is not a frivolous invitation, Claire. I want you to visit. A young woman who owns a construction company is an interesting person. I'd like to know you better."

"Thank you." Claire braced for the personal questions Tony had warned about, but Geneviève continued to talk about horses.

"Are you familiar with Tennessee Walking Horses?"

"I don't know if I've ever seen one."

"I'm sure you have. Remember the Lone Ranger and Silver? Roy Rogers and Trigger? Movie cowboys love Walkers. Even a clumsy rider looks good on a Walker."

Claire dredged up old memories of Saturday matinees, and an amused Geneviève swore that Dale Evans, Gene Autry, Hopalong Cassidy, Zorro, and Lash Larue all rode Walkers. Then she became serious.

"Walkers are gaited horses, and everyone wants their horse to have a big lick. It's the ultimate gait. Very few horses have a natural big lick, so trainers use padded shoes and chains to force longer and higher steps. It's perfectly legal, but it shouldn't be. Can you imagine a horse wearing high heels and ankle bracelets?"

"Only in a cartoon."

"Unscrupulous trainers go further. They apply irritants to the forelegs. It's called soring and is totally illegal but all too common. Done badly, soring can make a horse lame. In the worst cases, the damage is permanent. Those horses are sold for slaughter." Geneviève's eyes flashed indignation, and her voice rose with her outrage. "By the pound for dog food."

Several people turned to stare, and Geneviève lowered her voice. "I'm sorry, Claire. You ask a simple question, and I subject you to a ten-minute tirade."

"Don't apologize, please. Listening to you makes me want to help those horses, too." Tony had sneered at his mother's efforts, but Claire found her passion appealing.

"Well, I'm through preaching, and it's not all doom and gloom. Last fall I rescued a magnificent stallion—eighteen hands, black with a white blaze—that had been sored. I named him Fast Eddie after my favorite politician." Geneviève's smile became rueful. "I'm here because Eddie threw me. His forelegs have healed, but he's still skittish. I didn't realize how skittish."

"Will I see him when I visit the farm?" Claire had decided to accept the invitation. After a rocky start, Tony's mother had become good company, and the idea of riding again was tempting.

"He'll be there." Geneviève drew herself up. "Eddie's previous owner wants him back. Which will happen over my dead body."

"Let me give you my number," Claire said. "You can call when you're ready for a visitor."

"Why wait? You could go up this weekend. Kyle—that's my trainer—says everything's fine, but I'd like to hear from someone else that things are going well."

"I'm sorry. I'm tied up this weekend, and I really don't know enough to second guess your trainer."

"I'm not asking you to spy on Kyle. I just want reassurance. What about next weekend?" Geneviève took her hand. "You're a horse person, Claire. You understand. I rescue horses and they rescue me."

Claire did understand. She'd been a shy child, and for a few years, a quarter horse named Hershey had been her best friend. "I can't promise, but I'll try."

"Thank you." Geneviève's smile dazzled. "Now that I've taken up your afternoon with a lecture on horses, while giving you none of the help you came for, let me walk you to your car. I could use some fresh air."

Claire stood up. "I'll get your walker."

"Don't. Let me do it." She pulled herself to her feet, an effort that brought beads of sweat to her brow. "The sooner I can take care of myself, the sooner I can go home."

Geneviève's pace was slow but steady until they reached the front entrance. Then she stopped short. "Wait."

"Are you all right? Do you want to rest for a minute?"

"See them?" Geneviève jutted her chin toward a middle-aged blonde woman and an elderly man leaving the garden. "That man is Roger Devereux, my first husband. The woman is his niece Laura."

"He looks so much older." Claire had noticed this couple before. They'd been coming out the front door when she arrived, and she'd been touched by the woman's gentleness as she helped her companion navigate the doorway. He'd moved awkwardly, shuffling rather than walking, and when they passed, had cast a worried glance in her direction.

"I was twenty on our wedding day. Roger was forty." Geneviève snapped her mouth shut, as if biting back further comment.

The blonde woman glanced their way, a cool gaze that became a frown. She put her arm around the old man's waist and turned him back toward the gardens.

"Laura saw us. That's why she's hustling him out of here." Geneviève's voice dropped to a malicious whisper. "When I told Iris I'd been married to Roger Devereux, she told me there was a man by that name up on the fourth floor, what we call the batso wing. Iris doesn't work up there and couldn't tell me anything else about him, so I went to see for myself. Roger recognized me the minute I walked into his room."

"He must have been surprised to see you." Claire watched the couple walk away. It certainly looked as if Laura didn't want her uncle to see his ex-wife again.

"You bet he was. Watch. I'll show you what he did." She hunched over her walker, head down and hands covering her ears, then straightened up and said, "Roger great-God-almighty Devereux curled up like a big roly-poly bug and started humming. Isn't that a riot?"

Her venom left Claire speechless.

"When I left, he followed me downstairs and threw a tantrum outside my door. I had to call security. It took two men to haul him away."

"That's awful."

"Don't waste your pity. Roger understands a lot more than people around here think."

"Good-bye." Claire hurried down the walkway. She wasn't coming back. She wasn't going up to the farm. She never wanted to see this dreadful woman again.

3

Soft fingers slid across his stomach, and Tony opened his eyes. The clock radio said nine thirty-eight. He'd planned an early start, but another hour or so wouldn't make any difference. Dad's studio had been boarded up for twenty-five years. Another hour or two wouldn't make any difference. Kerri was demanding immediate attention. She nuzzled his neck.

"My plane leaves in three hours. Show me how much you're going to miss me."

Making love was Tony's favorite way to start the day, but this morning felt flat. He was able to perform, although more from duty than desire, and Kerri seemed satisfied. When she laughingly turned away his suggestion of a shared shower, he was relieved.

"I have to catch that plane, but hold the thought. The shoot is a week from Thursday. I'll call from the airport when I get in Wednesday night." She caressed his cheek. "We can pick up where we left off."

He called a car service while she dressed and gathered her belongings. He walked her to the elevator then stood at the window, watching her car pull away from the curb and wondering if he really wanted to see her again, so soon. Kerri's hasty departure reminded him of another morning, another woman who'd left his bed in a hurry...

It had been a house party in the lull between the European Grand Prix and San Marino. He'd wakened to the creaking of his bedroom door and the vision of Paula taking off her robe as she walked toward him.

"I was hoping." He threw back the covers and made room for her.

"You knew." She slipped in beside him. "But I don't mind. I like a confident man."

He covered her mouth with his, shutting off any further discussion of what she did or did not like in a man. Her husband was old, rich, and titled. Presumably she liked that too.

After Paula tiptoed back to her quarters, Tony lay in bed and surveyed his surroundings, the antique furniture and oriental carpets, the Murano chandelier, and the walls hung with tapestries that probably belonged in a museum. His luxurious bedchamber was one of many in this magnificent villa.

He walked, naked, to the window and admired the geometry of grape vines striping Tuscan hills the fresh green of April. A breeze carried the burble of a nearby stream and the musk of freshly turned earth. Beauty surrounded him, and every bit of it belonged to his host: the villa, the land, and the woman who'd just left his bed.

On the track, he was in charge. Off the track, he was a guest. He enjoyed temporary pleasures, committed to nothing, owned nothing, and owed nothing. It was what he'd wanted, that and New Orleans in his rearview. He'd spent the last decade telling himself to keep moving.

Moving targets are harder to hit.

He'd succeeded beyond his wildest dreams, advancing from mechanic to test driver to the pinnacle of Formula One racing. It had been a great trip, the road paved with beautiful women and fat paychecks, but the nomad's life was losing its appeal. He wanted his own place, something more permanent than the apartment in Modena. He watched a pair of hawks soar over the hillside and decided to buy a villa.

That summer and fall, he spent his free days crisscrossing the Italian Piedmont with eager real estate agents and his nights dreaming about raising his son in the house where his father had raised him. He lectured himself about self-pity and imaginary sons and kept moving. None of the villas he'd looked at—there'd been dozens—felt right.

The season's final race was Australia in November. He drove badly. When the team returned to Italy, he'd flown to New Orleans, hoping to repair his relationship with his mother, the only relative he had.

His old house had been an unhappy surprise. When he told Geneviève that he planned to sell it and buy something nicer with a guest suite she could use whenever she felt like staying in town, he got another surprise. She'd turned on him, eyes blazing fury.

"Don't you dare sell our family home."

He was still trying to make her happy, so he decided to keep the old house and fix it up. He could stay through February to oversee the renovation. His agent came up with a list of companies that could do the job. Claire's company had worked in the neighborhood, and her references were good, so...

He liked Claire, and he liked her idea about turning the restored center hall into a gallery for his father's art. Unfortunately, he owned exactly one of his father's paintings. He'd never seen one in his mother's house and was almost positive she didn't have any. Nor would he ask. Only a masochist would mention Jim Burke to Geneviève. His mother didn't remember either of her husbands fondly.

Claire, who didn't give up easily, had suggested looking in the studio. She offered to have her demo crew remove the boards blocking the door—the door itself if necessary. He'd remembered the canvases his dad had stacked against the wall and known that he wanted to open the studio himself. And he would—today—but first, with or without Kerri, he needed a shower.

Tony climbed the steps to the gallery, which looked one hundred percent better with the screens off. He unlocked the front door and walked into a disaster area with holes in the floor and chunks out of the plaster. Despite the mess, he could already see that getting rid of the half bath transformed the interior. He sorted through the tools Claire's crew had left him and carried a pry bar, a claw hammer, pliers, and a handsaw back to the studio.

The saw turned out to be useless. Whoever put up the boards had used more nails than a seventh-grade shop project. He picked up the pry bar and went to work. He'd tried to remove those boards before; this time he'd succeed.

A racecar driver is an athlete, and Tony stayed in shape even during the offseason, but removing the first board took fifteen minutes of hard work. He wiped the sweat from his face. One down and six to go before he could free the door, which was undoubtedly locked. Geneviève had ordered the studio sealed, and she didn't fool around.

Why she'd boarded it up was a mystery. She'd told anyone who would listen that she couldn't bear to go in, or have anyone else go in, now that Jim was dead. That was bullshit—she'd never gone in when he was alive—but it was her story and she was sticking to it. She'd always been weird about the studio. When she gave him the house, she told him not to open his father's studio until after her death, like it was some sacred trust.

He pulled a beer from the cooler that he'd had the foresight to bring along and rolled the icy bottle between his hands. A month ago, he would have been too intimidated by his witch of a mother to ignore her wishes, but falling off that horse had made her mortal. The woman who used to stride around like she owned the earth now took little baby steps while clinging to her walker.

The accident had humbled her in other ways. For Christmas, he'd suggested a holiday trip to a destination of her choice and tried to tempt her with promises of luxury accommodations. She'd declined without regret and bemoaned his transformation into a person with more money than sense. The prospect of six weeks in a low-rent nursing home had changed her attitude.

Sunny Gardens charged three times what her insurance covered, and he was paying the difference. Her thanks had been grudging, and he didn't expect her gratitude to last longer than it took the ink to dry on the final check. His fantasy about a mother and son reconciliation was long dead. He finished the beer and went back to work.

Tony's nail-removing and board-levering skills improved as he went along. One beer break later, he wrenched the last board off the doorframe. The rusted doorknob wouldn't turn—no surprise there. He hefted the sledgehammer like a baseball bat and swung for the fences. The frame splintered, and the door swung inward, hinges creaking just like they used to when Dad was alive.

Shaking off the memories, he stepped over the threshold. A musty odor, strong enough to trigger a gag reflex, caught in his throat. Holding his breath, he knocked the glass out of the closest window then took another big swing. The sledgehammer slammed through the plywood with a satisfying thwack.

He put his face to the hole and inhaled fresh air—fresher air. A dead mockingbird, feathers covered with dust and eye sockets empty, lay on the windowsill. It must have landed there and been trapped, unable to spread its wings for takeoff and too afraid to jump.

He smashed holes in the plywood covering two more windows, creating much needed cross ventilation and letting in more light. It still smelled bad, but he could breathe and he could see. The studio was as he remembered. His father's easel stood in the center of the room, the tall stool beside it. A stack of canvases leaned against the wall.

"Yes he stabbed the air with his fist.

Tony pulled the top painting free. Under dirt and cobwebs, vertical slashes of color depicted a beautiful woman, her hooded cloak open to show a long sliver of body. Memory brought tears to his eyes. He'd watched his dad brush on these colors. He pressed his finger against a corner of the canvas and gradually increased the pressure. It held. The studio smelled of mold and rot, but the canvas was sound. He set it aside, returned to the stack, and picked up another painting.

Lucky for him, a movement caught his eye. The shiny black spider crouched inches from his hand. He knocked the black widow onto the floor, stepped on it, and kept an eye out for others. He should have been more careful from the get-go. Spiders and webs covered the outside. Anyone could see they'd colonized the place.

One at a time, Tony carried his father's paintings to the door. He thumped them on the steps to dislodge any remaining spiders and took them around to the front gallery. When he finished, three more black widows had died under his shoe, and fourteen paintings of various sizes formed a line from one end of the gallery to the other.

He walked back and forth, admiring them, grinning from ear to ear. He was happier than he could remember being in his adult life, and he wanted to share his joy. Claire had said she'd stop by toward the end of the afternoon, after she finished her errands, but Tony wanted to tell someone now. He'd known better than to let Geneviève in on his plans to open the studio. Now it was a fait accompli. Why not tell her? He made another circuit of the gallery then went inside to use the phone.

"You won't believe what I've found," he said. "You might even want one or two for yourself."

"What are you talking about?"

He explained.

Nothing in Tony's troubled relationship with his mother had prepared him for her reaction. Incredulous, then furious, and finally sobbing with what she said was grief, she demanded that he immediately replace the boards and never again enter the studio. Unable to get a word in edgewise, he hung up, cursing his stupidity. He'd been so thrilled about finding the paintings that he'd forgotten what a bitch his mother was, how she'd rebuffed his every effort to appease her. Did he actually expect her to be happy for him?

People don't change.

He went back outside to look at the paintings, wanting to recapture his good mood. The phone rang, and through the closed door, he heard Geneviève berating his answering machine. He walked back around to the studio. His old toy box ought to be inside.

Claire parked behind the black Ferrari. She noticed the paintings that lined the gallery but resisted the temptation to take a quick look and walked around back, looking for Tony. She spotted him dragging an antique blanket chest down the studio steps.

"Hey, what are you doing?"

He stopped. "Did you see the paintings?"

"Just a glimpse. I was looking for you."

"You're not going to believe your eyes." He grabbed her hand and pulled her around to the front.

"Tony." Claire couldn't help laughing. This grown man was as excited as a child at Christmas.

"Look what I found." He practically carried her up the gallery steps.

Even covered with grime, Jim Burke's paintings were glorious swirls of color, the psychedelic sixties strongly influenced by art nouveau. Most were large, four or five feet tall, which would be perfect. The center hall was wide with a high ceiling. All but one of the paintings portrayed a beautiful woman, nude or semi-nude. Claire bit back a smile. His father's art would only enhance Tony's reputation as a lady's man. Perhaps it was genetic.

"I'm overwhelmed," she said. "All these were in the studio? Unbelievable."

"There might have been one more." Tony's brow furrowed. "Dad used to say an artist should keep everything—even when a picture doesn't turn out as planned, it has value—but it looks as if he burned one. There's canvas in the woodstove."

"Still, you have all these. They're stunning." She walked the length of the gallery again.

"Fourteen Jim Burke originals, and they're mine, all mine." Tony rubbed his hands together in a parody of a movie villain. "They need cleaning, but the canvas appears to be in good shape."

Claire listened appreciatively while Tony described his struggles with the pry bar. She expressed concern when he told her about the black widows. Then a stray thought brought caution.

"Are you sure these paintings don't belong to your mother? Did your father have a will?"

"Geneviève deeded me this property and all its contents years after Dad died. The paintings are mine." He set his jaw.

"Good, but don't you want to tell your mother about finding them?"

"I already did, and don't worry. She has no interest in them."

"I went to see her Thursday afternoon. Did she mention my visit?"

"The subject didn't come up."

"She was horribly rude, not to me but to other people living there."

"I warned you." He turned back to the paintings. "Let's talk about something else, like these pictures. I've been thinking about how they'll go in the hall. I want to display the sketch on the easel, where I found it, to show a work in progress."

"That's a good idea." She walked the length of the gallery again. "Your father was a talented artist."

"I'm fresh out of Prosecco, but there's cold beer in a cooler out back. Come on." He took her hand again. "I'll show you Dad's studio. You've been wanting to go inside since day one."

Tony was wrong. She did not want to go inside—the studio both fascinated and repelled her, and that was before she'd heard about the black widows—but she really didn't have a choice. Opening it had been her idea.

4

Light from broken windows laid jagged stripes on the floor; dust motes floated in air that reeked of decay. Claire put her hand over her nose and breathed through her mouth.

Tony pointed to an easel in the center of the room. "That's where I found the sketch. Right where Dad left it."

A tall table stood beside the easel, its top littered with tubes of paint, tin cans holding brushes, and a splotched palette. Age and grime had darkened all the colors. Charred remnants of canvas hung from the open door of a woodstove and fluttered when Tony walked past. He gestured toward a lighter-colored rectangle of wall.

"The others were stacked over there."

She nodded.

A thin paisley coverlet lay crumpled on an unmade single bed. A faded blue work shirt hung from a hook on the wall. Shelves of books, an old TV set, and a sofa defined the living area. Beyond that, dust coated a silent refrigerator and a long-cold frying pan still on the stove. The far corner had been enclosed for a bathroom, its sink and toilet visible through the open door.

Jim Burke had lived as well as worked in his studio, and when his life ended, all his belongings had been sealed inside. Like an ancient tomb, the studio contained everything the dead man would need in the hereafter.

Claire's throat tightened, and black spots danced in front of her eyes. Desperate for breath, she took a deep gulp of the foul air and tasted bile. She turned and ran outside.

"Are you okay?" Tony stood beside her, a supportive arm around her waist.

"I will be in a minute." She couldn't have a panic attack in front of Tony. Or throw up at his feet. She liked him and cared what he thought of her. Her company needed his business.

"The mold probably got to you. That place has been closed up for twenty-five years." He half-led half-carried her back to the house and helped her sit down on the back steps.

"Could you get me a glass of water and my purse, please?" The panic attacks that plagued her after Tom died had abated. She'd not had one in months. She'd worked her way off the anti-anxiety meds, but like an ex-smoker who always has a pack nearby, she still carried the pills. Just in case.

When Tony returned, she took the glass with both hands to keep from spilling. Carefully, she sipped the water. Little swallows slid around the lump in her throat. Her heart stopped pounding, and her breathing returned to normal.

"I'm okay now. Thank you." She found a Kleenex in her purse, wet it, and wiped her face. The pills stayed in their bottle.

Tony sat down next to her. "It's hard to believe, the way it looks and smells today, but I spent the happiest hours of my childhood in that studio." There was a smile in his voice. "It was light inside. The bushes weren't all grown up, and Dad kept the windows open. I was crazy about trains, and he let me run tracks all over the floor, as long as I didn't get under his feet. His models mothered me. Lisa was Dad's favorite and mine too. She gave me little wooden cows to ride in my cattle car."

Eyes closed, Claire lay back against the step. Tony, solid and comforting beside her, kept talking.

"I told you I had only one of Dad's paintings. I never told you how I got it. Do you want to hear the story?"

"Yes." *Stay here with me just a bit longer.*

"My junior year at Tulane, a bunch of us were on a gallery crawl, looking for women and drinking free wine, when a painting caught my eye. I looked again, and it was like a punch to the gut. Took all I had not to start bawling. I found the gallery owner and told him my father had painted that picture. The model's name was Lisa."

Finding his father's art should have been a happy discovery, but Tony no longer sounded happy. She murmured something about a surprise for everyone and waited to hear why.

"Howard Levine, the gallery owner, told me Dad's art sold well in New Orleans but rarely came on the market. People didn't want to sell. He thought Dad would have become nationally known if he'd just lived a little longer and had a bit more of his work in circulation."

"Your father was a good artist." All these paintings—why hadn't anyone taken them to a dealer after Jim Burke died? Shutting them up in the studio made no sense.

"Howard sold me that painting at his cost and let me pay for it on time."

"He sounds like a very nice person."

"He is, and he likes Chagall. When I started making real money, I bought him one as a belated thank-you present. Howard retired a few years ago, moved to Arizona, but we've kept in touch." Tony paused, and when he resumed speaking, anger roughened his voice. "The next morning I called Geneviève and asked why I had to learn from a stranger that Dad was a recognized artist and not just some wannabe living off his wife. She hung up on me. She's the one who had the studio boarded up with the pictures inside. She had to know they were there."

"Well, the paintings are out now."

"Other stuff got locked up inside, including the cows that Lisa gave me. When you arrived, I was wrestling with my old toy box, which for some reason weighs a ton. Tell me when you're ready to go back."

"I'm fine, but I'd rather wait here while you go on back and open it."

"Easier said than done. Someone nailed it shut, probably Geneviève." He shrugged. "I don't know whether to be baffled or indignant."

"If we're talking about the chest you were bouncing down the steps, I think it's an antique. Bring it here and I'll help you open it. There's a dolly in the back of my truck."

Minutes later, Tony dumped the chest at her feet. It looked to be early nineteenth century, probably from southern Appalachia. A pioneer family would have used it to carry blankets and linens to their new home along the Mississippi. Claire stroked the fine old wood. She pictured a young woman smoothing and folding the linens she had embroidered for her trousseau, preparing for a new life that would begin with a dangerous journey.

"It would be a shame to damage this old chest." She showed him how to extract a nail without denting the surrounding wood.

He pulled out all the nails, but the lid still wouldn't budge. He peered underneath. "It wasn't just the nails; it's glued shut." He reached for the pry bar.

"Wait. This really is a nice old chest. Let me try to break the seal. I'm good at this kind of thing. There should be a wood chisel among the tools the crew left you."

Tony returned with the chisel and watched while she tapped along the seam. The glue, brittle with age and applied with too heavy a hand, cracked and split. She sat back on her heels.

"It's your toy box. Do you want the honor?"

He eased over and lifted the lid. "What the heck?" He pulled out a square of decayed burlap, threw it on the ground and picked up another. "Sandbags?"

The bags smelled awful, worse than the studio. Claire held her breath waiting for the stench to dissipate. How could Tony stand it?

"Someone emptied a bunch of sandbags into my toy box. On top of my toys?" He ran his fingers through the sand then frowned and pulled out a long white bone. "What's this?"

Her stomach turned over. "Oh my God."

"What?"

"It looks like an ulna." She ran her fingers along the inside of her forearm. "This bone."

"From a human being?" He examined the bone. "Are you sure?"

"When my husband was in med school, I helped him study. It's been a while, so maybe not."

"But maybe yes?"

She made herself look more closely. "Probably yes."

A range of emotions played across Tony's face: bewilderment, disbelief, horror, and then anger. He held the bone against his forearm. "About my size. Right?" He laid the bone on the grass, sifted through the sand and pulled out a second long white bone. "Another one." He held it up for her to see.

"It's the other forearm bone." They'd found human remains. The studio really was a tomb. Tony's toy box was a coffin. She grabbed the stair rail and pulled herself up. "We'd better call the police."

Head bowed as if in prayer, Tony knelt beside the toy chest.

"We should call the police," she repeated.

He still didn't look up, but this time he responded. "Go ahead.

Phone in the bedroom works."

When she returned, he was still beside the chest but no longer kneeling. She sat back down on the steps and said, "The police will send a car as soon as one is available."

"The forearm was here." He drew a line in the sand. "So, the rest of the arm would be about here. Right?" He slid his hand over. "Someone my size, you'd have to fold him into a fetal position to fit him in."

"The police said not to touch anything."

He dug into the sand and uncovered another bone. "This is the upper arm, isn't it?"

"I think so." She looked away.

"What's this one?"

"Tony, don't. Those bones used to be a person." The med school skeleton used to be a person too, but this was different. She extended her hand. "Let's wait out front."

He shook his head and continued digging, using both hands to brush the sand aside, pulling out bones, and laying them on the grass. She couldn't stop him, but she didn't have to watch.

"I'll be out front."

"Don't go. Please. I want to put him back together, and I could use your help." He held a long bone parallel to his thigh, frowned, and then slid it below his knee. "It's part of the leg, but which part?"

"Stop it, please. This isn't a game."

"Trust me, sweetheart, I'm not playing. Tell me what this is."

"One of the lower leg bones." She pointed to a bone he'd set aside. "There's its partner."

"Which makes this the thigh." He put the bones in place.

Claire leaned back and closed her eyes. Where are the police? She felt Tony beside her.

"Look at this. Come on, Claire, help me." He was holding a human skull as tenderly as a mother with a newborn. He turned it sideways and pointed to an area of shattered bone. "Fractured skull. Probably what killed him."

She nodded mute agreement.

He returned to the skeleton and set the skull in place. It rolled onto the damaged side. He tried again, and again it rolled over. His head was down, and she couldn't see his face, but she could feel his tension. Tony had been eight or nine when the studio was sealed up—old enough that he'd remember things.

"Do you know whose bones these are?"

He looked up as if he was going to answer, but when their eyes met, he turned away.

"What?" she said. "Who?" But she was talking to his back.

Tony disappeared around the corner of the house, a car door slammed, an engine roared, and tires squealed.

Claire walked around front. She carried Jim Burke's paintings inside, where they'd be safe, and sat on the front steps to wait for the police.

5

Tony drove with the fury of an avenging angel, cutting through city traffic as if he was running through the pack at Le Mans. Claire's arrival had delayed his discovery, but Geneviève would have known it was inevitable. What would she do now? She was nothing if not formidable. She had dared to invoke his dead father's memory, to pretend grief for the man she'd killed. He swerved around a slow car and accelerated to make the yellow light, ignoring the chorus of angry horns.

Geneviève had killed his father. He was sure of it, although he couldn't imagine why. Not money. She was the one with money, the one who owned the house and the farm and God knows what else. Her first husband had been rich, and she'd fleeced him in the divorce. Not passion. She'd told him that his father was the love of her life, but he couldn't recall any sign of tenderness on either side. By the time Dad died, even a little kid could tell their marriage was in the toilet.

Why kill him? Why not just throw him out?

Hatred—that had to be it. Geneviève thrived on conflict. She loved a fight and nursed her grudges into full-blown hate. After ten years of a bad marriage, she'd hated her husband enough to kill him, enough to hide the paintings that were his life's work. Tony's hands tightened on the steering wheel as he remembered how she played the young widow role for all it was worth.

"I just don't know how I'm going to manage, and with a child to care for," she used say, wiping away a crocodile tear. But when she told him his father was never coming back, her eyes had been dry...

Geneviève had been alone in the house when he and Meemaw returned from Uncle Will's. He'd started to run out to the studio to say hi to Dad, but she'd grabbed his shoulder and held him back. It was past his bedtime. He started to argue, but her frown stopped him. He was all too familiar with his mother's ready slap, the blows that left stinging red handprints on his cheek.

He'd changed into pajamas and knelt beside his bed, so worried he'd felt like throwing up. Dad was supposed to follow Geneviève to Uncle Will's farm, but he never made it. Everyone said, don't worry, his father hadn't come up because the roads were out, hadn't called because the phones were out. But the grown-ups would stop talking whenever he walked into the room, and now he was back home, and still no Dad.

"I want Dad to listen to my prayers." He'd said, fighting back tears.

"Jim had an accident." Geneviève leaned against the door, her arms folded across her chest. "When the water went down, they found his truck in a ditch." She wrapped her arms tighter. "He must have been washed down river. He's gone, and this time he's not coming back."

He started to cry and she said, "Remember him in your prayers. He's up in heaven and he'll hear you." She'd turned and walked away...

Most women would have hugged a stranger's child, but Geneviève had left hers to grieve alone. Now, twenty-five years later, he knew why. She wasn't going to get away with it.

He parked in the Sunny Gardens visitors' lot and hurried up the walkway. Ahead of him, a middle-aged society blonde walked with her arm around a tall man who looked at least a hundred years old. Tony mumbled an excuse me and stepped off the sidewalk to pass them. The blonde's glance turned into a double take with narrowed eyes. He thought she was going to chastise him, but she turned back to her companion without speaking. He kept going.

He pushed the door open and stepped inside. The concierge looked up, and her face froze mid-smile. He saw his reflection in the mirror behind her desk and forced himself to slow down, relax his shoulders, unclench his jaw and fists.

"Hi," he said. "I'm hoping my mother will let me use her shower." His smile apologized for his filthy clothes and dirt streaked face.

"Good evening, Mr. Burke." The concierge remained cautious.

"If you don't mind, I'll just sneak down the hall to her apartment."

"Your mother is in the main parlor." She waved toward the big room on the right, where elderly men in sports coats and women in dresses sat around chatting, glasses in hand.

This was a surprise. Geneviève had been emphatic about not socializing with the other residents, whom she viewed with disdain. She must be looking for cover. Fine with him. If she thought he'd back away from a public confrontation, she was mistaken. He intended to tell the world.

"I'll just check in with her first." He moved on before the concierge could tell him he wasn't properly dressed.

Geneviève sat alone by a pair of French doors on the far wall, gazing out at the garden. Tony appraised her with a stranger's eye and saw an elegant woman, dark hair pulled into a chignon, clothing and make-up beautifully understated. She sat erect, as if riding one of her precious horses, and seemed unaware of the people around her or of him, standing in the doorway.

Is this what a killer looks like?

He studied her face, the features so like his own. She was still attractive, but after years of frowns and sneers, the ugliness inside had begun to show. In another ten years, if she lived that long, she'd look like a witch. His certainty, which had wavered at the sight of her, returned. He cut through the crowd and stopped in front of her chair, his feet inches from hers.

She turned and her eyes, hard with defiance, met his. She'd been expecting him.

Rage overwhelmed reason. Tony knocked the glass from her hand and hauled her to her feet. He pulled her so close that his breath mingled with hers.

"You bitch. You lying, murdering bitch."

"Have you lost your mind?"

He pushed the French doors open and dragged her, stumbling and clinging to her walker, into the garden.

"Let me go, damn you. I'm your mother."

"I'm damned *because* you're my mother."

"You're drunk." She raised her good hand to slap him.

He grabbed her wrist. "I just found Dad's bones."

"Let go. You're hurting my arm."

He loosened his grip but didn't release her. "All these years, it's been nothing but lies. Dad's body was missing because you hid it. In my toy box, for Christ's sake. That's why you boarded up his studio."

"You're crazy, drunk and crazy." She maneuvered her walker so that it was between them. "You must have found the skeleton Jim used for his drawings."

"Bullshit."

"Don't you talk to me—"

"I found his bones buried in sand in my toy box."

"Jim was afraid the skeleton would float away in the flood."

"Right, like his body floated away. There was no accident. You made it all up."

"His truck was found in a ditch ten miles south of New Orleans."

"You're lying."

"I have copies of the newspaper articles and the police reports. If you insist, I'll show them to you."

"I saw his skull caved in. Did you lose your temper and take a swing with the first thing you laid hands on? Like you used to beat the hell out of me. Or was it planned? I wouldn't put either past you."

"You're such a fool. How did I kill a man twice my size? And stuff his body in a little chest?"

"I don't know how, but I know you killed him."

"Do you really think I drove his truck into a ditch and then walked ten miles back to town in the middle of a hurricane?"

"I'm not giving up. I'll hire detectives. They'll find proof. There's no statute of limitations for murder. I'll see you hang."

Something akin to fear sparked her eyes. "I swear on my mother's grave that I did not kill your father."

"You'll say anything, won't you?"

"I swear on my mother's grave," she repeated.

All Tony's energy left him. He let go of her wrist—he couldn't bear to touch her—and turned around.

A room full of old people stared at him, their mouths agape. No one spoke or tried to stop him as he strode back through the parlor and out the front door. He didn't know where he was going or what he was going to do, but he could not spend another moment anywhere near the monster who was his mother.

6

Iris Burton left for work a few minutes early. She wanted to stop and buy beignets, a little treat for her favorite patient. Not that she was really a nurse, but aides have patients too, and Geneviève said she was better than the real nurses. "Iris, you're a breath of fresh air," she'd said the first time Iris brought her morning meds.

Iris carried the beignets back to her car, warmed by the bag of pastries and by the appreciative glances from the few tourists out this early on Sunday morning. The other aides, even the real nurses, wore those ugly pant sets that Geneviève said looked like cheap children's pajamas. Iris always wore a proper uniform: a white dress, white stockings, and high-heeled white shoes. Right now, those high heels were killing her feet—she'd waited tables until two last night—but she walked briskly, her head high and the trace of a smile on her face.

So what if she was tired enough to lie down and go to sleep on the sidewalk? Impressions matter. The people noticing her this morning didn't know who she was, but someday everyone would know her name. She'd be driving a big new Mercedes, not her parent's hand-me-down, eight-year-old Chevy Impala. No, better than that. Iris's smile became real. Her chauffer would be driving her limo.

Her parents didn't understand. Last time she talked to them, her father said what he always said about being ready to pay the tuition as soon as she was ready to go back to college. It wasn't as if she'd flunked out. Her mother had signed off with the usual dumb joke about moving back home. "I haven't turned your bedroom into a sewing room, not yet." Iris told Geneviève it made her want to sew her mother's mouth shut.

Geneviève had laughed and said her family never understood either. Geneviève understood. She'd been there and she knew. She warned Iris about men, not her mother's dumb story about free milk and a cow, but from a worldly perspective. "Men have their place," she'd said with a smile and a wink, "but never depend on a man to get you where you want to go. And for God's sake, don't let one knock you up."

She had promised caution, although she had neither a boyfriend nor the time for one. She wasn't living the life she'd imagined, but it was temporary, and she made the best of things. At the Blue Lantern, she practiced acting by adopting different personas for each table. Customers loved it and left good tips. The old people at Sunny Gardens were a less receptive audience. Half of them were too deaf to hear an accent.

She parked in the employee lot and checked her make-up in the rearview. She'd started working here last month, when her parents stopped helping with her rent, and she already dreaded Sunday mornings. Not only did they come after working late on Saturday night, but everything took longer because of all the friends and family either visiting or come to pick someone up for church. She tucked a stray curl under her little white hat and reminded herself to stay positive.

"*Buenos dìas*." She waved to the first person she saw, one of the gardeners who probably really did speak Spanish. She smiled a *bonjour* and a *guten tag* to two women out for a pre-breakfast walk. Although she didn't really know any language but English, she could say hello in several. The first impression is the most important.

At the front door, the security guard said, "How's our little Tower of Babel?"

"Vunderful, yust vunderful." She batted her eyelashes like a sultry Russian spy, and they both laughed.

Iris stowed the beignets in her locker and fetched her cart from the meds closet. She walked down the hall to Geneviève's apartment, singing softly to herself. "Fame. I'm going to live forever." She knocked lightly.

"Good morning, it's Iris."

Other people answered their door looking a mess and wearing frumpy housecoats, but even at seven a.m., Geneviève was dressed with her hair and make-up done. The others griped about this or that when all they were doing was getting old. Geneviève, who'd been thrown from a horse and seriously injured, never complained. This morning, however, she looked pale. Make-up couldn't hide the dark circles under her eyes.

"Are you all right?" Iris asked even though she knew Geneviève would never admit anything was wrong.

"I'm tired. That's all."

"It's nice out." She handed Geneviève her pain pills and a cup of water. "We could have coffee in the garden today. I brought us a treat."

"I don't know."

"I'll check back when I finish. You'll see. Once your meds start working, you'll feel better."

Iris's next stop was Mrs. Benoit, who usually treated her like a piece of furniture. This morning, the stuck-up old grouch actually smiled at her and spoke.

"Did you hear about last night?" Without waiting for an answer, she said, "Geneviève Burke had a big fight with her famous son. He stomped in looking like a bum, grabbed her right out of her chair and hauled her out into the garden. At the cocktail hour, in front of everybody, but no one was close enough to hear what they were saying."

Iris bit her tongue. Her hand itched to slap the smirk off Mrs. Benoit's ugly face.

"They argued for a few minutes. Then he stomped out, and she went back to her apartment. It was like a movie when the lone cowboy rides into the sunset, except she was thumping her walker down the hall."

"No one helped her?"

"It happened so quickly, we were too surprised to move. You would've been too. After he left, people tried to help, but she wanted none of it. She insisted she was fine and refused to call the police—not on her own son. Said he was her cross to bear."

Iris shook her head in dismay. *Poor Geneviève and what a horrible son. He's even worse than she said.*

"Someone sent for Dwight Chastain." Iris didn't want to hear anymore, but Mrs. Benoit wouldn't shut up. "I happened to be in the hall when he tried to talk to her. He's in charge of the whole place, but she wouldn't even open her door, told him to go away all she needed was a moment's peace. Have you seen her this morning?"

"I just gave Mrs. Burke her morning meds. Here are yours."

"I thought she'd open the door for you. You two are thick as thieves. Did she tell you what the argument was about?"

"You know the staff doesn't discuss patients, Mrs. Benoit." She disengaged herself and moved on. She knew nothing about last night, and if she did, she certainly wouldn't tell that nasty old biddy.

At the next apartment, Mr. Pasqua took his usual five minutes to open the door. He either didn't know about the argument or had better manners than to mention it. Several of the other residents were more inclined to snoop, and they all knew she and Geneviève were friends.

Having to evade questions without being openly rude made this Sunday morning even slower than usual, and it was ten-thirty before she finished her rounds. She locked her meds cart back in the closet and hurried into the kitchen.

The fifteen seconds it took the microwave to warm up the beignets felt like an eternity. She fixed a tray, coffee and beignets plus a flower snuck from one of the centerpieces to add a cheerful note. Satisfied that she'd done all she could to make a nice little picnic, she hurried down the hall.

Iris balanced the tray at shoulder height with one hand, like she did when making her way through the tables at the Blue Lantern—a gag pose that always amused Geneviève—and knocked on the door.

"Yoo hoo. Sorry I'm late."

No response.

She knocked harder. Still no response, so she tried the knob. The door was locked. Geneviève must have gotten tired of waiting and gone to get her own coffee.

It's my fault for being so slow.

She left the tray on a hall table and went to check the dining room. She looked in the parlors and took a quick spin through the garden. The gym didn't open until one on Sundays, but just to be sure, she peered through the doors of the weight room, the swimming pool and the sauna. Anxious now, she hurried back to the dining room and asked the servers if anyone had seen Mrs. Burke.

"Not today. She usually comes in for breakfast about seven-thirty," a waiter said. "Of course I could have missed her. It's been crazy, typical Sunday."

"It's not like she hangs around and talks to anyone," another added. "She isn't the world's friendliest person."

Iris gave him an icy glare. "She's friendly to me."

Poor Geneviève. She'd looked so pale. Everyone said her worthless son had manhandled her last night. What if she really was hurt?

Her imagination took flight. What if Geneviève had collapsed in her apartment and was too weak to call out or get to the door? She could have passed out and hit her head on something as she fell. She could be in a life and death situation.

She ran to the office and told the nurse that Mrs. Burke was missing. "We were going to have coffee together, I'm sure she didn't forget, but I can't find her anywhere. I'm afraid she's unconscious in her apartment."

The nurse followed her down the hall and, after confirming that no one answered, unlocked the door with her master key. Impatient and worried, Iris rushed into the apartment.

Geneviève was there. She lay crumpled on the living room floor, one end of her scarf covering her face. Iris knelt and lifted the fabric, an impulse she would regret for the rest of her life.

Blood colored the whites of Geneviève's bulging eyes. Her lips pulled back in a silent scream. The rest of the scarf was wrapped tightly around her neck. Iris clawed at it, trying to pull it off. Geneviève's skin felt cold and strange. Dead.

"No, no, nooooo." Someone kept screaming.

7

Tony called shortly after lunch. "I owe you an explanation."

"Yes, you do," Claire said.

"Not over the phone. Can I come see you? I'd invite you here, but my place is a mess."

"We could meet—"

"This should be a private conversation."

"Okay." Curiosity overcame annoyance, and Tony had a point. If they met in a bar or restaurant, people might recognize him. They'd come over to ask for an autograph or talk about racing. She gave him the address of the Clarke mansion. "Push the button beside the driveway gate, and I'll ring you in. Then follow the drive to the end. I rent their carriage house."

Half an hour later, he stood on her porch, a human wreck. He hadn't shaved and his eyes were bloodshot. Before she could say anything, he held up his hand.

"I know. I look awful. I feel awful. Do you have any vodka?" His words floated on a cloud of alcohol.

She stepped aside to let him enter. "Are you sure you don't want coffee?"

"I'm awake. What I need is a drink." He stopped in the middle of the living room.

"What's the matter?"

"I've been cleaner. You don't want me on your nice white sofa."

No, she didn't. "Why don't you sit on the blue chair?"

"There's a cat in the blue chair, and he looks big enough to do some damage." Tony staggered back, raising his hands in mock fright when Dorian's yawn showed sharp teeth.

"Dorian's harmless." Claire shooed the cat off the chair, and he stalked from the room, vertical tail conveying feline disapproval. The blue chair was Dorian's favorite perch, and sharing is not a cat thing.

"Dorian Gray?" Tony sat down.

"Uh huh."

"That's funny." He didn't laugh. "My dad liked that book. He told me the story, said it was about art revealing truth. I was just a kid, and I didn't understand what he meant, but I thought it was a cool story."

"I read it in college."

"I drank in college, majored in engineering and alcohol. Speaking of which, vodka's my first choice, but I'll be grateful for whatever you have."

"I have vodka. What do you want in it?"

"Three ice cubes. Please. Thank you."

When she handed him the drink, Tony held the clear liquor up to the light and swirled it around. *"Ah my beloved, fill the cup that clears today of past regrets and future fears."* He winked. "The Rubaiyat of Omar Khayyam, it's one of my favorite books."

Claire looked for clues to how much he had been drinking. He wasn't staggering or slurring his words, but he wasn't sober either. "I take it this is a hair of the dog," she said.

He tipped the glass to his mouth, closed his eyes, and let the liquor run down his throat. He repeated the process until the glass was two-thirds empty. "Did you know that vodka is Russian for little water?"

"You wanted to talk to me."

"Did the police ever show up?"

"About an hour after you left."

Two bored officers had followed her around the house. The sight of the skeleton, luminous in the twilight, brought them to attention. They told her that most calls about finding human bones turned out to be the remains of a pet dog that previous residents had buried in the back yard. They started asking questions.

She had answered, feeling increasingly cut off from reality, as if she'd wandered into a stranger's nightmare.

The bones had been in the outbuilding, she'd told them, in that chest with the sand in it. Tony Burke opened it, looking for his childhood toys. That's right, the racecar driver. He owns this house. No, she wasn't one of his girlfriends. Her company was fixing up the house for him. No, he reconstructed the skeleton, not her. No, she didn't know why. He hadn't explained. No, she didn't know where he'd gone. Yes, he appeared to be upset.

"Only an hour?" Tony said. "It must have been a slow night."

"They want to talk to you."

"I went back this morning. Everything was right where I left it." The joking tone had vanished.

"Another call came in, a crime in progress. They said someone would be back, but they didn't know when. So I left."

The policemen had raced off in a flurry of blue lights and screaming sirens If they'd stayed longer, asked more questions, or gone into the studio to see for themselves, she might have shared the possibility that Tony thought the skeleton was his father. She might have suggested that he'd gone to talk to his mother, to demand an explanation because she'd been the one to have the studio boarded up. But those were all conjectures. She'd been a murder suspect based on other people's conjectures, so maybe she wouldn't have said anything.

"I'm sorry about leaving you like that, but you're the one who called them." Tony lifted his now empty glass and rattled the ice cubes. "Be a good girl and get me another little water. Please."

She fixed him a second drink, heavy on the ice cubes. "Where did you go?"

"I went to ask my mother why she killed my father." From his calm tone, he could have been saying that he'd stopped by the drugstore to buy toothpaste.

"I wondered if you'd gone to see her."

"Not see her, confront her." He took another long sip of vodka and rocked back and forth in the chair. "The last time I saw my father was almost twenty-five years ago. He and Geneviève were arguing."

"That doesn't mean she killed him."

Tony pointed at Dorian, who had returned to sit in the doorway and fix him with an unblinking amber stare.

"I don't think your cat likes me. Hey big fellow, I'm friendly." He held his hand out, but Dorian kept his distance.

"You're sitting in his chair and you're rocking. That makes him nervous."

"Nervous as a long-tailed cat in a room full of rocking chairs.'"
Tony half smiled. "Meemaw used down-home expressions all the time. It
drove Geneviève crazy."

"Who's Meemaw?"

"Who's Meemaw?" He pretended shock. "You're not from 'round
here are you?"

"Michigan."

"Meemaw is your maternal grandmother. Mine was widowed. She
spent a lot of time at our house, and after Dad died, she moved in full-
time. Before then she lived with Uncle Will up in Burney. Geneviève's
from Burney, but she doesn't like to admit it." He stood and walked over
to the window.

Claire watched him apprehensively. His humor felt desperate, and
his mood changes were giving her whiplash.

"Meemaw was deathly afraid of hurricanes. Soon as one came into
the Gulf, she'd start nagging us to go up to Uncle Will's. Camille had her
terrified. Dad told her the storm looked to be going east of us, but she
kept fussing. Geneviève told Meemaw to shut up, and Dad told her not to
talk to her mother like that, so she starts yelling at him. After a few
rounds of this, Dad told Meemaw to take me and go. If Camille
threatened New Orleans, they'd follow." He turned back to face her. "My
father carried our stuff out to the car and kissed me good-bye. I never
saw him again."

"I'm sorry." There was nothing else to say. She knew his father had
died during Camille.

He pulled a worn snapshot from his wallet. "This is my dad, four
years before he died." The photo showed a broad-shouldered man sitting
on the floor helping a little boy put a puzzle together. Neither face was
fully visible as they bent over the pieces, intent upon the task, but the
picture captured a closeness that went beyond the physical.

"That's a lovely picture," she said and meant it. "Father and son."

"Meemaw gave it to me. It's the only one I have. " He studied it a
moment before returning it to his wallet. "Do you want to hear the rest of
the story?"

"Yes." Because he wanted to tell it.

"Dad phoned the next day, said they were coming up and should be
there sometime late afternoon. When they didn't show up, Meemaw
called the house, but nobody answered. It was dark out when Geneviève
finally walked in. Everyone asked her where she'd been and where was

Jim. She says traffic's terrible and Jim's helping a friend get his boat out of the water. He'll be right along.

"She went to bed, but Meemaw and I sat up waiting. The wind was blowing hard. A big tree went over in the yard, it didn't hit the house, but it knocked out the electricity." He turned back to the window and rested his forehead against the glass.

Claire wanted to walk over and hug him, but she didn't quite dare. He was telling her an intimate story but also holding himself at a distance. She waited, without speaking, for him to continue.

"The storm passed, and Geneviève went back to New Orleans. Meemaw and I stayed with Uncle Will for a few more days, a week at most, I don't remember. When we got home, Geneviève told me Dad was gone. They found his truck, but he'd been washed away."

"I can see why you think we found your father, but you don't know for sure."

He brushed her words aside. "You know what seals the deal? My trains. I brought my favorite engine to Uncle Will's house and left the rest in my toy box out in the studio. When I got back home, my trains were in a cardboard box in the laundry room, and the studio was boarded up."

Claire tried to find an alternative explanation but could only come up with possible extenuating circumstances. "It looked as if death came from a blow to the head. It might have been an accident."

"When I told Geneviève about finding the paintings, she went nuts. She screamed and cried, ordered me to put the boards back and never go near the studio again. I thought she was getting senile, but then I found Dad." He drained his glass. "That bottle's not empty yet, is it?"

"Let me get you some coffee and something to eat."

"I'm not hungry."

"You should talk to the police. I know the head of homicide. His name is Mike Robinson. He's a nice guy."

"No hurry. Dad's not going anywhere, and Geneviève has nowhere to go." He collapsed back into the chair and slumped forward, his chin on his chest.

"Tony? Are you okay?"

He lifted his head as if he was going to say something, but no words emerged. His eyes closed, and he slid from the chair to the floor, where he remained half-sitting, half-sprawled. Definitely not okay.

Dorian walked over and sniffed the unconscious man. He looked up at Claire, cat scorn on his face.

"Come on Dorian, give the guy a break."

She held on to Tony's shoulders and worked him around until he was lying on the floor. Then she put a pillow under his head, removed his shoes, and covered him with an afghan. Who knew how much alcohol he'd consumed before he got to her house. She hoped he wouldn't be a sick drunk.

Sometime around eight, Tony woke long enough to use the bathroom and drink a glass of water. He was in no condition to drive, so she made up the sofa.

8

Captain Mike Robinson started this Monday like every other, in the office by six. He fixed a pot of coffee and began reviewing reports of the weekend carnage. Drunkenness, drug dealing, gang warfare, and domestic strife had taken their toll. Seven people dead between six Friday evening and midnight Sunday—a new high. In a deviation from the usual pattern, one of the domestics involved mother and son rather than husband and wife.

Detectives Smith and Monroe caught the call, and according to their notes, it wasn't the usual no-question-who-did-it domestic homicide. Despite witness statements that the victim's son publicly manhandled her early Saturday evening, no one had considered the incident worth reporting. She hadn't appeared to be injured, an interpretation supported by the fact that she was alive and well Sunday morning when an aide brought her morning medications. Moreover, no one saw her son on the premises after their Saturday evening argument.

One glance at the crime scene photos told Mike that death resulted from strangulation, not a delayed result of whatever happened the night before. The door to the victim's apartment had been locked, and there was no indication of forced entry. A team from the Crime Scene Unit had found multiple fingerprints and fibers. Those analyses would filter in over the next couple weeks. He turned to the interviews and was surprised to find only three.

The first was with one of the people who discovered the body. A nurse employed by the assisted living facility had unlocked the apartment at the urging of an aide, a young woman named Iris Burton, the same one who'd brought the meds earlier. The aide was friendly with the victim and had become hysterical upon finding the body. She was under a doctor's care and would have to be interviewed later. The nurse had little to report beyond finding the body and confirming recent death.

Monroe had conducted a group interview of thirty some witnesses to the mother-son argument. That session degenerated into a verbal lynch mob as people vied to condemn the son in ever-harsher terms. To make matters worse, none of the quotes were attributed to a named individual. Any competent defense lawyer—hell, any first-year law student—would see every bit of this thrown out.

Smith had done no better. He'd learned that the victim had recently been involved in a confrontation with another resident, a man suffering from senile dementia. He'd questioned that individual with no guardian present. This interview, which should not have occurred, ended with the man's collapse and an incriminating statement that would never be admitted in any legal proceeding.

No one had made a serious effort to find the son, a man named Tony Burke. The manager of Sunny Gardens had phoned Burke, intending to inform him that his mother was dead, but had not been able to reach him. A patrol car sent to his house found no one home, nor did it appear that he was actually living there.

Disgusted, Mike closed the file. Smith and Monroe worked for him, but layers of seniority and connections protected them from any serious disciplinary action. Suspending either or both would use up big chunks of time and political capital. They weren't worth it. His best option was to chew them out, put memos in their files, and reassign the case. He decided to give lead responsibility to his newest detective.

Until recently, Beatrice Washington had been a uniformed officer riding around in a black and white. Superintendent Vernon, who personally intervened to secure her promotion, said she was sharp as a tack. Cynics said Vernon was sucking up to the politicians and their diversity agendas. Black and female, Beatrice Washington was a two-fer. Mike hadn't seen enough of her to form an opinion. She'd been learning the ropes and assisting where needed. There'd been no problems so far, and this already muddled case would be a good test.

She'd need a partner. Mike checked the roster and saw that Bill Lukas had a relatively light load. A solid and experienced investigator, Bill would be a good choice to work with Detective Washington on her first case. He left messages on her voicemail and on Bill's, asking them to call him as soon as they got in, and picked up the next file. Minutes later, Beatrice Washington knocked on his door.

"I got your message, sir. I was at my desk, but my phone isn't working. Incoming calls go straight to voicemail, and I can't call out."

"Come on in. We can talk now."

"Yes, sir." She folded her lanky frame into a chair.

Detective Washington looked like a college basketball player, but according to her file, she was thirty-two years old, and her college degree had been earned with six years of night school.

"How long has your phone been out of order?" he said.

"It's never worked, sir."

"I'll look into it." There was no excuse, but there was a likely explanation. "Let me know if you have any more problems."

"Yes, sir, but I don't want to cause trouble."

"I'll make it clear the complaint originates with me." He'd also make it very clear to the good old boys that harassing their new colleague would not be tolerated.

"Thank you, sir."

"Here's your first case." He handed her the file. "Because you came in early, you have time to familiarize yourself with it before the staff meeting."

She glanced at the summary and looked up, wide-eyed. "Tony Burke?"

"Do you know him?"

"I know who he is." Her mouth turned up at the corners, the beginnings of a smile quickly concealed. "You must not read gossip columns, follow Grand Prix racing, or buy fancy cars. Sir."

"Right on all counts. But now that you mention it, his name rings a bell. Tell me why."

"Tony Burke drives racecars for Ferrari and dates beautiful women, models and actresses." She rolled her eyes. "One after another and half of them married to other men."

"Does he live here?"

"Tony grew up in New Orleans. He moved to Italy years ago, but now he's come back and bought a car dealership."

"And gotten mixed up in a homicide."

If Mike had realized their prime suspect was a celebrity, he wouldn't have assigned the lead investigative role to a rookie. Because taking it back would be interpreted as a vote of no confidence, he let the assignment stand. But he modified his staffing plan. "It's your first case, and I'll work with you. My time is limited, so tell me if you need more resources, and I'll assign another detective to work with us." He hoped her rapid promotions had been based on merit and not political expediency.

"Yes sir."

"And now that we're partners, why don't you call me Mike."

An hour later, she stood in the door to his office, holding a file. "Excuse me, sir. I found something that might shed light on Tony Burke's confrontation with his mother."

He glanced at the clock. Five of eight, they had thirty-five minutes until the homicide division's Monday morning staff meeting. He waved Beatrice to a seat. "What did you find?"

"Late Saturday afternoon, a woman named Claire Marshall reported finding human remains on property belonging to Tony Burke. The patrol officers confirmed it."

He held out his hand. "Let me see."

How many women named Claire Marshall lived in New Orleans? According to the report this one was a thirty-four-year-old Caucasian about five-eight and 125 pounds, with red hair and green eyes. He would have described her hair as auburn or, when the sun caught it, copper. He scanned the incident report.

"The timeframe fits," Beatrice said.

"That it does." He turned the pages over to see if he had missed something but found no mention of impounding the remains, no effort to contact Tony Burke, no follow-up of any kind. Smith and Monroe didn't have a monopoly on shoddy work.

"Well done, Beatrice. How'd you find this so quickly?"

"I told some guys I used to work with that I had my first case, and it involved Tony Burke. They told me they'd answered a call at a house he owned, and I asked to see the report."

"Did you tell them to get over there ASAP and secure the scene?"

"Yes, sir." She bit her lip. "I hope this isn't going to cause any problems for anyone."

"Not unless I read about this incident in the papers. In which case, heads will roll. Pass it on."

"Yes, sir."

"And get an Crime Scene team to Burke's house, this morning if possible. If it's really been twenty-five years, they probably won't find anything, but it's a starting point."

Monday morning and he was already up to his neck in compromise and bad news. He sent Beatrice on her way and called Detectives Smith and Monroe into his office. He had just enough time to chew them out before the staff meeting.

Mike was wrapping up the staff meeting when Superintendent Vernon walked in, a sour expression on his face. "Smith, Monroe, don't go anywhere." He turned to Mike. "I want to discuss their response to the Geneviève Burke homicide."

"It was unsatisfactory."

"Tell me something I don't already know."

"They're off the case. I've assigned it to Detective Washington. I'll be working it with her."

"Then she better stay, too."

Although Mike wasn't a Henry Vernon fan, he sympathized with the man responsible for making the police department look good when every indicator pointed in the wrong direction. Crime was up, clearance rates were down, and officers kept getting caught on the wrong side of the law. The drug dealers had more and better weapons than the police. Street slang for Uptown was *Chopper City*, after the AK-47s and M-16s chattering in the night. Vernon must feel like Sisyphus, rolling a rock uphill every day and knowing it was going to roll back down overnight. But that neither justified nor excused micromanagement.

"I've already spoken to Detectives Smith and Monroe," he said.

"I'm sure you did, Mike, but you're new here, and there are issues you might not be aware of." Vernon took a packet of chewing gum out of his pocket, unwrapped a piece and shoved it into his mouth. He chewed savagely, all the while glaring at the two detectives. The tension in the air lessened only slightly when he finally spoke.

"Monroe, you had your eye on the door the whole goddamn time you were there. Since when do we conduct group interviews? In a homicide! Was your Sunday dinner getting cold?"

"No, sir," Monroe said.

"The victim was seen alive a little after seven. Her body was found shortly before eleven. We're looking at a window of less than four hours. Did anyone notice?" When neither Monroe nor Smith responded, he repeated the question.

"Yes, sir. We did," Monroe said, "and we talked about it."

"Really. What did you say?"

Vernon's tone should have warned him, but Monroe plowed ahead. "Seven come eleven, but it wasn't a lucky roll for the old lady."

"Life is a crap shoot," Smith added helpfully.

Incredulous, Vernon looked from one to the other. "You think that's funny?" He added another stick of gum to the wad in his mouth before returning to the attack. "Why, Detective Monroe, do I see no indication that you asked what people were doing or what they observed during those four hours?"

Without giving Monroe a chance to defend himself, Vernon shifted his attention. "Smith, you make Monroe look brilliant. You were told that Roger Devereux was legally incompetent, but you couldn't wait for his doctor to show up, much less his legal guardian. You browbeat a senile old man who just happens to belong to one of this city's leading families. Have you ever heard of Devereux Chemicals? Devereux Petroleum? Devereux Engineering?" With each corporate name, Vernon's face grew redder and his attack on the chewing gum, more ferocious.

Mike gritted his teeth. The case file for the Burke homicide described the sort of sloppy police work that made the whole department look bad. Smith and Monroe deserved criticism, but delivering it was his job. And he had. He glanced at Beatrice to see how she was coping. She was staring, her expression impassive, at the table. He caught her eye, saw a glimpse of despair, and understood.

"Excuse me, sir," he said to Vernon. "Detective Washington and I would be happy to come back when you're ready to talk to us." The Super would resent the challenge to his authority, but he had to speak up for his new detective's sake. Smith and Monroe would be slow to forgive her for witnessing their disgrace. Young, black, female, and new to homicide, she had a tough enough road without that.

"I want you to hear this, too, both of you," Vernon said, but he dialed it back. In a calmer voice, he assured Smith that the Devereux Family was on a first name basis with both the Mayor and the Governor and wouldn't hesitate to accuse him of abusing Roger. The manager of Sunny Gardens would be happy to back them up. "But you are one lucky SOB. The Devereux family can't go after you without revealing their connection to the victim." He looked around the table. "Anyone know what that connection is?"

When no one hazarded a guess, Vernon told them. "Geneviève might be an old lady today." He flicked Monroe a dirty look. "But she was hot stuff back in the fifties and sixties. Beautiful and wild before wild became the new normal. Of course, that was after her divorce. Anyone want to guess who she divorced?" This time he didn't wait for an answer. "Roger Devereux."

Mike raised his eyebrows. "That was a long time ago."

"Forty years, which is ancient history to the children of the media." Vernon's lip curled in contempt. "Reporters run in a pack, gangbanging the obvious. No one will discover the Devereux connection, unless the investigation drags on and some lucky idiot trips over it. For a change, time is on our side, but it won't stay there forever." He pounded on the table. "I want a fast resolution. We have a suspect. Everyone told you Tony Burke killed his mother. Smith and Monroe, you knocked on his front door, and when he didn't answer, you went on home."

"His house is being rehabbed," Smith said. "We got the company's name off their sign. We'll call them this morning."

"Last I heard you and Monroe were off the case."

"They are," Mike said.

"Then get the hell out of here." Vernon tore the wrapper from another piece of gum. "Mike and I have things to discuss."

Smith and Monroe jostled each other in their hurry to get out the door.

Mike put a hand on Beatrice's arm, letting her know she should stay. "Detective Washington has found additional information."

This time, Vernon listened without interrupting. Only the increasing speed of his gum chewing revealed his emotions. When Beatrice finished, he said, "Claire Marshall. It doesn't rain but it pours."

"The responding officers have been warned not to discuss the call, and I'm sure Claire doesn't want her name in the paper." Nor did Vernon. The Frank Palmer-Claire Marshall fiasco was only a few months in the past. Vernon had put himself center stage when the investigation appeared to be going well, and he was stuck in the spotlight when it went very wrong. No matter how short their collective attention span, the media would remember.

"Have you talked to her yet?"

"No. Detective Washington learned of Claire's involvement just this morning." He'd been debating whether to call himself or have Beatrice do it. Vernon's assumption, tipped it. He and Claire had a history, possibly a future. He'd make the call.

"Good luck." Vernon's sardonic smile said luck would be needed.

"And good luck finding Tony Burke. He could have left the country by now."

"He's unpopular at Sunny Gardens, but—" Mike began.

Vernon raised both hands in mock surrender. "I read the file. We don't know if Tony Burke killed his mother or not, and I'm trusting you not to jump the gun. If we arrest him, he'll hire ten slick lawyers, and the media will be on our doorstep twenty-four seven. We don't move against him until we have an ironclad case."

9

Claire sprinted to get the phone before it woke Tony. She recognized Mike's hello, and a smile spread across her face. She'd been afraid he'd never call again. It would have been her fault.

"How nice to hear from you." She said. "How've you been?"

"I'm calling on police business. We're looking for one of your clients, a man named Tony Burke."

"He's here, but he's still asleep." She felt like a fool.

After Claire hung up, it occurred to her that things must be unusually quiet in New Orleans if the head of homicide was investigating twenty-five-year-old human remains. Hope rekindled. Mike could be using this as an excuse to see her again. She went into the living room and leaned over the sofa.

"Wake up, Tony. It's almost ten."

"I don't care." His voice scraped like gravel.

"The police want to talk to you. They're on the way."

He sat up. "Do I have time for a shower?"

"I've put out clean towels. Coffee will be ready by the time you're finished."

He asked for a Coke with lots of ice and carried it with him into the bathroom.

Tony wasn't the only one who needed to clean up. Claire changed from jeans and a work shirt into nice slacks and the new green silk blouse that brought out the color of her eyes. Her make-up was in the bathroom with Tony, so she had to make do with combing her hair and putting on fresh lipstick.

Her living room reeked of stale alcohol. She opened the windows and started to clear the sofa but changed her mind and left the sheets right where they were. There had been an awkward pause on the phone after she said Tony was still asleep. She'd been too irritated with herself to clarify the situation. And exactly what would she have said?

She pushed the button to open the driveway gate then carried her orange juice outside to wait on the porch. "Mike called. Big deal. It's Tony he wants to see, not me. He took me out a few times because he felt sorry for me, just like I feel sorry for Tony." She said it aloud to prove to herself that she'd be fine if it were true.

Dorian, who had followed her out, wasn't listening. He had turned into a cat statue, his attention focused on a male cardinal that was eating from her bird feeder.

"Don't even think about it." Her voice startled the bird, which flew off in a flash of red.

She picked Dorian up and settled him on her lap. He allowed her to scratch behind his ears briefly then hopped down to investigate a rustle in the bushes.

The cardinal returned to the feeder. The dowdier female would be around somewhere. Cardinals mated for life, and this pair, frequent visitors to her feeder, lived in a big oak behind the carriage house. Claire watched him peck at the seeds and, for maybe the tenth time, replayed her last date with Mike.

They'd been at Sweet Lorraine's, chatting while they waited for the musicians to return from break. She became conscious of his hand close to hers on the table, so close that she felt its warmth. Something inside her froze. As if it had a will of its own, her hand slid back onto her lap and stayed there. Mike didn't seemed to notice, but of course he did. After the next set, he took her home, thanked her for a nice evening and wished her a Merry Christmas—four weeks early.

She should have said something. She could have told him that she really liked him and enjoyed his company and maybe wanted to be more than friends. Someday. But she just wasn't ready yet.

The next morning she'd thought about calling him to explain and ask for his understanding. He knew she'd had a hard time since her husband died, that it had been only sixteen months. He might have understood, might have been patient with her. She had lifted the receiver more than once but each time put it down without dialing. She'd never called. Nor had he, until now...

An unmarked police car crunched down the gravel drive and

stopped in front of her porch. Mike emerged from the driver's side. His dark hair, a little longer than the last time she'd seen him, curled against his shirt collar. Sunglasses hid his eyes, but she remembered their intense, almost electric, blue. She liked and respected him, trusted him implicitly, and enjoyed his company. How long would the space left inside her when Tom died stay cold and empty?

The passenger door opened and a slender African-American woman appeared. In her high heels, she was taller than Mike's six feet. They walked up the steps together, and he introduced her as Detective Beatrice Washington.

"Bea," the detective said with a wide smile.

Claire offered them coffee or juice, which both refused. "I hope you don't mind if I finish my juice out here. My living room smells like a flophouse." She sat in the swing and gestured toward the rocking chairs. "Have a seat."

"Is Burke still here?" Mike said. Neither sat down.

"He's in the shower." She could hear the water running. They must hear it too. Not one but two investigators, it really was police business. "I guess this is about the skeleton?"

"You're working on Burke's house?" Mike said.

Answer my question with one of your own. Just like old times. "We were. I called everyone off the project to give you time to get those bones out of there." Jack had been horrified when she explained the reason for the delay. If the demolition crew glimpsed the skeleton, they'd walk off the job and never come back.

"Can you tell us any more than you told the responding officers Saturday afternoon?"

"I'd rather let Tony do the talking." She pushed the railing with her foot, setting the swing in motion. "I'm surprised old bones are getting such high-level attention."

No one offered an explanation. Moments later, a loud clank signaled that the hot water had been turned off.

"Old plumbing," Claire said. She stood up, opened the front door, and gestured for them to enter. "Please make yourselves comfortable. I'll tell Tony you're here."

"We have some bad news for him." Mike said.

Bad news? What could be worse than thinking your mother had murdered your father. She knocked on the bathroom door. "Tony, the police are here, and your coffee's ready. How do you want it?"

"Hot and black, please."

She poured a cup and carried it into the living room. Mike and Bea were sitting in the two chairs, which left only the sofa with its crumpled sheets. She put Tony's coffee down.

"I'll be outside. Let me know if you need anything."

"Don't leave, Claire, please. I could use some moral support." Tony walked in looking amazingly good, clean-shaven, eyes clear, and hair combed. He winked at her. "I owe you a fresh razor blade."

The implied intimacy brought color to her cheeks. She pictured Tony rummaging around in her bathroom and outrage joined embarrassment. She couldn't look at Mike or Bea. Apparently oblivious to her reaction, Tony pushed the sheets onto the floor and sat down. Too angry to speak, she sat as far from him as possible, which wasn't far. He'd sat in the middle, and it wasn't a big sofa.

Mike introduced himself and his partner. No first names now, it was Mr. Burke, Detective Washington. "I'm afraid we have bad news for you, Mr. Burke."

"Bad news?"

"Yes." Mike paused. "Your mother died yesterday morning."

"Geneviève's dead? What happened? She was healthy Saturday night."

"She was murdered."

Tony stared into his coffee cup. All irritation forgotten, Claire tried to imagine what he must be feeling. His relationship with Geneviève had been strained, but she was still his mother.

"I'm so sorry, Tony."

"Would you like a few moments to gather your thoughts?" Mike said.

"No, I'm okay. It's a shock—death is—but my mother and I weren't close. Claire can tell you, we didn't even like each other."

She winced. She'd never heard Tony or Geneviève say a kind word about the other, but she didn't really know either of them and didn't want to judge their relationship.

To her relief, Mike changed the subject. "We have some questions for you." When Tony nodded, he said, "Let's start with Saturday afternoon. You and Claire found human remains."

"If you have time, I'd rather start at the beginning."

Tony repeated the story of his father's disappearance and his mother's sealing the studio. Mike asked an occasional question. Bea observed and took notes. Claire wanted to leave, but Tony kept reaching over and touching her as if she was some kind of talisman. He kept his hand on hers as he described finding the bones.

"I realized they were Dad, and I knew Geneviève had killed him. I drove to Sunny Gardens." He grimaced. "I'm sure you've heard about our conversation. It was heated, and we had a large audience."

"We'd like to hear your side of the story," Mike said.

"It's not complicated. I accused. She denied. I left. The end." He finished the last of his coffee, put the mug down and massaged his temples.

"Did you have any contact with your mother after that?"

"No. I went back to the apartment and started drinking. I should say started drinking seriously. Earlier, Claire and I had a beer to celebrate finding Dad's paintings." He rubbed his temples again. "Hard to believe that was the same day."

"And yesterday morning?"

I woke up around noon and drank some more. Then I came over here. He gestured toward the crumpled sheets. "Claire was kind enough to let me spend the night on her sofa."

"You spent the last thirty-six hours either drinking or sleeping it off?" Bea's question shaded into rebuke.

Mike gave his partner a sharp look. "Mr. Burke, do you know of anyone who might wish your mother harm?"

"Harm? Lots of people. But you're really asking who might have killed her." Tony picked up the coffee mug, realized it was empty, and stared into it as if looking for truth in the dregs.

"Saturday night, when I confronted her, Geneviève pointed out that she couldn't have driven dad's truck into the ditch, left it there, and gotten back to New Orleans by herself. Nor could she have maneuvered his body in my toy chest. He was a big man, my size." He looked up. "All of that is true, but it doesn't make her innocent. It means she had help. Her accomplice would have been a man, probably a lover. That's who killed her."

Bea started to say something, Mike shook his head and she closed her mouth.

"I can guess what happened," Tony continued. "Geneviève told him I'd found Dad's bones. They'd gotten away with murder for twenty-five years, but the jig was up." He took a deep breath and let it out slowly.

"She would have told him to kill me. She'd know that was the only way to shut me up. Instead, he killed her."

Mike broke the stunned silence. "That's quite an accusation."

"Look at it from his perspective. She's the one who can identify him, not me. I don't have a clue who he is."

"I meant accusing your mother of trying to arrange your murder."

"Really? She killed my father. You think I might have killed her. You don't appear to have many illusions about human behavior." Tony's flat stare challenged Mike to disagree. "If I were you, I'd check her phone calls. Anything after four o'clock Saturday when I told her I'd been in the studio."

Listening, Claire felt like an intruder in her own living room, a spectator on an intimate drama she had no right to observe. Tony had moved his hand from her arm, and she took the opportunity to get up. She walked over to the window and watched the birds at her feeder, blocking out what anyone was saying until a sharp tone caught her attention.

Bea was asking Tony questions, referring to her notes, bearing down on details, and demanding proof. Could anyone confirm his activities after he left Sunny Gardens Saturday evening? Was there anyone who might have seen him Sunday morning between seven and eleven o'clock? Mike stayed on the sidelines and, when he did speak, used a sympathetic tone.

Their interplay reminded Claire of how she'd been treated when she was a murder suspect. The police went after the closest person, someone plausible to accuse, and then they tried to find incriminating evidence. That's what they'd done with her. Mike had played the good cop then, too. Was being the good guy a privilege of rank? She turned to face them.

"Excuse me. Are you almost finished?"

Everyone looked at her.

"I have an appointment," she said.

"Just a few more minutes and we'll be out of your hair." Mike spoke in his official voice, wore his official face, and acted as if they'd just met. Next he'd be calling her Ms. Marshall. He was a policeman first and a human being second. How could she have thought that they might someday be more than friends?

"Okay." She kept glancing at her watch until he and Bea left.

"Thank you seems inadequate," Tony said, "but that's all I've got." He carried the coffee cup into the kitchen. "I'm on my way. Don't let me make you late for your appointment."

"There isn't one. I just wanted them to leave. I'd had enough. Hadn't you?"

"They expected me to care that my mother was killed. Or at least pretend to care." He walked over to the window. "A bird feeder. I wondered what you were looking at. Did I tell you about the mockingbird?"

"I don't think so."

"It was trapped by the boards covering one of the windows and died on the sill. Another of Geneviève's victims." He stared into the middle distance, just as he'd done when he found her looking at the studio. "I know it sounds off the wall, but I believe my dad's soul was trapped, too. In his studio, along with his art. Do you think I'm crazy?"

"No." The studio had felt haunted.

"I'm going to show those pictures to the world," he said. "Howard will help me. I can't do anything about Geneviève, but I'll find her accomplice. Twenty-five years isn't that long a time. Someone knows who she was seeing, who her friends were. The trick is finding that someone."

"When I visited, she mentioned photographs showing the artists and writers who were their friends. They might be in a sideboard up in your attic."

"She told you about *Chez Geneviève* and how her life was wonderful until I came along?"

"That's not exactly what she said."

"Close though. Don't look so guilty, sweetheart. I've heard it a million times."

"If you can find those photos, you could give them to the police. And I bet they'll check her phone calls."

"They're not looking anywhere but at me. You heard them."

"If there's anything I can do to help." She raised her hands in a hopeless gesture.

"How about some more coffee?"

"How about a real breakfast?" She hadn't heard anything about eating in his recital of yesterday's activities. "Are you hungry?"

"Starved."

10

Mike drove slowly up the driveway, reluctant to leave Claire alone with Tony Burke, which was ridiculous. She'd just spent the night with the man.

"What do you think?" he said.

"Claire was lying about the appointment."

"Let's find out." He drove halfway down the block, turned in a driveway, and parked looking back at Claire's driveway. "I was asking what you thought of Tony Burke."

"I don't know. I've seen him on TV, climbing out of his racecar, pulling off his helmet and grinning, pretty girls hanging on him while he holds a trophy in one hand and a foaming bottle of champagne in the other. Tony Burke on top of the world, the man who has everything." She shrugged. "This morning blew all that away."

"Forget before. What did you observe this morning?" His dislike of Burke had been immediate and visceral. He usually went with his gut, but this time he wasn't confident of his objectivity. Watching Burke with his hands all over Claire had been hard.

"That I didn't expect?" She thought a moment. "First, intelligence. He's smart and articulate. Arrogant might be unfair, but he makes his own rules. And he has no more illusions about human behavior than you do. If he's our killer, we've got our work cut out."

"The story of his father's disappearance, do you think that was a performance?"

"It will be easy enough to check, but no, I think it was genuine. That doesn't mean his story is true. Memory is tricky, and he was a child." She chuckled. "He certainly knows how to make an entrance. Did you see Claire's face when he said he'd used her razor? Lucky for him we were there."

"You did a nice job."

"I didn't enjoy playing the heavy, and he really resented it." She frowned. "Do you think he's right about his mother killing his father?"

"We have a concealed body with a fractured skull. It looks like homicide, but we haven't identified the victim, forget any suspects."

"Two murders twenty-five years apart," she said. "Where do we start?"

"The recent one. Concentrate on Geneviève Burke, starting with everything she did after four o'clock on Saturday."

"As Tony suggested."

"We're not going to ignore good advice no matter the source." Personal feelings had no place in a homicide investigation. "Ask residents and staff at Sunny Gardens where they were during the four-hour window Sunday morning. That's a lot of interviews, and I'll assign Bill Lukas to help you. Stay away from Roger Devereux. I'll handle him. As for the bones, I'm going to put Smith and Monroe on them." The assignment would combine the punishment of wading through old records with a chance to redeem themselves if, as seemed likely, the two murders were related.

"I don't want to step on anyone's toes, but what if Bill and I work from both ends?" He gave her a quizzical look and she explained. "Ask the other residents when they met the victim. Did they know her back in the day? Do they remember any gossip about her?"

"Good idea." It was a very good idea and, he hoped, an indication that Detective Washington was as sharp as Vernon had promised.

He called the office, briefed Bill Lukas, and asked him to meet them at Sunny Gardens in half an hour. He left messages for Smith and Monroe to meet him in his office at three. By the time he finished, fifteen minutes had passed since they left Claire's house. Neither she nor Burke had driven out the gate. He pulled away from the curb.

"You're right," he said. "She lied."

"But she's not sleeping with him, and she wanted you to know."

"Why do you say that?" Claire hadn't flinched when Burke put his hand on her arm, her shoulder, even her knee.

"Everything was tidy except for the sheets on the sofa. She knew we were coming, she had plenty of time to clear them off, but she didn't. The only reason to leave them was to show us where Tony spent the night."

Mike caught her fleeting smile. His new detective had either sensed or been told that he and Claire had a history. Whether or not they had a future was up in the air, but he wanted to believe Bea was right about the sleeping arrangements.

"What's waiting for us at Sunny Gardens?" he said.

"I faxed over the list of names from the group interview with a note saying we wanted to talk to each person individually and would also be interviewing staff members. The manager—his name is Dwight Chastain—called back. He and his staff will do all they can to assist in our investigation. However, he hopes it won't be necessary to disturb Roger Devereux again."

"Devereux is my problem," Mike said. "You and Bill take care of the others."

Lushly landscaped grounds surrounded an L-shaped mid-rise building. Sunny Gardens looked more like an upscale apartment complex than an assisted living community. Mike parked in a space designated for visitors and followed signs to the main entrance. A balding middle-aged man with a decided paunch intercepted them at the door. After introducing himself, Dwight Chastain said they'd set up two interview rooms as requested. His assistant would show them the way.

"The second interview room will be used by Detective Lukas, who will be here shortly," Mike said. "I'm looking for information about Roger Devereux. Can you tell me how to contact his guardian?"

"The family was afraid this would happen." Chastain stuck out his lower lip, and his already downturned mouth became an inverted U. "Their attorney is in my office."

Bea left with the assistant, and Mike followed Chastain to an office behind the elevators. Paul Gilbert was inside, talking on a mobile phone. His well-groomed presence both reinforced Vernon's warning about the Devereux family's position in the community and raised new questions. Did Gilbert, and by extension the Devereux family, realize the seriousness of the situation? Paul specialized in defusing scandal, not criminal defense.

Chastain started to introduce them, and Paul said they'd met.

"It's nice to see you again, Mike. I only wish it were under more auspicious circumstances." They shook hands, and Paul explained his presence. "Roger Devereux's niece is his legal guardian. I'm her personal attorney and here at her request. I've known Roger all my life. He and my father have been friends since grade school. Of course, now..." He shook his head.

"I'd like to interview Mr. Devereux. Is now convenient?"

"Roger has been declared legally incompetent. I've been told that he was distraught after the first interview. I wouldn't be doing my job if I didn't question the need for a second."

"The Police Department is aware of his condition and sensitive to it, but we're conducting a homicide investigation. There's no alternative, Paul, and if this is a good time."

"As good as any."

Chastain led them to the elevator. Once inside, he pointed to a keypad beside the door and a sign saying the Memory Garden code was DD-MM-YY. "The elevator won't open on the fourth floor until you enter the correct code. This system allows access while maintaining the security of our residents, all of whom suffer from dementia severe enough to require round-the-clock care."

"According to a report in your files, Roger Devereux left the fourth floor on his own last Wednesday," Mike said.

"Neither Roger nor any other Memory Garden resident has the capacity to translate those directions into the proper code, and no one on my staff took him out." Chastain wiped sweat from his forehead. "There are fire stairs, but if those doors are opened, an alarm sounds. The alarm did not go off Wednesday."

"But Devereux did leave the fourth floor." Mike reminded him.

"The Devereux family is extremely concerned about the recent incident, and so am I," Chastain said. "If our insurance company ever decided our security was inadequate, they'd cancel our liability coverage. We'd be out of business that day."

"What did your insurance company say about the murder of a resident in her locked apartment?"

Their arrival at the fourth floor saved Chastain the embarrassment of answering. He punched in the date, and the elevator doors opened onto a large room with a glass-enclosed office at its center. On the left, a dozen elderly people dozed in wheelchairs arranged in a semicircle in front of a TV. On the screen, a young Julie Andrews skipped across an alpine meadow. The area to the right was set up for dining with plastic chairs at square tables for four. Vaguely Italian food odors lingered from the noon meal.

A stocky, dark-skinned woman wearing lavender scrubs emerged from the office. Chastain introduced her as Tamika, lead caretaker for the Memory Garden. Round eyes and a wide mouth that tilted up at the ends gave Tamika an amiable appearance, but her expression hardened when Chastain explained the reason for their presence.

"Roger is in his room," she said. "Resting."

"Please take Mr. Gilbert and Captain Robinson to see him." Chastain retreated to the elevator. "I'll be in my office if you need me."

Her gait stiff with disapproval, Tamika led them down a wide, carpeted hallway. Most of the doors were closed, but the last one on the right stood half open. Inside, an elderly man sat in an armchair beside the window. The people not watching television had worn sweatpants, jogging clothes, or bathrobes; this man was dressed in a businessman's suit and tie, wearing shoes not slippers. Tamika rapped on the doorframe.

"Roger, you have visitors."

Roger Devereux turned to look at her but didn't speak. His empty expression contradicted the initial impression of normalcy.

Tamika stepped aside, and they walked in. Paul sat on the bed, leaving Mike the other chair, and Tamika stood sentry beside the door. Roger returned his gaze to the window. Paul broke the ice.

"Hello Roger. It's Paul Gilbert. How are you today?"

"I think it might rain."

Paul made repeated attempts at conversation, but Roger Devereux showed no interest in anything but the weather. When Paul conveyed his father's best wishes, Roger looked worried for a moment then, once again, pointed out the dark clouds gathering on the horizon.

Mike cleared his throat—they didn't have all day.

Paul took the hint. "Roger, I'd like you to meet my friend, Mike Robinson. Mike works for the New Orleans Police Department."

Devereux ducked his head between his shoulders and turned away, muttering something about being tired.

"Mike wants to talk to you. It will only take a few minutes."

"I'm going to bed." Roger stood up, still averting his gaze, and started to remove his jacket.

Tamika stepped forward. "It's not time to get undressed, Roger. Please sit back down." She settled him in the chair.

"I'd like to ask you a few questions about Geneviève," Mike said.

Roger lurched to his feet. "No, no, no," he cried. "Don't say that."

He grabbed Tamika by the shoulders and shook her as if she were a rag doll.

Immediately, Mike was on his feet and behind Roger. He put the man in a hammerlock, forcing him to release Tamika who fell back against the wall. Paul leapt to her assistance. She brushed him off and pushed a button by the door.

"Let him go. You're hurting him." She glared at Mike. "I've called for support."

"No-one is hurting anyone." Mike maintained his hold until two orderlies hurried into the room.

Released, Roger collapsed onto the bed. "I'm sorry." Sobs shook his body. "I'm so sorry. I didn't mean to hurt you. Get up. Please get up."

"Go. Just go." Tamika pointed to the door. "Let us take care of our patient."

Mike and Paul returned to the main room, leaving the staff to settle Roger. A few residents looked at them curiously, but most ignored them. Paul smoothed his jacket and straightened his tie as if they'd been rumpled by his proximity to the struggle.

"You and I both know any statement Roger made is inadmissible as evidence," he said.

"Has anyone told you that he said essentially the same thing yesterday when a detective interviewed him?" Mike noted the flicker of surprise on Paul's face. No one had. "That one is on tape. I can play it for you if you'd like." It, too, was inadmissible, but Paul should know of its existence.

"What is the public interest in prosecuting a mentally incompetent old man? He's already locked up here."

"My job is to find out who killed Geneviève Burke. Roger's guilt, whether he's charged or not, would prove someone else's innocence. You saw what happened, and you heard what he said. I have to follow up." *Before your client hurts anyone else.* Roger Devereux looked frail, but he was surprisingly strong when agitated. He belonged in a more secure facility.

A few minutes later, Tamika, flushed with anger and exertion, joined them. Before anyone could ask if she was all right, she said, "I hope you're satisfied. That poor old man had to be sedated again."

"That poor old man could have broken your neck." Mike looked around. "Is there a quiet place where we can talk?"

She pointed to the glass-enclosed office. "It's a fishbowl, but no one can hear what we're saying. Not that anyone would understand or care."

They sat down and he cut to the chase. "Is the violent behavior we just observed typical of Mr. Devereux?"

"You can't ask her to draw a medical conclusion from a single event," Paul said.

Mike suspected the interruption was intended to give Tamika time to think about her answer and to be sure she understood its importance. If so, the ploy was successful.

"People suffering from Alzheimer's often exhibit inappropriate behavior, including misdirected anger." She spoke as if repeating words from a training brochure.

"You have a bruise on your arm and scratches on your neck." Mike had noticed them when she went to soothe Roger. "Did one of your patients do that?" She looked stricken, and he amended his question. "Did Roger do that to you? Last Wednesday, after he tried to break into Geneviève Burke's apartment?"

"I object to a discussion of anything your department learned by reading medical records that should have been kept confidential." Paul said.

"Objection noted." Mike didn't argue, although the medical records in question had been Geneviève Burke's, and he doubted that Paul's objection would hold up in court. He turned back to Tamika. "What can you tell me about Mr. Devereux's whereabouts between seven and eleven yesterday morning?"

"I wasn't on duty, but I've talked to people who were."

"We'll talk to them later." He wasn't interested in hearsay.

"They'll tell you exactly what I'm saying. Last Wednesday was the first time Roger has ever exhibited any violent behavior. Today was the second."

"You weren't here Sunday."

"I know Roger." She looked close to tears. "He's a sweet and gentle man."

Mike thanked Tamika for her cooperation. She was distressed, and there was no point in badgering her. Tomorrow, he'd send Bea back with a subpoena and orders to gather more information about Wednesday afternoon's incident, including verification that Roger Devereux was responsible for Tamika's injuries.

"I'm through if you are," he said to Paul.

Mike waited until the elevator doors closed. "Roger isn't the victim, but you'd never know it from talking to the people who work here. I'm still looking for someone who cares that a woman was murdered."

"I'm the person you're looking for." Sadness shadowed Paul's face. "When I was a boy, she was my Tante Geneviève. I adored her. She was beautiful, lively, and fun. Unlike most other adults, she paid attention to me. After she and Roger divorced, she was no longer welcome in my parents' house. It broke my heart."

"She became *persona non grata* just like that?" Mike snapped his fingers.

"I don't know all the details, but as a divorcée and after she remarried, Geneviève created one scandal after another. To my eye, she was a free spirit, bursting the bounds of conventional society. My parents had a different perspective. Looking back, I suspect some of the men she bedded were married to friends of my mother."

"Could any of them, her lovers or their wives, be living here?"

"It's certainly possible."

They exited the elevator on the main floor. Curious stares followed them through the reception area.

"I'd like to hear more," Mike said. "Let's find somewhere private."

"I can't, not now. I squeezed this in as a favor to the family. I have to get back to the office."

"I'll walk you to your car." Outside and out of earshot of the curious, he asked, "What else can you tell me about Geneviève's life post-divorce?"

"The short version. She married an artist and gave birth to a son who's a wild one in his own right. Her second husband died young, but she never remarried. Her son grew up, and she moved to a farm north of town."

"When was the last time you saw her?"

"The summer after I graduated from high school—that would have been 1966. I contacted her, and we met for lunch." He paused, and when he resumed speaking, regret shaded his voice. "Geneviève charmed and sparkled and asked about my plans. Unlike most of my friends, I'd chosen a college out of state. She approved. In fact, she advised me not to return to New Orleans. There are days I wish I'd listened. Today is one."

"Paul, I've never seen this side of you."

"Geneviève was my first love. You have a soft side hidden

somewhere, don't you?" Paul chuckled, his usual equanimity restored. "When my parents found out about our lunch date, they were not pleased."

"That was your last contact?"

"Years later, she called my office. I did some legal work for her, for her son really. It's been ten years since we last spoke, but I care that Geneviève was murdered."

"What about her son?"

"I represented him several times, nothing too serious, really, and nothing recent. He moved to Europe and became a successful racecar driver. Tony Burke. You've probably heard of him. I believe he's back in town."

"That he is," Mike said. "And he had a very public argument with his mother the evening before she was killed." He didn't press for information about Tony's old legal problems and none was forthcoming.

"Is Tony a suspect?" Paul didn't sound as surprised as he should have.

"Everyone's a suspect until we find the killer. That includes ex-husbands and old lovers. Those husbands of your mother's friends, do you know any of their names?"

"You're serious?" Paul said. When Mike nodded, he shook his head. "I don't."

"Your parents might."

"I'm not at all sure they'd tell you."

"You could ask them for me. I'm most interested in the late sixties."

"That's twenty-five years ago." Paul looked skeptical. "I'll ask, but I'm not sure they'd remember."

"Ask about Roger and Geneviève's relationship post-divorce. They should remember that."

After Paul left, Mike checked in with Bea and then drove himself back to headquarters. When he met with Smith and Monroe, he'd tell them to look for Tony Burke's name in files from ten to fifteen years ago. Paul's involvement meant a conviction was unlikely, but if they were lucky, they'd find an arrest record that would tell them if Burke had a history of violence.

Paul Gilbert returned to his office in a somber mood. Today had been a day for ghosts. Memories of Tante Geneviève had haunted him since he'd learned of her death. An early client had been among the curious residents of Sunny Garden, standing apart except for a middle-aged woman, clinging to his arm. Their eyes met briefly, and the other man nodded but didn't smile.

Paul had needed a moment to recognize Edward Cantrell and hoped his shock at the man's deterioration hadn't shown. Many years ago, he'd defused a potentially messy situation for Edward, who'd left his wife and family for a woman a generation his junior, perhaps the woman beside him now. He thought he remembered gossip about Edward and Geneviève. He'd ask his father.

Suzanne was still at lunch. She'd left a pink message slip on his chair, a treatment reserved for the highest priority calls. He picked it up. Tony Burke wanted to talk to him. It was urgent.

Et tu Tony?

Paul had neither seen nor spoken to Geneviève's wayward son in a decade, and he was in no position to help him today. He dialed the number and left a message conveying his condolences. He didn't approve of Tony, but he felt sympathy for the child he'd been, the man he'd become.

That last lunch, back in 1966, was the first time he'd seen Geneviève from an adult perspective. He'd inquired about her husband and son, and she'd responded with an airy wave of her hand. She had no idea what Jim was up to, and she didn't care. "Don't follow in my footsteps, Paul," she'd said. "Marriage is a trap, and children are bloodsuckers." Tony had been six at the time. Poor little tyke might as well have been an orphan.

He walked over to the window and stared out at the darkening sky. Roger was right; it looked like rain.

11

Claire tossed the dirty sheets into the washing machine and added bleach along with the detergent. She pulled the vacuum cleaner, the mop, the broom, and an array of cleansers out of the closet. She opened the windows wide, swept and scrubbed, cleaned and wiped, shook out rugs and pillows, but the funk lingered. Only time would banish the miasma left by Tony's terrible accusation and Bea's sharp questions.

She put the last load of washing in the dryer and drove over to Tony's house. He had asked her to look for the old photographs. She parked at the curb because three unfamiliar vehicles, two sedans and a van, sat in the driveway. The police, probably.

No one was out front, and she walked through the house and out the back door without encountering anyone. The skeleton, still lay on the grass its skull askew. She gave it a wide berth and followed the path to the studio. A man stood by the studio steps, smoking a cigarette. Sounds of activity came from inside.

"What are you doing here?"

"I was about to ask you the same thing," he said.

"My company's working on the house. At least we will be once those bones are gone."

"Ah, Claire Marshall. I should have guessed." He introduced himself. "Don Sherrill, NOPD Crime Scene Unit." He nodded toward the studio. "The scene, we think."

"There are some things I want to do in the house."

"No problem, and we'll be taking those remains with us when we leave this afternoon. But we're going to want you and your workers to stay out of our crime scene for a while longer."

"We're not working on the studio. There's no reason for us to go in there." She looked up at the eaves where the big spiders still tended their webs. "Watch out for black widows. Tony killed several."

"Everyone's wearing gloves and protective clothing—standard protocol—but thank you."

Claire returned to the house and climbed the stairs to the second floor. A door concealed in the master bedroom closet provided access to the attic, a half floor under the eaves that was crammed full. Dim light coming through shuttered vents revealed a jumble of boxes, chairs, side tables and cabinets. How on earth had they gotten all this furniture in here? She turned on her flashlight and surveyed the clutter.

Geneviève had said the photos were in an old sideboard. The likeliest candidate stood beside the back chimney. A search of its drawers produced an array of tablecloths and napkins, yellowed Christmas wrapping paper, and an envelope containing a dozen black and white photos, group shots taken in the living room. Small print in the borders dated the pictures from June 1958, and names scrawled on the back identified the people.

Geneviève Devereux—these pictures had been taken before her marriage to Tony's father, but not long before. Jim Burke was on the scene, usually beaming at Geneviève and once with a possessive arm around her. Claire recognized several other names: a local fiction writer who'd gone on to write several best-selling novels, a prize-winning poet. One of the women was a painter of some note. *Chez Geneviève* had been real, and Geneviève had been stunning.

The old snapshots captured her beauty and vitality. Claire had seen few traces of that woman during her visit to Sunny Gardens. Geneviève's eyes sparkled only when she talked about her horses. They'd glittered with malice when she looked at the other residents of Sunny Gardens, with hatred when she saw her ex-husband. She had disparaged her only child and might have killed his father.

Whatever had happened on Geneviève's life's journey had transformed that laughing young beauty into a bitter old woman and, in the end, a murder victim. Saddened, Claire returned the pictures to their envelope. Certain stones are better left unturned; certain doors, better left closed. Opening the studio, which Tony wouldn't have done if she hadn't pushed it, had destroyed a delicate balance and brought fresh tragedy.

She couldn't go back and change anything that had happened, but she could go to the farm as Geneviève had asked. She could help exercise the horses and be sure they were being well treated. She still had the trainer's phone number—Kyle somebody, that was his name. Back downstairs, she rooted through her pocketbook until she found it.

He was happy to hear from her. "Geneviève told me you were going to call, but with everything that's happened I forgot."

"What if I come up this afternoon?" In her present mood, she wasn't going to get any work done.

Claire parked Felicia under a spreading oak. There were three rings between her and the barn. In the farthest one, a sandy-haired man sat erect but easy in the saddle, a skilled rider putting his horse through its paces. She leaned against the fence and watched.

The horse with its arched neck and prancing walk reminded her of a drum majorette. The rider, who had to be Kyle, touched his heels to the horse's flanks. The horse sped up but, instead of breaking into a trot, walked with ever-longer steps while vigorously nodding his head up and down. His front legs lifted so high their movement appeared circular, while his back legs reached forward in an almost horizontal thrust. This strange gait must be the big lick Geneviève had talked about.

Kyle slowed the horse and walked him over to where she stood. They exchanged names and he said, "I'm glad to see you."

"I'm glad to be here. Who's this handsome fellow?" She nodded toward the horse.

"Tomfoolery. Did you see the big lick?"

"Yes." She wasn't sure what she thought about it. From the side, it might be graceful, but from the back it looked awkward, like the horse was about to sit down. "He's gorgeous."

Tomfoolery neighed and pranced as if he understood the compliment.

"Gorgeous and high-spirited. He's been out on approval, but they brought him back last week. Too much horse." Kyle said. "He needs a confident rider."

"Out on approval?" He made it sound as if Geneviève sold horses. "What for?"

He gave her a funny look. "Most people want to try a horse out before they buy it."

"I thought Geneviève rescued Tennessee Walking Horses."

"She did. Then she nursed them back to health, retrained them, and sold them."

"She never mentioned selling them." Claire felt betrayed and then a little foolish. Of course, Geneviève had to find homes for the horses she rescued. Otherwise, she'd have no room for new horses. And she had to cover her costs, which had to be significant. Besides, everyone knew it was better not to give an animal away. People take care of what they pay for.

"The best horses that come through here go back to the show ring. That's where the money is, and that's where Tomfoolery is headed." He patted the big horse's neck. "Soon as we find the right rider."

"Geneviève wouldn't sell a horse to show. She hated the chains and padded shoes."

"There are flat-shod classes, a flat-shod circuit, two associations of flat-shod owners and breeders. Geneviève sold horses. That's how she made her living."

"Oh."

He frowned. "Knowing Geneviève, she was afraid if you realized this operation was a business, not a charity, you'd expect to be paid."

"Paid?"

"Exercising horses is work, hard work. I get paid, and you should be too. I can set it up."

"I don't want to be paid. I want to help." Claire felt like crying, which was stupid. A simple misunderstanding was nothing to cry about. Kyle couldn't know that she was here because she wanted to honor what had been good in Geneviève, whose death was partly her fault.

"Hey, I'm sorry. Don't take offense."

"No offense." She forced a smile. "I had this fairy tale vision of Geneviève rescuing beautiful horses and everyone living happily ever after. But horses take money. Food, shoes and tack aren't free. Vets cost a fortune. I know that. I just didn't think about it."

Kyle returned her smile. "Nothing's wrong with fairy tales, and yours wasn't so far off the mark. The horses go to good homes or they don't go." His smile faded. "Geneviève abused people, but she took good care of her horses."

"What happens to them now?"

"Her lawyer called this morning and told me not to sell any horses until he can talk to her son. He's in charge now, but the lawyer hasn't been able to reach him."

"I know Tony. My company is working on his house. Give me the lawyer's contact information and I'll pass it on."

"Okay, thanks. Meanwhile, if you want to start with Memphis, the bay gelding in stall three, I'd appreciate it. He's next in line. You'll see his tack has his name next to it."

"I haven't ridden in years." Geneviève had said her body would remember, but Claire wasn't so sure. What if Memphis, like Tomfoolery, needed a confident rider? She didn't feel at all confident.

"Then what are you doing here?"

"I don't know." It had been an impulse and probably a dumb idea.

"I have a lot of work to do."

"I can saddle Memphis for you." She felt Kyle's eyes on her back as she walked to the barn.

The mingled scents of fresh hay, horse sweat and manure evoked childhood memories. She had loved that smell and still did. She'd never minded mucking out Hershey's stall, and she had loved grooming him, brushing his coat until it shone. She found the proper tack and carried it to stall three where Memphis waited. He stood quietly while she slipped the bridle over his head and threw the saddle on his back. Then he nickered softly, as if inviting her aboard, and rubbed his velvet nose against her cheek.

"I like you too." She rested her forehead against his neck and decided that she would ride him after all. She adjusted the stirrups to her length, led him to the mounting block, and swung up into the saddle.

Kyle watched their approach with an expression that mixed confusion and annoyance. "I thought you didn't know how to ride."

"It's been a while," she said, "but I used to ride dressage, and it's coming back. What do you want me to do?"

Three hours later, Claire finished putting a mare named Tia Maria through her paces. The afternoon was getting late. As much as she wanted to stay, Tia Maria would have to be her last horse.

Kyle was setting out fresh hay. "You had me going there, but you're good. Long as I'm here, you're welcome to come back. And if you change your mind about being paid..."

"Thanks, but I feel as if I should pay you, especially for letting me ride Tia Maria. If I were going to buy a horse, this is the one I'd want." She dismounted. "Before I go, let me get that lawyer's card, and I'd like to say hello to Fast Eddie."

He gave her a sideways look. "Who?"

"Geneviève's favorite horse." Claire smiled. "Named after the

Governor."

"I don't know which horse you're talking about." He folded his arms across his chest.

"A black stallion with a white blaze." When Kyle shook his head, she said, "The one that threw her."

"Tomfoolery threw her. He's a black stallion, but he doesn't have a white blaze, and I've never heard him called Fast Eddie."

"Where are the other horses?"

"The ones we just rode are either in the stable waiting to be groomed or if they're done, out in the pasture with the ones I worked before you got here. Another three are out on approval."

Claire abandoned an argument she couldn't win. On her way out, she drove slowly by the pasture, looking for a tall black stallion with a white blaze. Geneviève might have sold other horses, but she would never have sold Fast Eddie. "Over my dead body," she'd said. Now Geneviève was dead, and Fast Eddie was missing.

Kyle had lied. He'd known which horse she meant. When pressed, he'd tossed out the first name that came to mind, but Tomfoolery had been out on approval. He couldn't have thrown Geneviève. Kyle was a lousy liar. Was he also a horse thief? A killer? She remembered his hands, strong yet gentle on the reins, and couldn't imagine them tightening a scarf around Geneviève's neck. But what did she know about Kyle? Nothing.

That evening, Claire called Tony. "I found photos from 1958. Later would have been preferable, but there are names on the back."

"You're doing better than I am. I'm dodging reporters who want to know how I feel about my mother's murder and playing telephone tag with a lawyer. After that chat with the police, I want some legal advice."

"I can drop the pictures off at the dealership or leave them at your house."

"Are you going to be home tomorrow night?"

"Yes, but—"

"I'll come over about seven. You don't have to do a thing; I'll bring dinner. After we eat, we can look at the pictures."

"Okay. Sounds like a plan." She'd wait until tomorrow night to tell him that his mother's most valuable horse was missing. It would be easier to explain in person.

Claire's next phone call was to her mother. She'd told her about Tony Burke, Authentic Restorations' celebrity client, and if reporters were harassing Tony, the national news might pick up the story about his mother's murder...

"I was just about to call you," her mother said. "I saw on the news about Mrs. Burke. What a tragedy. Did you know her?"

"I met her once."

"I don't know Tony, but if you think it's appropriate, please give him my condolences."

"I will."

"I can't believe you're mixed up in another murder." Before Claire could deny being mixed up in anything, her mother said, "Are you still seeing that homicide detective?"

"I was never really seeing him."

"Wouldn't it be funny if he investigated Mrs. Burke's murder?"

He was, and there was nothing funny about it. Claire changed the subject by asking about the weather—not very imaginative, but it worked. Michiganders love to complain about snow, and in January, snow is a sure thing.

Unfortunately the diversion proved brief, and her mother turned to her new favorite topic, Claire's social life or lack thereof. When she'd gone home for Christmas, her mother had pointed out that a year and a half had passed since Tom died. Wasn't that a long enough period of mourning? Claire had countered with Mike Robinson, a mistake if ever there was one.

"I wish you knew some nice men," her mother said.

"I'm surrounded by nice men: carpenters, plumbers, electricians. My business partner is a nice man, my accountant's a nice man, and so is my lawyer. Even my cat's a male, but I'm not sure how nice he is."

Then there were the not-so-nice men. She'd spent the afternoon with a horse thief. Tomorrow morning, she had a meeting with a potential client who was a total jerk. Tomorrow night she'd be having dinner with a notorious womanizer and possible alcoholic suspected, unjustly she thought, of killing his own mother. Despite his character flaws, she liked Tony. He'd sounded okay on the phone. She hoped he really was.

12

Paul Gilbert toyed with his letter opener, an ivory antique worth thousands of dollars. Today had been an ordeal, but it was over. He could go home, yet an odd lethargy kept him at his desk. He had a nagging sense that there was something he should have done. Or more likely, should not have done.

After returning to New Orleans, he had built a successful career on others' sins and misdemeanors. When a client or the child of a client did something foolish, he negotiated an arrangement that appeased the victim and, if necessary, satisfied the authorities. He worked behind the scenes, dealing with incidents the world would never know had happened. His efforts provided him satisfaction, often colored with amusement, and a healthy income

Homicide is a felony, the most serious of crimes. You're in over your head.

He'd been led into the swamp one step at a time, beginning with yesterday evening's phone call from his father, a man who rarely asked for a favor...

"I cannot imagine why the police browbeat Roger," his father had said. "All I know is Laura wants you to see it doesn't happen again."

"Why did she contact you and not me?"

"I don't know, but please do what you can to help her. And Roger."

Refusing his father's request was out of the question, so Paul had called Laura. Roger's niece said the incident with the police had occurred in the context of a homicide investigation.

"Homicide? In that case, you, as his legal guardian, should engage a criminal defense attorney."

Before he could explain why, she was explaining why not. "I knew you'd say that, Paul, but it has to be you. Strangers upset Roger. He was so distraught after that policeman questioned him that he had to be sedated. Just because he used to be married to that bitch."

And so he'd learned that Geneviève was dead. The news shocked and saddened him. As a boy, he'd been dazzled by Tante Geneviève. As an adult, he'd admitted her flaws: the recklessness that he'd confused with courage and the narcissism that demanded love from everyone— even the young son of her husband's best friend. He'd seen that she'd been neither a good wife nor a good mother, neither kind nor compassionate, but nothing since had warmed him like the glow of her attention.

He'd swallowed his sorrow, aware that any expression of grief would infuriate Laura. "A decades old divorce is an unlikely motive for murder. There must be something else."

"I don't know what's going on. Aren't there people you can call?"

"I'll do what I can." He had noted Laura's non-answer, so his first call was to the manager of Sunny Gardens.

Dwight Chastain's reluctant admission explained the police interest in Roger. Chastain apologized profusely for the unnamed staff member who'd allowed a detective to read the murder victim's file, which, unfortunately, contained a report of Roger's attempt to enter her apartment. No, he had not given them a copy.

By the time he'd finished talking to Chastain, it was getting late, but both his father and Laura had emphasized the urgency of the situation, so he soldiered on. He contacted a highly placed friend in the police department and learned that Roger was indeed a suspect. There would be more interviews. He extracted a promise that no contact would occur without his presence, which, he'd pointed out, was simply the police agreeing to obey the law.

The police had complied. He'd been present, and nothing he'd said or done had made one iota of difference. Early this afternoon, he and the head of homicide had witnessed Roger's anguished outcry, apparently the second one, which could easily be interpreted as a confession. They'd both seen Roger attack his caretaker. Worse, Roger's violent behavior appeared to be triggered by mention of Geneviève. If he had encountered her in the flesh, he might well have strangled her...

Paul tapped the letter opener against his open palm. The situation was fair neither to Roger nor to him. From a legal perspective, Laura was his client, and he had two messages on his desk asking him to call her. From his personal perspective, the real client was his father. He put the letter opener down and dialed his parents' number.

"You're at home? I thought you ate at the club on Mondays," his father said.

"I'm still at my office. Did Laura explain why the police wanted to talk to Roger?" When his father said no, Paul told him. The explanation provoked a rare curse.

"Damn Laura. She knows I would never knowingly involve you in anything to do with Geneviève, dead or alive."

"If Laura had called me directly, I'd have agreed to help," Paul said. It was probably true. The Gilbert and Devereux families belonged to a small world of old New Orleans families whose friendships endured through generations. Although they saw less of each other these days, when he was a child, Laura had been like a big sister. The decade that separated them was enough to prevent squabbles but not an unbridgeable chasm.

"I'm hoping you can give me some information, Dad. The police want to know if the relationship between Roger and Geneviève survived their divorce." His father would know. He and Roger Devereux had been confidants until dementia stole Roger's mind.

"You've seen what's left of the man. He's not capable of sustaining a relationship of any kind. We were friends for more than sixty years, and he doesn't recognize me."

His father's anguished but evasive response solidified Paul's intention to extricate himself. "The police talked to Roger again this morning. He became violent when Geneviève's name was mentioned."

"Roger violent? Ridiculous. Who told you that?"

"I was there—at Laura's request. Her accusation of police misbehavior during the first interview should be taken with a spoonful of salt." Paul let it sink in. "I saw what happened, and I heard Roger make statements that could be interpreted as a confession."

"Roger had nothing to do with Geneviève's murder. I don't care what he said. He's not living in the same world you and I live in. He was probably referring to something that happened decades ago, if at all."

"The nurse who cares for Roger agrees with you," Paul said. "And the police are looking at Geneviève's past, at all the men in her life, not only Roger. I suspect they were numerous, but I don't know any names. I was hoping you could help me."

"No. You're asking me to open Pandora's box," his father said, "and I will not do it. Nothing I can tell you will help in this situation. Good people could be hurt. You, as a lawyer working for the Devereux family, could be compromised."

"Not helping the police would compromise me. I have a legal and ethical responsibility."

"I doubt you remember—you were a child and smitten with her—but after the divorce, Geneviève became the angriest person I've ever encountered. She was determined to destroy anything resembling another person's happiness. A happy marriage represented a challenge to her seductive powers, particularly if the husband was one of Roger's good friends. The damage she caused was incalculable. Try as I might, I cannot mourn her death."

"None of that matters, Dad. If you have any relevant information, it's your responsibility to tell the police."

"A gentleman does not divulge that sort of information."

Paul had been afraid of this. His father was the same age as Roger, still *compos mentis*, but clinging to an old-fashioned code of honor and ill equipped for an encounter with homicide investigators. Paul could envision him defying a subpoena, daring the police to put him in jail for refusing to answer their impertinent questions. He would do everything in his power to keep that from happening.

"If the police contact you, let me know. Immediately. Please, Dad, don't talk to them without me."

"Roger's not capable of murder. He was declared legally incompetent years ago."

Laura had said two years, but the length of time was irrelevant. Paul tried again to make his father see the seriousness of the situation.

"Legally incompetent isn't a free pass. There are institutions for the criminally insane, and they have little in common with Sunny Gardens."

"Criminally insane? Have *you* lost *your* mind?"

"I'm about to call Laura. Roger's situation requires a criminal defense lawyer. Don't let her—" Paul started to say "use you" but stopped. "Don't let her persuade you otherwise."

"I'm sorry I involved you in this mess." His father's normally firm voice quavered and broke. "Dear God, what have we come to? If there is such a thing as mercy, make the police leave Roger alone."

Laura was waiting for his call. "Roger's nurse said he had to be sedated again today," she said. "And you were there. How could you let the police browbeat a helpless old man? Why didn't you protect him?

When he could fit a word in edgewise, Paul described what had happened.

"I don't care what he said. Roger didn't kill her. He's not capable of hurting a fly. This is all Geneviève's doing. She never forgets a slight. She'll do anything to get back at us."

Paul started to say that Geneviève was dead and not doing anything to anyone, but he stopped mid-sentence. Laura was distraught beyond reason. He relayed the only positive news he had. "I spoke to Dwight Chastain again this afternoon. The staff will swear that Roger is incapable of leaving the floor on his own."

Chastain had told him that every morning, the man who once ran a major corporation and sat on the boards of several others dressed in a suit and tie as if he was going to his office. Then he sat on his bed waiting for someone to lead him down the hall to breakfast because he was afraid to leave his room by himself. It was a heartbreaking vision and one he wouldn't share with Laura, although he suspected she already knew.

"Someone needs to tell that homicide person," she said.

"He knows. His name is Mike Robinson. We're acquainted, and it's a relationship of mutual respect. Mike is a skilled detective and a decent human being who is simply doing his job." He continued to soothe. "There's no vendetta against Roger and no desire to prosecute an incapable individual."

A stray thought pierced Paul's reasoned arguments. Mike would recognize him as a skilled lawyer, but did he also consider him a decent human being? He shrugged off the self-doubt and warned Laura to expect a call from Mike or someone working for him. The police wanted to know about Roger's post-divorce relationship with Geneviève.

"Their relationship ended with their divorce."

Paul couldn't tell if she was lying or if she really believed what she said. He was fairly certain that his father knew otherwise. Laura resumed cursing Geneviève, and Paul abandoned tact.

"Laura, listen to me. I cannot, in good conscience, continue to represent Roger in this matter. You should engage an attorney who specializes in criminal defense. I can recommend several for your consideration. And please do not ask my father to intervene on your behalf with me or with the police."

"I thought I could count on you, Paul." She hung up.

13

Claire limped up the walkway to Tony's house. Her thigh muscles howled despite last night's long hot bath and the two aspirin she'd taken with breakfast. An afternoon on horseback when she hadn't ridden in years might not have been smart, but she was glad she'd done it, and she planned to go back.

She checked the backyard before calling Jack. "The bones are gone. Pick up where you left off but stay away from the outbuilding. The police are treating it as a crime scene."

He exhaled loudly. "I'll have the demo crew there in an hour."

"I don't know where Tony is. I hope he's okay." She'd half expected to find him prowling around his father's studio. He wouldn't have cared what the police said.

"I hope he doesn't change his mind about us fixing up that house. By the end of next week, everything else will be finished or close to it."

She could chastise Jack for worrying about business when he should be feeling compassion for the murder victim and her son, but she understood. Jack's world began and ended with his family. His responsibility as their breadwinner weighed heavily, and his brush with financial disaster had left its scars. He'd never met Geneviève. He'd only seen Tony in passing and viewed him with awe and disapproval, a perspective shaped by sports pages and supermarket tabloids.

"I'm meeting the Curriers and their financial advisor at ten," she said. "I thought we were out of the running, but maybe not. And I'm well into the talking stage with three other good prospects. If they all come through, you can worry about being too busy."

"I don't mind that kind of worry." He chuckled. "The crew won't mind a bit of overtime, and if you get us all those jobs, I know some good boys who are looking for work."

"Don't hire anyone yet."

"Don't worry. I'm not going to jinx anything. Where are you now?"

"About to leave Tony's. I'll catch up with you after the meeting."

The offices of Levy and Jackson Financial Advisors occupied the fifth floor of an office building in the financial district. The offices were nondescript, more functional than chic, and certainly without the luxurious aura of Paul Gilbert's law office. Claire smiled to herself. Dave Currier wouldn't want to do business with a firm that "wasted" money on decor.

The receptionist said the Curriers weren't there yet and directed her to a comfortable waiting area. Too sore to sit when she didn't have to, she walked over to the window. Movement in the adjacent building caught her eye.

A young woman was conducting an animated conversation with someone out of sight. No, she was holding a cordless phone to her ear. She paced back and forth, talking and laughing, gesturing with her free hand. Watching her was like watching TV with the sound muted. Now she was listening. Her pacing slowed, and a smile softened her face. When she resumed speaking, she held the phone against her cheek in a two-handed caress. Without hearing anything, Claire knew her voice had dropped to an intimate whisper. She looked away.

Will I ever feel that way again?

The door burst open. Dave and Anne Currier hurried in, full of apologies about traffic and parking problems. Claire assured them she hadn't been waiting long, and the receptionist ushered them into a small conference room where Ron Jackson was working on a laptop computer. His manner was efficient but pleasant as he made sure everyone agreed that the purpose of the meeting was to evaluate her proposal. In other words, Claire thought, to ensure the Curriers did not, once again, pay too much.

They had purchased a house overlooking a small park not far from Tony's property. Theirs was also a villa, but larger and intrinsically nicer, with architectural flourishes that remained intact because the house had never been renovated. They'd jumped at it the moment it came on the market and paid the asking price. Hindsight said they'd paid too much.

Original architectural details are a plus; original systems are not. The rusted cast iron plumbing leaked through pinprick holes which the previous owner had covered with Band-Aids—as if they were skinned knees. The electrical system was a 110-volt fire hazard with old-fashioned fuses that blew at the slightest provocation. Space heaters in non-working fireplaces provided heat, and a previous owner had installed a window air conditioner in the master bedroom.

Retrofitting new systems in an old house is expensive, and Dave Currier had expressed shock at her estimate. She hadn't heard from him since before the holidays and assumed he'd found someone to do the work for less. Then, last week, he'd called and asked for another meeting, this time with his financial advisor.

She'd thought about it and seen an opportunity to save money. Whether or not the savings would be enough to swing the deal remained to be seen. She made her pitch.

"Since we last spoke, my company has begun work on a house in your neighborhood. If we start yours right away, our subcontractors can move between the two jobs. I can package the work and negotiate better prices for the plumbing, electrical, and HVAC. It will save you a minimum of three thousand dollars."

Dave wasn't impressed. "Three thousand, is that all?"

"It could be more, but I don't want to promise what I might not be able to deliver. And the other client also saves money." Tony's contract was cost-plus, but she wasn't going to cheat him in order to get this job.

"Your estimate was ten percent higher than any other. You need to come down more than a few thousand."

Before Claire had time to frame her response, Ron said, "I checked your references, Claire. People rave about the quality of your work, but Dave's issue is cost."

"We restore historic houses, which is both more difficult and more expensive than simply gutting the inside and rebuilding. On the plus side, preserving the architectural integrity adds value." And she'd told Dave this several times already.

Ron cleared his throat. "You asked me for due diligence on this proposal, Dave. I thought it looked good. It just got three thousand dollars better."

"Can I count on a profit when I sell?"

Dave's question was directed to Ron, but Claire jumped in. "I guarantee the quality of our work; no one can guarantee your return on investment." She wasn't going to work for nothing because he'd paid too much for that house. And if he was planning to flip it, he'd paid way too much.

Anne, who'd spent the meeting gazing out the window with the resigned air of a princess imprisoned in the tower, turned to her husband and spoke for the first time since saying hello.

"We can start right away, can't we?"

The door closed behind the Curriers, and Ron's face broke into a grin. "For a minute there, I thought Dave was going to get a carefully chosen piece of your mind."

She thought about denying it, but he was right. If Jack weren't counting on her to bring in new business, she might have suggested that Dave go waste someone else's time.

"Haggling over the numbers is no fun. Thank you for your help."

"I doubt you need help with numbers. One of the things the due diligence turned up is your previous work as an actuary. You made a big career change."

She nodded. Her job with the insurance company had paid the bills while Tom was studying to be a doctor, but she hadn't enjoyed the work. And then Tom died...

"I hope you're not offended that I looked into your work history."

"Not at all," she said. "Small construction companies are often on shaky financial ground."

"Construction's a tough business, especially for a woman. How'd you get into it?"

Claire appreciated Ron's help with Dave Currier, and she knew he was just being friendly, but she was sick to death of this question. She rolled out her usual response, a bit more detailed than usual. If he'd done due diligence, he already knew about Jack's financial problems, and she'd be wise to acknowledge them.

"So you pulled him out of the hole and now you're the managing partner."

"In a business I love. And Jack is a marvelous craftsman. Our partnership works well." She stood up to leave. "Thank you for your help with the Curriers."

Ron scrambled to his feet. "Dave comes on strong," he said. "But all you have to do is keep Anne happy. He worships the ground she walks on."

"Anne is a lucky woman." Her expensive clothes and heavy gold jewelry had provided an interesting contrast to her husband's skinflint attitude. The Curriers could prove to be challenging clients, Anne wanting the best and Dave unwilling to pay for it.

"Would you like to join me for an early lunch?" Ron said. "There are several good places within walking distance."

"Thank you, but Jack is waiting for me. He'll be pleased to hear we have this job. Thanks again for your help." She shook his hand and made her escape.

Jack was in the shambles that had been Tony's kitchen. When she walked in, he told the demolition crew to break for lunch. "But don't take too long. Staying off the job yesterday put us behind, and February is a short month."

"It's only Tuesday." Claire said. "Barring a new disaster, we'll finish demo this week, which is right on schedule. And the Curriers signed the contract."

"Nice work, partner." He gave her a high five.

"I'm on my way downtown. Permitting the Currier project should be a breeze. We're not touching the exterior. No architectural review." She stepped around shards of kitchen cabinet, heading for the back door. "But first I want to take a quick look at the studio."

She followed the now well-worn path to Jim Burke's studio. The door was padlocked and plastic sheeting covered the broken windows. The police had left, but big spiders remained. They watched her from behind yellow crime scene tape. She suspected some of their smaller cousins still lurked inside.

Carefully, she knelt and looked underneath the building. The supporting piers were cement block and appeared to be dry-stacked. Several were so far off plumb that their tilt was visible to the naked eye. Her vantage point also revealed floor joists several inches lower in the center than on the edges. The studio had started to fall in on itself.

14

Superintendent Vernon looked up from his cluttered desk. "You wanted to talk about the Burke case?"

"Based on witness statements, we could arrest Tony Burke for assaulting his mother. Period," Mike said. "There's no evidence to support a murder charge."

"So, what's new?"

"The victim had skin fragments under her fingernails. Odds are it belongs to the killer. DNA analysis could identify him."

"DNA analysis? Give me a break. This is 1994, not 2094."

Mike had come prepared for resistance. "Ten years ago, the Defense Department used DNA to identify remains returned by the North Vietnamese. Oregon used it in '89 to convict a child rapist. The Feds are running a pilot program with a dozen states. They're compiling a database of DNA collected from crime scenes, unidentified remains, and convicted criminals. They'll use it to—"

"Louisiana isn't one of those states." Vernon unwrapped a piece of chewing gum and stuffed it into his mouth. "My dentist says every tooth in my head is going to fall out if I don't stop grinding my teeth. I told him if he had my job, he'd grind his teeth."

"DNA could break this case wide open." Mike didn't add that a bill before Congress would make the DNA database nationwide with or without Louisiana's approval. Louisianans prided themselves on not doing what the rest of the country did, and he didn't want the discussion to wander down that byway.

"DNA won't convince a New Orleans jury," Vernon said. "You put some egghead professor up on the stand to talk about science, they won't like him, they won't listen to his theories, and they'll acquit."

"Forget the science. People understand odds. If there's a match, we can swear the odds are more than a million to one that the skin under the victim's fingernails came from Tony Burke. She fought back when he strangled her."

"What if there's no match? What if she tried to claw the scarf from her neck, and it's her own skin? We've wasted time and money."

"We'll continue the investigation while we're waiting for results. If there is a match, it will end up saving us money. I've got four detectives working full-time on this case."

Vernon continued to play the devil's advocate. "Say it is his skin. His lawyer will say she scratched him during their altercation."

"We have thirty plus witnesses who will swear she didn't put a hand on him. She held on to her walker with both hands while he dragged her outside. She tried to slap him, and he grabbed her wrist."

Vernon's chewing sped up as the argument intensified. "Burke's not going to give us a DNA sample, and you're not going to convince some peckerhead judge to make him."

"I think he'll cooperate. He says the skeleton is his father. DNA analysis is his chance to prove it."

"Okay, okay. If Burke goes along, I'll approve the expenditure. How long before we get the results?"

"The lab says a week or two. We'll need to test Burke, the skeleton, the skin from under the victim's fingernails, and the victim herself. I'd like to get a sample from Roger Devereux as well." He knew he was pushing his luck, but a match with Tony Burke was no sure thing, and Devereux was their other suspect.

"You want DNA from Roger Devereux?" Vernon's eyebrows approached his hairline.

"DNA can prove innocence as well as guilt."

"Tell that to Paul Gilbert."

"Paul is no longer representing Roger Devereux."

"Where'd you hear that?"

"From Laura Bethea, who is Devereux's niece and guardian."

"I know who she is."

"She called yesterday, wanting to discuss her uncle. I suggested we meet in Paul's office, and she told me he was off the case. I'm due at her house in forty-five minutes. Just me—she insisted upon a private meeting."

The message had been one of many waiting on his desk when he returned from Sunny Gardens. Someone named Laura Bethea claimed to have information relevant to Geneviève Burke's murder. In every high-profile case, the police are swamped with calls from attention seekers, Messages like Ms. Bethea's are a dime a dozen, but this homicide hadn't been in the news. He'd returned her call.

"I wonder why she summoned you. The mayor takes her calls." Vernon glanced at his phone. "Tread carefully. She could cause you and me both a world of trouble."

"I'll keep you posted." He left Vernon to his paperwork.

The Bethea house was in Lakeview, a short block from Lake Pontchartrain. A vaguely Spanish structure, it stood well back from the street, sheltered by well-tended plantings. Mike was a few minutes early, but the door opened as he climbed the front steps. A slender blonde woman greeted him. Both she and her house radiated luxurious good taste. Even he recognized her long-sleeved ivory dress as expensive.

She ushered him into a sitting room and, in a soft voice, laid out her rules for their meeting. "I do want to help with your investigation. However, if anything I tell you becomes public, I'll see that you lose your job."

Mike felt a flicker of sympathy for Vernon who dealt with this kind of crap every day. He nodded.

"Paul Gilbert told me you've been asking questions about my uncle's marriage."

He nodded again, another ambiguous response she could interpret as she wished.

"Paul can't help you—he was a child at the time—but I can." A little hitch in her voice hinted at suppressed sorrow. "Poor Roger, poor Geneviève." She passed a hand over her eyes, as if wiping away a disturbing vision.

The display struck Mike as calculated. He didn't say anything, and after a pause, she resumed her story.

"Geneviève was my sophomore English teacher at Saint Agnes. She was fresh out of college, enthusiastic, brilliant, and beautiful. I immediately developed an adolescent crush on her and insisted she be invited to the family's celebration of my sixteenth birthday." Roger

Devereux's niece smoothed her skirt over her knees and crossed her ankles. Her story put her well into her fifties, but she looked a decade younger. "You've met Roger," she said, "but not really. All you've seen is the dry husk of what was a charming and vibrant man."

"Alzheimer's is a terrible disease," he said.

"Roger was twenty years older than Geneviève but still handsome and vigorous, a natural athlete who won the club tennis championship every year. He was intelligent, well-travelled, the perfect man except..." She passed her hand over her eyes again. "I'm getting ahead of myself."

Mike shifted in his seat. He wondered when she would get to her point—if she had one. He felt as if he was watching a play. Laura Bethea had written the script and chosen the setting. What role had she assigned him? He sat back and waited for enlightenment.

"Roger was my favorite uncle, Geneviève, my favorite teacher. Their first meeting was a success, and so I created other situations to bring them together. I fantasized about them marrying and Geneviève becoming my aunt. You could blame me for their tragic marriage. Others have, but once they met my role was minor." Her words tumbled over each other as if she'd sensed his impatience and was determined to speak her piece before he stopped listening altogether. "You could be crass and say that Geneviève wanted financial security, while Roger wanted the respectability and stability of marriage. He was forty and still a bachelor. There is truth in that, but they also answered each other's emotional needs. She wanted a father figure who would adore her. He loved beauty, and she was beautiful. Her youth made him feel young."

Laura shifted her gaze from his face to the rug by his feet. When she spoke again, her voice was barely above a whisper. "Roger thought she understood his situation, but she had no idea. It was a disaster." This revelation was followed by a dramatic pause while she blotted what might have been a tear from her cheek.

Mike didn't need a script to know his line. "What situation?"

"Roger was sexually attracted to men, not women. Geneviève mistook his disinterest. She thought he was a gentleman, respecting her virtue and waiting until marriage."

Mike was less sure of his line this time, and Laura's assertion contradicted all he'd heard about Geneviève Devereux Burke. He opted for an honest expression of skepticism. "I doubt—"

She cut him off. "Remember, this was 1950. Nice girls didn't have sex before marriage. They didn't know about homosexuality. If she'd grown up in New Orleans, perhaps, but Geneviève was a nice girl from a small town in Northern Louisiana and barely out of her teens. I truly believe both married in good faith. She was able to carry through. Roger was not." She folded her hands in her lap, tightly as if they were the only things holding her together.

"They hadn't been married a year when Geneviève walked in on Roger engaging in an intimate act with a young man. There was a horrific scene." She shuddered. "I wasn't there, but I saw the scratches on his face. She literally tried to claw his eyes out. Of course, the marriage was over. She received substantial compensation in exchange for her silence."

Is she accusing the victim of blackmail? Mike nudged the conversation in that direction. "Did your uncle continue to support her?"

"All contact ended." She sighed. "Roger loved Geneviève, not as she wished to be loved but as he could. He blamed himself for taking away her youth and her innocence. He said he'd bear that guilt forever. It was the greatest sorrow of his life."

"I appreciate your frankness, Ms. Bethea, but the events you describe occurred decades ago. I'm not sure how relevant they are today."

"Not to you and me, but the past is the only thing Roger has. When you mention Geneviève, if he understands at all, his mind goes back to their marriage and its ghastly end. If he says anything, he's talking about forty years ago, not last weekend."

Now Mike understood why she'd wanted to talk to him. Paul had told her about her uncle's "I didn't mean to hurt you" outburst, and her story was designed to counter it. He tried to salvage some value from their meeting.

"Did you remain close to Geneviève after the divorce?"

"We no longer traveled in the same circles. She became notorious, carrying on blatant affairs with any man who would have her." Laura seemed to find this promiscuity more distasteful than her uncle's luring a naïve young woman into a hollow marriage.

"Do you remember the names of those men?" *If you do, this meeting won't have been a complete waste of my time.*

"No, I'm sorry. It's been too long. And it was nothing I wanted to know."

She was probably lying, but there was no point in saying so, not now. If he had the opportunity, he'd ask again, when she was under oath. He moved on. "We'd like to take a DNA sample from your uncle. It could clear him of any suspicion."

Laura jumped up, eyes blazing. "Absolutely not. You've already done more than enough to that poor old man."

"It's a simple procedure, a cheek swab that could be taken by one of his caretakers."

"Roger had nothing to do with your murder. Please. Leave him alone." She drew a ragged breath.

"We don't want to disturb your uncle, but we have to pursue our investigation. A woman was murdered."

"Roger couldn't have done it. He was with me the morning Geneviève was killed."

Mike kept his expression neutral, but this was a big surprise. Why hadn't she started here? Why go through the ancient history of a failed marriage? His detectives had interviewed the staff. Why hadn't anyone mentioned Laura Bethea's visit?

"When did you arrive?" he said.

"A little before eight, just as Roger finished breakfast. I brought him downstairs for church. After the service, we went back upstairs. I stayed and talked to him for another thirty minutes, until eleven-thirty or so. I'm sure the staff can verify my visit, that Sunday and most others." Laura walked to the door. "Thank you for coming, Captain Robinson. I appreciate your taking time to meet with me."

Mike drove away, a serf summoned to the manor then dismissed, unsure if he'd learned anything of value or not. Laura Bethea, like Tony Burke, seemed to believe the motive for Geneviève's murder lay in her past. Mike was willing to be convinced, but not by the fairy tale he'd just heard.

The interview had followed her script, except her outrage when he requested a DNA sample. That had thrown her off her game, but only briefly. All in all, Roger Devereux's niece had accomplished her objectives. She'd explained away any confession her uncle might make, provided him with an alibi for the crucial time period, and drawn a line in the sand. He'd better have a rock-solid reason and high-level backup before talking to Roger again.

15

Tony was bringing take-out and due any minute, but Claire's thoughts were with Mike. Yesterday's lie about having an appointment had been childish. She'd been disappointed that he wasn't there to see her. Looking back, she thought that, maybe, he really was. His job was primarily administrative, only high-profile cases required his personal involvement, but Geneviève's death wasn't news until someone realized Tony was her son. Even then, the newspaper put the article in the sports section. That didn't strike her as high profile.

If Mike was there because of her, he wouldn't have liked what he saw. He would have noticed that she didn't recoil when Tony put his hand on hers. Tony had been reaching for comfort, and she was all he had. His touch meant nothing. That night in the club, Mike's touch would have meant something, possibly led to something she wasn't sure she wanted—not yet.

The doorbell interrupted her deliberations. She pushed thoughts of Mike aside and let Tony in. He walked straight into the kitchen and set two white paper bags on the counter.

"Thai One On, the best take-out in New Orleans. I hope you like spicy." He didn't appear to have been drinking, nor did he seem troubled, which was amazing considering what he'd been through.

"Spicy is good." She opened the larger bag, and delicious aromas wafted into her kitchen. "I made a pitcher of iced tea. That will cool things off."

He leaned against the counter and watched her set out the containers. "As you will soon see, the other bag contains a cold six-pack of Sapporo, which goes well with Thai food, even if it is Japanese beer."

"I'm going to have iced tea. Can I get you some?"

"You're afraid I'll get drunk." He put his hands on her shoulders, and turned her to face him. "I'm properly embarrassed about Sunday night. I apologized the next morning. If you want, I'll apologize again. But you could cut me a little slack, given the circumstances."

Tony's non-apology made him the wronged party. Claire felt a tick of annoyance. She'd just been well and truly manipulated, and she didn't remember any apology Monday morning. Still, he had a point. She slipped out of his grasp.

"No apology needed. Are you ready to eat or do you want to look at the pictures first?"

"Are we through squabbling?"

"What?"

"I'll take that as a yes." Using chopsticks with surprising expertise, he suspended a generous serving of pad Thai above her plate. "Let's eat first. You're not one of those women who nibbles are you?"

"No. And I'm hungry."

"Good. I appreciate a woman with a healthy appetite."

The food was delicious, and when they moved on to the spicy beef, Claire had to admit that beer really was the better complement.

"Thank you," Tony said. "I like winning an argument with a beautiful woman." He grinned like a man without a care in the world.

"You're in an awfully good mood."

"It's been a good day. I took two of my father's paintings to a gallery Howard recommended and told them I had more. They're going to stage a Jim Burke retrospective."

"Congratulations." She raised her beer in a toast.

"The gallery knows that none of the paintings are for sale, and they're okay with that as long as I help them publicize the show."

"Do you have a date?"

"Last two weeks of June. They can't fit the opening in before racing season begins, but I'll be back on this side of the pond in June. The Grand Prix du Canada is June 12. We're looking at opening the next Friday."

"I'll mark my calendar."

"That's the good news. The bad news is that Howard never met Geneviève and has no idea who her friends were. She and Dad were leading separate lives by the time he signed with Howard's gallery."

"Maybe we'll find something in the pictures."

They finished eating and after putting the dishes in the dishwasher, a task Tony insisted upon sharing, adjourned to the living room. Dorian, who was in his favorite chair, opened one eye but closed it when Tony sat on the sofa.

"Do you think the big fellow likes me?" Tony said.

"He's tolerating you." Claire handed him the photographs.

"Look with me." He slid over. She sat beside him, and he laid the photos out on the table, pausing to study those that included his father. "The only people I recognize are my parents."

"There are names on the back. One or two might ring a bell." She pointed out the people she'd been able to identify.

Tony had heard of the writer. "But he's dead, killed himself years ago." He flipped through the photos again. "A dozen people having a good time at a party, and no one has any idea what awaits. Two murders and a suicide that we know of. Everyone in these pictures is probably dead by now."

"Not everybody. This one's a poet, currently living in London." She tapped the photo. "We can try to reach him through his US publisher. Tonight, we'll look the others up in the phone book."

"The phone book?"

"I made a list. We have eight names."

"Of people who may or may not be alive and if alive may or may not still live here. And who knows how many people in New Orleans have the same names."

"Do you have a better idea?"

"Say we actually find someone, what makes you think they stayed friends with Geneviève after I was born? According to her, life changed, fun stopped, and misery began. Even if they stayed friends, would they remember who she was sleeping with in 1969 as opposed to 1968 or 1970?"

"People remember Hurricane Camille," she said. "That's our reference point."

"You don't give up do you?"

"Not without even trying. I'll call. People might recognize your name. I'll say I'm researching local artists and ask about Jim Burke."

"Have at it, but I don't think you're going to find anyone." Tony leaned back, legs stretched out and ankles crossed, a patient but not optimistic observer.

The first three names didn't pan out. Of the eleven possibilities, eight answered their phones, but none of them had heard of Jim Burke. Two people hung up on her.

"Okay, on to Bill Boaz," she said. "There are five Boaz possibilities in New Orleans, a B, a Bill, two Williams, and a W."

"Do you know what a snipe hunt is?"

"Look, I'm trying to help you."

Her irritated tone woke Dorian, who jumped out of his chair and left the room, tail held high.

"And I appreciate it, but this is—" Tony searched for a word. "—haphazard, and I don't have time to fool around. The police are building a case against me. I'm innocent, but innocent men have been convicted before. There's a lawyer in town who has helped me in the past. I've been trying, without success, to reach him. I'm beginning to think he's avoiding me."

"I'm not a lawyer, but this is how I find previous owners. Let's finish what we started." She dialed the next number.

B. Boaz didn't answer, but Bill Boaz listened to her explanation then said, "You're trying to reach my Dad. He died four years ago. But you might want to talk to my mother. She modeled for Jim Burke back before she and Dad got married."

Claire, who'd been about to offer condolences on his father and apologize for disturbing him, bounced to her feet. "Do you think she'd be willing?"

"Is water wet? Mom loves talking about the good old days, and my poor ears wore out long ago. Tonight's her bingo night, but give me your number, and she'll call you back tomorrow."

"Just a minute." Claire put her hand over the receiver. "Bingo." She laughed. "We found one of your father's models, and she's out playing bingo. This is her son. Do you want to talk to him?"

Tony shook his head. "Just her. Can you get her number?"

"Judy," Tony said after Claire hung up. "I don't remember a Judy."

"She's in one of the photos, Judy Harmon. She was early sixties; you would have been a toddler. Her husband also knew your parents, but he died several years ago."

Suddenly Claire realized how tired she was. "Do you want to keep going or are you ready to call it a night?"

Tony stretched and yawned. "I can take a hint. Tell your cat goodnight for me."

Claire stood to walk him to the door, and the muscles that had loosened up over the day ached again, reminding her of horses. "I almost forgot." She handed Tony the business card Kyle had given her. "This man is your mother's lawyer. He's been trying to reach you."

"Where did you get this?" He frowned and turned the card over.

"I went up to the farm yesterday afternoon."

Tony's frown deepened. "We spoke last night," he said. "You didn't mention being at the farm or talking to my mother's lawyer. I've been here for hours, and you don't mention it until I'm on my way out the door?"

"I went up to the farm to help exercise the horses because I'd told Geneviève I would. Kyle, her trainer, mentioned that her lawyer was trying to reach you. I offered to pass on his card. That's all." *No good deed goes unpunished.*

"The horses." Tony smacked his forehead with an open palm. "I forgot the horses. Are they mine now?" He collapsed back onto the sofa. "Please, say no."

"I didn't mention it last night because I wanted to tell you in person. I was afraid you wouldn't understand."

"Good call, sweetheart." He sat up, all business. "What's going on?"

"The lawyer wants to know if he should sell the horses, but I think Kyle already stole one." She told him what Geneviève had said about Fast Eddie and how Kyle denied the horse ever existed.

"The lawyer can sell the horses, or the trainer can steal them," Tony said. "I don't care as long as they're gone."

"That horse is valuable. The previous owner tried to buy him back, but Geneviève refused. Now she's dead and the horse is gone. What if she was killed because of this horse?"

"That's not what happened."

"You don't know for sure. Someone should tell the police."

"Go ahead and tell your boyfriend. Get him off my back."

"He's not my boyfriend."

"I'm glad to hear that, but I'm not sure I believe you." He put his arm around her shoulders and gave her a quick half-hug. "Sorry, Claire. You mention Geneviève's horses, and I act like a horse's ass. Thanks for putting up with me and for tracking down Dad's old model. Now I'm really leaving."

16

Mike and Bea met in his office first thing Wednesday morning. He brewed a fresh pot of coffee, and she opened a box of glazed donuts she'd brought with her.

"Mmmm. Still warm. Help yourself." She pushed the box across his desk.

He took one, confident that she'd finish the rest before the day was over, probably before the morning was over. As far as he could tell, Detective Beatrice Washington ate constantly. His previous partner had a weakness for beignets and the waistline to prove it, but Bea was slender as a greyhound. What a metabolism she must have.

"How's it going with the DNA samples?" she said. "Any trouble getting Tony on board?"

"None, but Roger Devereux is a no go. I'll tell you about it after you tell me about Iris Burton."

"Iris is an aspiring television personality. Sunny Gardens is her day job. Seven to ten every morning, she distributes medications under the direction of a real nurse. Nighttimes, she waits tables in a supper club. She sees both jobs, and as far as I can tell everything else in her life, as playing a part. Our interview began with a dramatic monologue followed by tears."

"You didn't find her convincing?"

"I found her sorrow overdone. She'd known the victim for what? A few weeks. She just started at Sunny Gardens the beginning of the month."

"She was the last person to see the victim alive and the first one to find her dead."

"Which might make her a suspect, but I don't see it," Bea said.

"What's she like?"

"Young. I think she's led a sheltered life until very recently. She's also ambitious, shallow, and totally focused on her appearance. She sleeps in her false eyelashes in case there's a fire."

He chuckled. "Is she attractive?"

"Extremely. But at the end of the day, I feel sorry for her. It's as if she doesn't exist unless someone is looking at her. She boasted that, unlike the other aides, she had memorized the names and faces of everyone living in the apartments. She always greets them by name because, and I quote, very encounter is an audition."

"She sounds like a monster."

"She's immature and self-absorbed, but actually quite pleasant in a ditsy way. I'm not sure how smart she is."

"Did she notice anything unusual during her rounds Sunday morning?"

"She says no, and no one else I've spoken to did either. Sunny Gardens isn't as buttoned down as they'd like us to believe. Visitors are supposed to sign in at the door, and while no one actually came out and said it, I'm pretty sure that rule isn't enforced. Sunday morning is an especially busy time. The receptionist estimated there were twenty or thirty visitors. I checked the book; three people actually signed in. "

He finished his coffee. "What else?"

"Iris had nothing good to say about Tony Burke, but when I pressed, she admitted they'd never met. She was repeating things Geneviève had told her. What a family." She looked down at the half eaten donut in her hand. "I've been doing all the talking."

"Okay, I'll take a turn. You interviewed the young ingénue while I talked to the old pro." Mike summarized Laura Bethea's story while Bea finished her donut and ate another.

"You weren't convinced either," she said.

"The only time she stepped out of character was when I said we'd like a sample of Roger's DNA. Her outrage appeared genuine. Still, the interview was useful. I came away with two big questions. First: was Geneviève still, or again, trading silence for money? Second: why has no one told us that Roger Devereux left the secure unit Sunday morning?"

"I can answer the second question. No one on the staff believes Roger could possibly have killed Geneviève, and everyone is afraid of the Devereux family's wrath. As for the blackmail, do you want me to look into the victim's finances?"

"I've already asked Bill to do it. For now, I want you to stick with the interviews. You're doing a nice job, and your description of Iris raises another question."

"Sir?"

"Why were she and the victim close? Everything I've heard tells me that Geneviève Burke was sophisticated and intelligent, although not particularly likeable. Why would she befriend a nineteen-year-old whose highest ambition is to become a personality?" In his world personality was something a person had, not something they became. "And why would Iris want to spend time with such an unpleasant old woman?"

"I think I understand." Bea folded her napkin and laid it beside her empty plate.

"Mother-daughter?" he prompted.

Bea shook her head. "More like comrades-in-arms. Both were small-town beauties whose ambitions brought them to the big city. There's insecurity in leaving your roots for a better place and a fear of not quite belonging even if you become a success. You don't know the secret handshakes, and you'll never be able to share jokes about what happened in Miss so-and-so's cotillion class. Things like that. But there's also a sense that you're better than those who've never had to struggle or make their own way. You had to be."

"I think I understand." *More than you're saying.* He sensed that Bea's insights were hard earned and very personal.

"They bolstered each other in what was an uncomfortable if not hostile environment," she said. "When Iris finished her shift, they'd have coffee and exchange gossip about the other residents. Iris described current carryings-on, and Geneviève told about old scandals."

"What about old lovers?"

"Geneviève didn't tell tales on herself, but others did. Sunny Gardens is full of people with long memories and hatchets to bury. One woman bragged about cutting her dead. Another called her trash." A frown creased Bea's forehead. "They were talking about a murder victim."

"Tony said his mother wanted to stay at Sunny Gardens but, after she got there, did nothing but complain. Bumping into old enemies could explain her change of attitude. Do these women have alibis?"

"With big holes." Bea shrugged. "Which means nothing."

"Run their names by Vernon. See what he says. He remembers Geneviève well."

"He said so with a gleam in his eye and—" Bea clapped her hands. "Why haven't we asked him about Geneviève's old lovers?"

"More to the point, why hasn't he volunteered any information?" They looked at each other.

"I'll ask him," he said. "You go over to Sunny Gardens and continue the interviews. We'll compare notes again at the end of the day. My office at five."

17

Iris dreaded going back to Sunny Gardens, but if she didn't work, she didn't get paid, and her parents wouldn't give or lend her another penny. She never should have told them what happened to Geneviève. Her father had threatened to drive right down and bring her home. "You'll have to drag me into the car," she'd told him, "kicking and screaming." Iris Burton was not about to leave New Orleans with her tail between her legs.

She staggered into the bathroom, patted her cheeks with cold water, and gave her reflection a pep talk. A little before seven, she pulled into the Sunny Gardens employee parking lot, ready for work in her clean, crisp nurse's costume.

Being back here made her stomach feel all queasy, but a personality is at her best no matter how she feels on the inside. When she was famous, the old people would remember when Iris Burton brought their morning meds. They'd talk about how nice she'd been, always well dressed with a pleasant word for everyone. She retrieved the meds cart and, on feet that felt leaden despite her best effort, started her rounds.

The yellow crime ribbon strung across the door of Geneviève's apartment brought tears to her eyes. She dabbed a Kleenex to catch any mascara smudges and bowed her head in a brief prayer before moving on to Mr. Pasqua. He opened his door the minute she knocked.

"How are you doing, Iris?"

Oh no, he's been waiting for me. He's going to ask questions. I can't stand it.

"Everyone's sorry about what happened to Mrs. Burke. We know you two were friends." He patted her shoulder. "You take care of yourself now."

Mrs. Benoit stepped out in the hall. "It's just terrible what happened, murdered in her own living room. And you poor thing, you found her." She put her hand on Iris's arm. "Please accept my condolences."

The door across the hall opened, and Mrs. Martin came out to join the conversation. Another person came out, then another. People who'd never bothered being nice offered their condolences. They gathered around her and asked questions, not because they were nosey, but because they were sympathetic.

Iris told them about buying beignets and how she had searched high and low for Geneviève before getting the nurse, but she couldn't bear to talk about what she'd seen in the apartment.

"I bet her son came back. You saw how he treated her," Mrs. Benoit said.

Mrs. Martin shook her head. "Not her own flesh and blood. I think it was someone come to rob people."

"You weren't in the parlor Saturday night," Mrs. Benoit said. "What do you think, Iris? Did Geneviève ever talk about that son of hers?"

Iris had told Detective Washington what Geneviève said about her worthless son, but she wasn't going to tell anyone else. Mr. Pasqua saved her from having to answer.

"I think it was an intruder," he said. "Did you see anything unusual Sunday morning, Iris? Anyone who looked like they didn't belong?"

"No. I wish I had, but I didn't." She was being truthful, but as she continued on her rounds and everyone kept asking, she remembered the old man by the elevator.

He'd been dressed for church and looked like he belonged, but she'd never seen him before. She'd first noticed him after she finished the first floor. When she smiled and said good morning, he'd just turned away. The elevator came and she got on. When she came back downstairs, after finishing her rounds, he was gone.

At the time, she'd thought him rude—like too many other people who looked right through her—and put him out of her mind. But now, the more Iris thought about the man, the more suspicious he became. As soon as her shift ended, she called Detective Washington.

"I remembered something," she said. "Sunday morning, there was a man I'd never seen before. He didn't look suspicious, just like he was waiting for the elevator, except he didn't get on when I did. I'm sorry I didn't mention him before. I'd forgotten all about him."

"Don't be sorry. I understand. What time was this?"

"A little before eight."

"About twenty minutes after you gave Geneviève Burke her meds?"

"Maybe half an hour."

"Did you see his face?"

"Just for a second, but I think I'd recognize him if I saw him again."

"I'd like you to come in and work with one of our sketch artists." They made an appointment for four-thirty that afternoon.

Iris drove home feeling a lot better than she had on the way to work. Detective Washington had been nice as could be and very interested in what she had to say—not at all mad because she'd forgotten about the man. The old people at Sunny Gardens had listened to her, too. *When I'm a personality, the whole world will care what I say.* That thought reminded her to touch base with her agent. She hadn't spoken to Danny since last week.

"Where were you?" Danny said. "You missed the audition. I tried to call you but your phone must have been off the hook."

"Ohmigod, I forgot."

"You forgot?" His voice rose an octave. "All the time I spend trying to get you into auditions and you forget to show up. I thought you wanted to be someone. I can't do this by myself, Iris."

"I'm sorry. I know how hard you're working for me, and I really wanted that job." She felt the sting of fresh tears. "Something awful happened. That's why I forgot."

She told him about Geneviève being murdered and finding the body and just getting so upset that the doctor put her under sedation, and how she slept practically around the clock and woke up too groggy to think. And yesterday morning, she finally calmed down enough to talk to the police, but talking about what happened got her upset all over again, and she forgot about the audition.

"How come I didn't see anything about this on the news?" Danny broke in. "Sorry, dumb question. Who cares about an old lady in a nursing home?"

"I care. I know some people said she was a B I T C H, but they didn't know her. She was beautiful and smart and funny, and we were friends from the first day we met." Iris told him how Geneviève understood and encouraged her and how she knew lots of important people. "She used to have a salon in New Orleans just like Gertrude Stein did in Paris, and all the famous artists and writers hung out there. She was married to an artist and before that to Roger Devereux, they're one of the richest families in New Orleans."

"Wait a minute, Iris." Danny cut her off again. "Tell me again. Who was your friend who got murdered married to?"

"Roger Devereux. And I think I saw the killer. I might be the only witness."

"Whoa. Really?" Danny whistled. "We could have something here. Where are you, baby?"

"Home. I just got off work."

"Well hustle on over to my office. I hear opportunity knocking."

Danny was on the phone, so Iris waved hello and sat down to wait. She couldn't help overhearing what he was saying and then listening closely when she figured out that he was talking about her and Geneviève.

"The victim was married to big money," he said. "I'm surprised no one else has picked it up." The person on the other end said something Iris couldn't make out, and Danny said, "Still you got the connection. What makes it fresh and great for TV is the witness. The only person who actually saw the killer is a very, very sexy young woman. Trust me, she's got it all."

"Danny," she whispered. "What are you doing?"

"Of course you can't reveal her real identity until the cops have arrested the killer, but as soon as this afternoon, you can do an interview. Just keep her face out of it. A mystery witness, you gotta love it. She'll wear her nurse's uniform, show a little leg, half the guys in the audience will —"

"Danny, I can't." She spoke louder this time.

He held one hand up like a traffic cop and kept talking into the phone. "Hey man. I'm not going to tell you how to do your job, but you can run with it. Anything involving the Devereux family is news in this town. Think about a follow-up, interviewing the scared old rich folks at this Sunny Gardens place. Toss in something on the local murder rate. Then, when the cops get the guy, you can do another interview with the mystery witness, showing her face this time, and she's a beauty. The camera is in love with her. And she loves the camera."

Bad as she felt, Iris couldn't help smiling at that, but she had to let

Danny know that she couldn't do an interview this afternoon. She wrote him a note and held it in front of his face.

He waved her back to her seat. "I'm a friend of hers. She's understandably nervous, so she asked me to call you. Put yourself in her shoes. The last thing she wants is for the killer to find out who she is. The cops aren't giving her any protection." He paused, listening, then said. "She wants the killer brought to justice. I told you. The victim was her friend. And she's upset that the cops aren't giving this case any kind of priority."

Iris nodded her head. She was upset for sure, except the police really did seem to care.

"No one is asking for a dime, and you get the television exclusive. I'll be honest with you: she's an actress, just starting out, and she wouldn't mind the exposure." Danny listened then said, "Oh it's real. You ought to read the papers." Another pause. "Okay. Three o'clock at the studio? See you then." He hung up the phone and grinned at her.

Iris held up her note. "I can't, Danny, not this afternoon. I'm meeting Detective Washington at police headquarters. I told her about maybe seeing the killer and —"

"Iris, listen to me. You're talking to the paper at two and TV news at three. You can talk to the detective tomorrow. If you talk to her first, she might tell you not to talk to anyone else, and all my hard work will be for nothing."

"She already told me not to say anything."

"Don't give her a chance to tell you again. Look, Iris, do you want big-time exposure or not? Opportunities like this don't happen every day."

"I don't know. It doesn't feel right."

"Baby, when this is over, everyone in New Orleans is gonna know who you are. I can see you getting a regular spot on the morning show."

"You don't think this is doing something wrong, like using what happened to Geneviève?" Iris felt herself wavering. Getting a spot on the morning show would be fantastic.

"Didn't you just tell me how she encouraged you to go after what you want?"

"And not waste time worrying about what other people think." She finished the sentence. "You're right. I'm doing what Geneviève would want me to do."

18

Judy Boaz called Claire's office, burbling with excitement and "absolutely dying" to talk to Jim Burke's son.

"I remember him, a cute little kid. Jim was crazy about him. Tony, that's his name. I guess he's all grown up now."

"He is indeed." Claire bit back a smile.

"Tony Burke." There was silence from the other end then a shriek. "Tony Burke. Oh my gosh, Tony Burke. It's been so long, I never put it together. Oh. My. Gosh." Another shriek.

Claire held the phone away from her ear until the squealing stopped.

"Tony Burke, the racecar driver. That's him? That really is him?"

"Yes."

"Oh my gosh. I've seen him on TV. He's gorgeous, even better-looking than his Dad."

"If you'll give me your phone number, I'll pass it on. Tony has several appointments today, and I don't know when I'll be able to reach him. It might be tonight or even tomorrow before he calls."

"I'll be home all day, sitting by my phone. Tomorrow, whenever, I'm sitting there until he calls."

"Are you still in touch with any of Jim and Geneviève's old friends?"

"I don't know anyone who was friends with both of them. Um. It wasn't the world's happiest marriage if you know what I mean."

"Do you keep in touch with any of Jim's friends?"

"Not in years. I kind of dropped out after I got married. It was a wild crowd, and my Bill was the jealous type. He made me stop modeling, said he didn't want any other man seeing me in the altogether, especially not Jim Burke." Judy giggled. "Jim was a rascal, a lady's man with a silver tongue and a weakness for fine whiskey." She giggled again. "From what I've read about Tony, the acorn didn't fall too far from the tree."

"I'll give him your number." Claire was ready to end the call. Judy Boaz coherent was no better than Judy Boaz squealing.

"You know, Jim's art had started to sell, and I heard he was finally going to leave her. But he died first, a car wreck. It was a real tragedy."

"Tony has fond memories of his father." *And so, it seems, do you. I hope you're not going to say anything to tarnish his.* After more promises that Tony would indeed call, Claire signed off.

Tony checked in a little before noon. Claire told him that Judy might not be the source of information they'd hoped for and warned that she'd made the connection and was giddy with the excitement of meeting him.

"I wouldn't necessarily believe everything she says. You know how people embroider things."

"I'll call her when I get back to the dealership. She might have caller ID, and I don't want this number to get out."

"While I have you on the phone... Jack says the old heart pine floor in your kitchen can be salvaged. I think it would look better than tile." Tony's vision for his kitchen was pure Italian villa. Some aspects translated into New Orleans villa, but some didn't. "Where are you? Can you stop by and take a look?"

"I'm up by Tulane Hospital. I just gave them a DNA sample."

"Tulane Hospital." She used to go up there all the time when Tom was a resident. He'd worked long hours, and some days, she dropped by to say hello during his breaks. Sometimes she'd bring food, and they'd have a picnic.

"Claire, are you there? Have I lost you?"

"I'm here." She pushed memories aside and said the first thing that came to mind. "How do you give a DNA sample?"

"What are you imagining, young lady?" Tony chuckled. "You'll be disappointed to learn that all they did was run a swab inside my cheek."

"Oh." She felt herself blushing and was glad he couldn't see.

"Your friend Mike Robinson says he wants to be sure the skeleton was my father. I half believe him."

"Why only half?"

"I suspect he wants to check me against evidence they found in Geneviève' apartment. If so, he's wasting his time. I was there helping her move in. I didn't kill her."

"I know you didn't."

"Go ahead on the wood floor. I trust your judgment. If I have time, I'll stop by later this afternoon."

Claire passed Tony's decision on to Jack and spent the next hour negotiating with subcontractors. It looked like coordinating the two projects would save even more than she'd hoped. Dave Currier would be happy—or as close to happy as he could be when something was costing him money. By the time she finished the paperwork for the subs, it was five o'clock, and she still hadn't called the police about Fast Eddie. She dialed police headquarters and asked to speak to Detective Washington. A click said the call was being forwarded.

"Robinson here," Mike's voice.

"It's Claire Marshall," she said. "I'm trying to reach Detective Washington."

"She's here in my office. Just a minute, please." There was no "Hello Claire," no "Why are you calling?" He acted as if they barely knew each other, and maybe he was right.

"Hi Claire. What's up?" Bea said.

"I'm calling about Geneviève Burke."

"Let me put you on speakerphone. That way, I won't have to tell Mike what you said." Another click then shuffling background noise. "Okay, go ahead."

"Do you know that Geneviève rescued Tennessee Walking Horses that had been abused? She nursed them back to health, retrained them, and sold them to good owners. That's how she made her living." Kyle's words, not hers, but he was in a position to know.

"We're putting together information on her life," Mike said. "We didn't realize that you knew her."

"I met her once. We both like horses, but that's not why I called." There was silence from the other end, so she plowed ahead. "I was at her farm Monday afternoon, helping exercise her horses."

"Monday, after we questioned Burke at your house?" Mike's voice again.

"Yes." More silence. She imagined Mike and Bea exchanging puzzled looks, possibly passing notes. She ploughed ahead.

"Geneviève's most valuable horse is missing, and her trainer is pretending it was never there. I think you should talk to him. His name is Kyle Winslow." She gave them the phone number for the barn.

"Are you sure this horse is missing?" Bea this time.

Claire relayed Geneviève's story about buying Fast Eddie for pennies on the dollar and the previous owner wanting him back. "'Over my dead body' were her exact words. And now she's dead, and the horse is gone."

"Have you ever seen this horse?" Mike said.

"No, but Geneviève described him. Before I left, I checked the barn and both pastures. No horse there fit her description. Three or four horses are out on approval, but he's not one of them."

"Is there any reason you think there's a connection between her murder and the apparent disappearance of this horse?" Mike again.

"The timing and the fact that Kyle lied about him." She had liked Kyle, and he seemed too proud, too decent, to be a common thief, but he had something on his conscience. She was sure of that. "The horse is a three-year-old black stallion with a white blaze. He's eighteen hands, tall for a horse."

"Do you think the original accident could have been an attempt on Geneviève's life?" Bea again.

"I don't know." This was a new thought, and it was possible to tamper with a saddle or intentionally spook a horse. Kyle was in a position to do either. "Fast Eddie is the horse that threw her. It could have been an attempt to make her sell him."

"We'll talk to the trainer," Bea said.

"Rescuing Tennessee Walking Horses was important to Geneviève. I feel as if I owe it to her to help find her horse. I know you consider Tony a suspect, but..." Claire left it there.

"We don't have suspects yet, just people of interest, and he is one." Mike said. "However, you might want to maintain a bit more distance."

"I beg your pardon?"

"Claire, the last time I saw you, it was ten o'clock in the morning, and Burke was taking a shower in your bathroom."

Claire saw red. "Perhaps you should stop minding my business and concentrate on finding Geneviève's killer. And Fast Eddie is not *apparently* missing. He is missing." She slammed down the receiver, mad at Mike for his assumption and outraged because he hadn't listened. Fast Eddie had been important to Geneviève, someone had stolen him, and no one cared.

Mike winced as the bang of Claire's irate sign-off bounced off his office walls. He wondered if he could have handled it worse.

"Not tactful, boss. Not tactful at all." Bea was biting her lip, but she couldn't keep the laughter out of her voice.

He glared at her.

"There's nothing wrong with being human," she said. "I've been wondering about you and Claire ever since we went over there. You both played it cool, but I'd heard rumors."

"As you already know, Claire and I met last year when she was kidnapped by a psychopath. Like many victims, she blamed herself. I kept in touch because I was concerned about her and felt some responsibility for what had happened." Even to his own ears, he sounded like a pompous ass, and there'd been a lot more to the story. He amended his statement. "You're right, I like her, but there's nothing between us."

In the weeks since their last date, he'd thought several times about calling her. He'd picked up the phone more than once but never dialed her number. They'd reached a turning point in their relationship, and he wasn't sure either of them wanted to proceed.

Claire still carried a lot of baggage from her marriage, baggage he didn't want unloaded on his doorstep. His marriage had died a slow death. From neglect, his wife had said. She'd accused him of being married to his job. He wasn't sure the new job had changed that, and Claire would require a man who paid attention.

He picked up Tony Burke's file. Smith and Monroe had uncovered a history studded with arrests for DUI, public drunkenness, drunk and disorderly, assault and battery. The arrest reports painted the picture of a young man with a drinking problem, an anger management problem, and a good lawyer. Thanks to Paul Gilbert, there'd been no convictions.

"I've read it," Bea said. "Penny ante stuff and nothing recent."

"Would you want your sister to go out with this guy?"

"Both my sisters are happily married. But if Tony Burke offered to take me round the track, I'd hop right in his car."

Mike's double take caught her wide grin. She was laughing openly this time, and he had to laugh with her. Working with this young woman was a breath of fresh air. His previous colleagues had been men, both in the military and here in the homicide division. When he started, he'd worked most closely with an old cop on his way out the door. Detective

Beatrice Washington was a lot smarter and much better company.

"Burke also has a juvenile record," he said, "which has been sealed. We could seek a court order, but I can't think of a valid reason, not yet anyway, and we know enough without it. Trouble is his middle name."

"Trouble on a small scale, and nothing for the last decade. It looks like he grew up."

"Do you believe that or are you playing the devil's advocate?"

"Both. Murder is a long way from getting drunk and fighting over women, which is what he used to do." She pulled a granola bar out of her pocket and unwrapped it. "Want some?"

"No thanks but go right ahead." She was right, but he pushed on. "Burke's adult record shows a tendency to violence when he's been drinking heavily, which he admits doing during the relevant timeframe. We also have a motive, revenge for his father's death."

"Tony's not the least bit stupid, and these files," Bea pointed to the papers spread over his desk, "show that he's all too familiar with the criminal justice system. Yet he tells us that he believes his mother killed his father. He tells us he doesn't care that his mother was murdered. He tells us he was drinking or sleeping it off during the time she was strangled and hours on either side. And he agreed to give us a DNA sample."

"He could be taunting us, or he could be innocent. I'm reserving judgment." He was a good cop and good cops don't let personal animosities shade their investigations. "If it's Burke's skin under the victim's fingernails, I'll be convinced he's our killer."

"Yes, sir." She put the last of the bar in her mouth and tossed the wrapper into his wastebasket. "Two points."

Maybe she really did play basketball. Someday, he'd ask her.

19

Mike was surprised to see Walt Smith leaning against his office door, a newspaper in his hand and a smirk on his face. Smith had been sulking since Vernon's tongue lashing. He'd taken the assignment to search old records with bad grace, seeing only the punishment and not the opportunity for expiation. But something in this morning's paper had made him happy enough to come in early and lie in ambush.

"Looking for me?" he waved Smith into his office and toward a seat. "Nice job tracking down Burke's old arrests. How about a cup of coffee?" He began making a fresh pot. Both of them could see the message light blinking on his phone. "It's not great, but it's better than the swill they sell downstairs."

"Aw, man, it's not your fault," Walt said.

"What's not my fault?"

"Vernon. It's not your fault he tore me a new one. Sorry, Mike. I'm leaving." He dropped his newspaper on the desk. "Read it before you check your messages."

Walt closed the door behind him, and Mike unfolded the paper. A headline halfway down the front page read *Socialite murdered at upscale retirement home.* Geneviève Burke's murder had been worth a short paragraph buried deep inside Monday's metro section and a slightly larger article in the Tuesday Sports Section once the connection to Tony became known. Today, Geneviève Devereux Burke made the front page.

Mike skimmed the story, looking for a clue to the reporter's source. He found it in the last paragraph. "Despite an eyewitness who saw the murderer, the police have made no arrests." Iris? She'd called Bea yesterday, something about a man near the victim's apartment. A teaser at the end of the story directed the reader to *Reunited lovers* on page B-1. He turned to it.

With growing disbelief, Mike read the story of Roger and Geneviève Devereux, who married briefly when they were young and foolish and reunited in old age only to be separated by violent death. The story was a ludicrous fantasy that could have been designed to infuriate the Devereux family. No wonder Walt was laughing. If he weren't standing in the shadow of the guillotine, he'd be laughing too. He checked his message. No surprise. Vernon wanted to see him ASAP. He called Beatrice.

"The cat is out of the bag."

"Out of the bag and peeing on the carpet. It has to be Iris. I'm sorry, Mike."

"It's not your fault, nor is it mine, but I want a briefing on your meeting with Iris before I talk to Vernon."

"Let me go with you. I'm the one who interviewed her."

"Come on then. Can you brief me en route?"

"It won't take that long. I've told you about the interview. She rescheduled the meeting."

Vernon gestured toward the now familiar newspaper lying on his desk. "Have you seen this? If not, you're the only two people in New Orleans who haven't." Before either could respond, he continued, "What about the interview? On the fucking ten o'clock news? Did you see that?" He clenched and unclenched his jaw.

Mike looked at Bea, who shook her head. He answered for both of them. "This is the first we've heard about a television interview."

"No one told me until this morning, or we'd have had this meeting last night. Watch." The Super pointed at a screen set up behind the conference table. "I had a copy of the tape sent over."

After a short series of sputters and crackles, the picture emerged. A young woman sat in silhouette, her face blurred, and answered the reporter's questions in a soft voice. As she spoke, the camera moved from the long hair falling across her face to the hands folded demurely in her lap then lingered on her shapely legs, crossed and tucked to the side. The gist of the interview was that she had seen a well-dressed older man lurking near the victim's apartment at approximately the time of the murder. It was nothing definitive, but she and the reporter made the most of it.

"I saw the killer." She shuddered, and the camera panned to the newscaster.

Vernon muted the sound. "What the hell's going on?"

Bea answered. "The woman is Iris Burton, an aide at Sunny Gardens who was friends with the victim. She discovered the body. I interviewed her Tuesday, but she didn't mention this man. She called yesterday, told me about seeing him, said he'd looked as if he belonged, so she'd forgotten about him.

"I set up an appointment with a sketch artist. Yesterday afternoon, but Iris cancelled. Something had come up and she couldn't make it." Bea shook her head in dismay. "Her description is vague enough to fit any number of men who could have any number of innocent reasons to be there, but if I were the killer and I saw that interview..."

"We're stretched thin right now, but we have to consider protective surveillance," Mike said.

"Start by bringing her in." Vernon reached in his pocket for a fresh piece of chewing gum. He looked ready to explode.

"She's coming here after she gets off," Bea said. "Which should be soon. Her shift ends at ten."

There was a knock on the door, and Vernon's secretary stuck her head in. "Sorry to interrupt, but there's an urgent message for Captain Robinson. A man named Doug Chastain says Iris is dead. He's holding on line three."

Bea gasped. Vernon shoved his phone across the desk, and Mike picked up.

"Have you called 911?"

"I called you," Chastain said. "I don't want a bunch of sirens screaming in here like they did Sunday morning."

"I'm going to dispatch an ambulance."

"Don't bother. The girl is dead. If you don't believe me, I'll put our nurse on. She checked for vital signs and found none."

"What happened?"

"Someone shot her." Chastain emphasized *shot*, as if such a thing was beyond belief.

"Where is she?"

"In the employee parking lot. A group of our early-morning walkers found her lying beside her car."

"Don't let anyone near the body. Keep people out of the parking lot. A patrol car will be there shortly. Detective Washington and I are on our way." He hung up.

"That was fast," Vernon said.

"Again," Mike said. The first victim had been killed less than twenty-four hours after the discovery of the old bones.

"That poor foolish child," Bea murmured.

"If she'd met with you instead of that reporter, we'd know what the killer looked like, and she'd still be alive." Vernon's words were harsher than his tone. "Keep me posted."

Mike used the phone while Bea drove. He briefed Bill Lukas and gave him Tony Burke's contact information. "See if you can find him, see how he reacts to the news of Iris's death. I don't expect him to say anything incriminating, but we'd be remiss if we didn't follow up. Detective Washington and I are on our way to the scene. Meet us there when you finish with Burke."

"The killer knows his or her way around Sunny Gardens," Bea said.

"Another employee or a resident," Mike agreed. "Or a frequent visitor. For example, Tony Burke. Regardless of what he said about his mother, he helped her move in and visited her twice before the Saturday night argument."

"Iris told me she'd never met Tony."

"That doesn't mean he didn't know about her and couldn't find out when she came to work."

"What about Roger Devereux?"

"It's hard to believe he's capable of such organized behavior or has access to a gun. But we know he's capable of violence."

Two patrol cars, blue lights flashing, blocked off the far side of the Sunny Gardens employee parking lot. Bea took the closest parking space, and they walked over to the two uniformed officers.

Mike showed his badge. "Where is she?"

The officer gestured toward an aged sedan, its driver-side door ajar. "On the ground next to that old Chevy. He must have popped her the minute she exited the car. Crime Scene Unit is on the way."

"I want to take a look before they get here."

A young woman lay on her stomach, her face turned to one side. Blood puddled around her head, and streaks of dried blood showed where she'd slid down the side of the car. Mike knelt for a closer look. Two exit wounds, one in her forehead and one on her cheek said she'd been shot twice from behind. He'd guess at close range; forensics would probably find powder burns on the white cap she was wearing. Despite the wounds, he could see that she had been pretty. He looked up, and Bea answered the question written on his face.

"It's Iris." She turned away, head bowed.

"We're going inside," he told the uniformed officer. "Don't let anyone—I don't care who they are or who they know—near the body until the crime scene unit gets here. Refer any questions or objections to Detective Washington. She's in charge." That he was standing behind her went without saying.

He kept a firm hand on Beatrice's arm as they walked up to the building. "Are you going to be okay?" As far as he knew, this was her first homicide victim.

"I hope she never knew what hit her."

"I doubt she did."

When they entered the building, the crowd in the reception area parted like the Red Sea before Moses. The receptionist's face was tight with shock.

"Mr. Chastain is in his office," she said. "I'll call him."

"We know the way, thank you." He kept walking.

Dwight Chastain greeted them with an angry outburst. "She never should have talked to reporters."

Mike responded with a cold stare; Bea's glare could have burned a hole through steel.

"I don't mean to be unsympathetic," Chastain said, "but I'm in a very difficult situation. I have to explain Iris's indiscretion to the Devereux family."

"Would you rather talk to Iris's family?" Mike said.

The last of Chastain's bluster melted. "She was so young, such a pretty little thing."

"Detective Washington is in charge. She and Detective Lukas will each need a room for interviews. They'll start with the women who found Iris's body, the security guards, and any other staff or residents who think they've seen or heard something relevant."

"Of course, we'll do all we can to help in your investigation."

"I'll want to talk to the Memory Garden staff," Bea said, "whether or not they think they know something relevant."

Chastain started to object, and Mike assured him that the police department would not initiate contact with Roger Devereux without first notifying his family.

"Do you object to Detective Washington interviewing your staff?"

"I'm trying to do the right thing." Chastain's expression was defensive, his voice a grating whine.

"The right thing is to help us find the killer," Mike said. "Can you get me a copy of Iris's HR file? I'm looking for information on her next of kin."

"Of course." Chastain hurried off to fetch the file.

Mike got the car keys from Beatrice, who could ride back with Bill Lukas. "Soon as I get the file, I'm going back to headquarters. Call me if you need me."

Mike flipped through the stack of messages on his desk. Nothing that couldn't wait. He opened Iris's file, found a current address on her job application, and sent a team to secure the site. Further down he found next of kin. Her parents lived in Catahoula, a very small town in Northwest Louisiana. There was no phone number listed, so he called the Catahoula police station. The desk put him through to the chief.

"I'm looking for contact information," he said. "William and Carol Burton, they have a daughter named Iris." *Had, not have, but sharing that sad fact would come later.*

"Carol Burton taught me high school English, and I know Bill from Rotary." The chief's worried tone said he didn't expect good news from New Orleans Homicide. "Why are you calling? I hope nothing's happened to that little girl of theirs."

"Iris was murdered early this morning. I'm looking for help notifying her family."

"I'll do it. Fill me in." His tone was grim.

"Thank you." Mike passed on what they knew. "It appears that her assailant surprised her and that death was instantaneous."

"She was their only child."

"We'll hold her body until we hear from them." Mike thanked the chief again before hanging up. He didn't envy him the next several hours.

He fixed himself a fresh pot of coffee and turned to the message slips. Paul Gilbert had called on an urgent matter concerning Laura

Bethea. *Urgent according to who?* He returned the call, and Paul delivered the expected message.

"The Devereux family is furious about the publicity linking them to Geneviève Burke, and Laura blames you, personally, for that newspaper story. She's demanding your head. Apparently you and she had a tête-à-tête."

"I met with Mrs. Bethea at her request. However, neither I nor anyone else working here was the source of that story. *And you should know that.* Have you or she seen the television interview?"

"Apparently Laura has. I've only heard about it. I presume the woman interviewed was employed by Sunny Gardens."

Mike remained silent.

"She'll lose her job over this. The family won't be satisfied with less."

"She lost her life. She was shot dead in the Sunny Gardens parking lot early this morning."

It was Paul's turn to be silent.

"Which is where I was when you called."

"Yours is a brutal business, Mike."

"Homicide is brutal. My business is to arrest and convict the brutes."

"I'll do what I can to keep the family appeased. At the moment their greatest outrage is directed within, at poor Laura. When you have time, I'd like to talk to you about her."

"I have time right now."

"What I have to say is really an *apologia.* Laura is a good person doing her best in a bad situation. She and Roger have always been close. He was an indulgent uncle and, after her father died, a surrogate father. When Roger became ill, their roles reversed. She's been a devoted caretaker, but I'm sure it's taken a toll." He paused. "I'm no longer representing Roger."

"She mentioned that."

"I understand why you had to talk to her. I also understand that you have no obligation to inform me about the conversation."

"She discussed Roger and Geneviève's divorce." And how she could link that sad and sordid tale to the romantic drivel in the newspaper story was beyond him.

"As I told you before, I was a child when they divorced. I don't know anything about the circumstances."

"I imagine your father could tell you. Have you asked him about Geneviève's lovers?"

"I'm working on it, but surely after this latest killing…"

"The question becomes more urgent."

"I'll speak to my father again."

"Let me know what he says."

Mike poured a fresh cup of coffee and gave himself a five-minute break before addressing the case files on his desk. Once he had satisfied himself that everything else was moving ahead, he turned back to the Burke—now the Burke-Burton—homicide and the notes he'd written during Claire's call.

He doubted that horses had anything to do with Geneviève Burke's murder. If someone stole a horse up in Saint Helene, it was the concern of the local sheriff's office, not New Orleans Homicide. But he owed Claire an apology, and it would carry more weight after he'd talked to Winslow. He dialed the number she'd given him and, when a man answered, identified himself and asked to speak to Kyle Winslow.

"Speaking." Winslow's voice was tight with nerves, a not uncommon response to a call from the police.

"I understand that you worked for Geneviève Burke."

Silence.

"What exactly did you do for Mrs. Burke?" Claire had said he was a trainer. Talking about his job should settle him down and lead to a discussion of horses. Instead, the innocuous question produced a surprising response.

"I've been expecting your call. The neighbor copied down my license plate, didn't he?"

20

"Good morning, Walkers, Elaine Reed speaking."

"I'm hoping you can help me." Claire said. "There's a horse I'm considering, and I want to check his background before I commit to buying him."

"Are you a member?"

"No, but I'm hoping you can help me anyway." She'd found them in a directory of organizations.

"I'll try." The woman confirmed that the association maintained a registry of Tennessee Walking Horses. They also kept records of competitions, at least the major ones. "Is the seller one of our members?"

"I don't know. That's really my problem, I don't know anything about the seller, and he says the horses' papers are in a safe deposit box over in Georgia." *My real problem is I didn't think this through. What a lame story.* "He says the horse has won several shows, but he hasn't anything to prove it. I'm not sure he's telling the truth, and I wondered if there's a way to check."

"It sounds to me as if you'd be better off buying a horse from a seller you trust. Or at least waiting until this seller can produce the papers."

"But I really like this horse, and the price is so good that I'm afraid someone else will come along and buy him if I drag my feet."

"No papers and a very good price. Are you sure this horse wasn't stolen?"

"Oh, no." Claire almost dropped the phone. That was exactly what she thought. "The seller is a reputable businessman. He just doesn't have time for a horse."

"Do you know the horse's name? Which shows he won?"

"I know what he looks like." Silence from the other end. "He's a three-year-old stallion, black with a white blaze, eighteen hands tall. He won his first show when he was just a colt. Like eight weeks old."

"Have you ever owned a horse before?"

"No." This was true. Despite years of determined efforts she'd never been able to convince her parents to buy her one.

"Purchasing a horse is nothing to be done lightly." Elaine Reed shifted into lecture mode. "You're taking on a great deal of responsibility, expensive responsibility. The initial price is just the beginning. And stallions can be particularly difficult. I suggest you learn more about what it takes before you buy this horse or any other."

"I've been riding all my life. I know what's involved in caring for a horse, but I didn't know about Tennessee Walking Horses until I looked at this one. He's gorgeous, and he has an amazingly smooth gait, a natural big lick." Claire was talking fast and thinking faster. "If I came to your office, could I try to find him in your files?" She probably knew enough to find Geneviève's horse among the registered three-year-old stallions. Worst case, she could narrow it down to a few horses.

"Are you nearby?"

"I live in New Orleans, but I'll be keeping the horse on a farm a few miles out. I've already made arrangements." What began as a simple lie was growing into a complex fabrication, and Claire had never been a good liar. If she never had to make another call like this one, she'd be a happy woman.

"If you want to drive all the way up here, I'll try to help you. We're open weekdays nine to twelve and one to five. Anyone in town can direct you to our offices."

Claire thanked her and hung up. Going to Tennessee was a last resort. First, she'd give Kyle another chance to tell the truth about Fast Eddie. She called him, but his line was busy. She was meeting the plumber at the Currier's house in fifteen minutes; Kyle would have to wait.

By early afternoon, Claire had walked through both houses with the plumber and was back in Tony's kitchen, waiting for the electrician.

Things were moving along nicely. The demolition crew should finish knocking down the back stoop today, which would put everything on schedule. The men were taking a break, and she took advantage of the quiet to try Kyle again. This time, he answered. She asked if he could use help exercising the horses.

"Saturday morning, I have to run errands, but I should be done by noon."

"Come on up. I'll be here all day."

"I'll get there at two or a little before. Okay?"

"Two's fine." Kyle never wasted words, but today there was a different undertone. Claire couldn't tell if he was in a bad mood or just had other things on his mind. She asked if he'd sold any of the horses.

"We can talk about horses when you come up. See you Saturday."

"Okay."

As soon as she hung up, her phone rang. The electrician was running late; he'd be there in forty-five minutes. The demo crew resumed their attack on the back stoop, and Claire retreated to the front room. She was thinking about how to approach Kyle when she felt someone watching her. She turned around, and saw Tony.

"Sorry I didn't make it by yesterday afternoon," he said. "I stopped by late, after you'd left. You're right about the wood floor, but I still want real furniture in the kitchen, no built-ins."

He had given her pictures of a kitchen in an Italian villa, saying it showed the look he wanted. His budget was whatever it would take—he trusted her. Adapting Tony's vision to the smaller dimensions of his kitchen would be a challenge. It was also more consistent with the house than any modern kitchen with its walls of matching cabinets could ever be, and Claire was enthusiastic about the prospect.

"I've already located some cupboards and an armoire that might work. They will look terrific with the wood floor."

"I talked to Judy Boaz last night."

"And?"

"Let's go outside where we can hear ourselves think."

They sat on the gallery steps, and he said, "She kept telling me what a cute little boy I was and how much she'd like to see me all grown up. She was angling for me to take her out to dinner. Like my Dad used to, she says. When I dodged, she started whining." He scowled. "One phone conversation was more than enough of her."

"Did you ask about Geneviève?"

"She said Geneviève's affairs never lasted long, but there was one guy with money who was always in the background. She called him Geneviève's 'sugar daddy'. Judy talks like a character in an old b-movie."

"Did she remember his name?"

"She never knew it, says it was a secret even from Dad. But she's sure that this sugar daddy gave Geneviève land where, he knew, a highway was going through. She sold it for a fat profit. We find the deed." He snapped his finger. "We have his name."

"Easier said than done." She explained that land records were organized not by the names of owners but by location. Unless he knew what piece of land was involved, they'd be looking for a needle in a haystack.

"I thought you researched the deeds for the houses your company restores."

"I do, and I know the addresses. Did Judy tell you anything else, like what road we're talking about, what year this happened, something to narrow it down?"

"No, but I can get back in touch. I ended our conversation on a positive note, just in case." He groaned. "I'll take her out to dinner if I have to, but trust me, I'd rather go out with you."

"I certainly hope so. You just finished telling me how awful she is."

"Let me rephrase my comment. There's no one in New Orleans I'd rather take to dinner." He looked her over. "It takes a special woman to look good in baggy jeans and a work shirt, but I'm hoping you own a dress."

"I own several dresses. Did you call the lawyer?"

"I'm meeting with him Monday. Are you busy Saturday night?"

"Saturday I'm going up to the farm to help exercise the horses and staying to talk. I think Kyle is ready to tell me the truth about Fast Eddie. If not, I've found an organization of Walking Horse owners and trainers in Tennessee that can help us find the horse."

"Claire, the missing horse is a snipe hunt for the police, not for you. I really want them off my back. A detective woke me up this morning to ask if I'd killed Iris somebody."

"Iris, who worked at Sunny Gardens? Someone killed her? When?"

"This morning. Did you know her?"

"Your mother mentioned her—positively. Iris was the only person working there that she liked. And she's dead? Tony, something really weird is going on."

"No kidding. And look who's here to talk about it." He pointed to the curb where a car had just pulled up. "Your pal the policeman."

Mike was alone this time. He got out of the car and walked toward them.

"Hi Mike," she said. "What brings you here?"

"I've been looking for your friend." He nodded toward Tony.

"I haven't been hiding." Tony's eyes had turned the cloudy gray of a winter storm.

"Is there somewhere more private where we can talk?" Mike said.

"What's wrong with right here?"

Several bangs followed by a loud crash came from inside the house. Mike's raised eyebrows asked for an explanation.

"We're demolishing the back stoop," Claire said. "Let me see if they can't keep the noise down for a few minutes." She started to rise, but Tony grabbed her hand.

"Stay, Claire, please. You know as much about this as I do, and I could use a little moral support." When she sat back down, he used his leverage on her hand to pull her closer.

Mike took a tape recorder out of his pocket. "Do you mind if I record our conversation?"

"Record away," Tony said. "I have nothing to hide."

Finding Claire and Burke together had been an unpleasant surprise, and Mike was annoyed with himself for not anticipating the possibility. He returned to headquarters, cleared some paperwork, and then stopped by Bea's office. She'd just returned from Sunny Gardens.

"I got your message about the horse trainer," she said. "It looks more and more like Tony is right about his mother's involvement in the old murder."

"She knew that skeleton was there."

"Have you told Claire? Or thanked her for the tip?"

"I just saw her. I should have mentioned it."

"I bet she was happy to see you." Bea smiled.

"She was with Burke, and neither was happy to see me." They'd been deep in a conversation that stopped the minute they spotted him.

"I don't believe it. She likes you, Mike."

Bea was going to tease him about Claire Marshall every chance she got. Well, he'd gathered a little ammunition this afternoon and he was going to use it.

"Burke asked about you."

"Really?" She raised her eyebrows.

"He wanted to know if you were back at the office, pulling wings off butterflies." He gave it a minute to register. "If you're still interested in this guy, Beatrice, you're going to have to do something about that first impression."

"He said that? Really?" She laughed. "I guess it's back to charm school for me." She took a package of cookies out of her jacket pocket and waved them at him. "Want one? Oatmeal raisin. Practically health food."

"No, thanks."

"What else did he say?"

"He never met Iris Burton, but he thinks she must have been the 'little friend on the staff' who told his mother that Roger Devereux was at Sunny Gardens, in the batso wing. Claire backed him up. Geneviève told her the same thing, used the same term."

"The batso wing? That's cold."

"He thinks the management might have another name for it." Burke had a sense of humor, albeit a dark one. "Our celebrity suspect is not happy about the publicity surrounding his mother's murder, and he isn't sure whether we or the reporters are more annoying. But he was amused by the newspaper story about Geneviève being reunited with her lost love. The funniest part was anyone thinking she had the capacity to love."

"He's not backing off is he?"

"Not an inch." Burke had been defiant, and he'd manipulated the situation beautifully, Tony and Claire united against the evil intruding policeman. "Nor has his arrogance abated. He's going to give us the killer on a silver platter. It's all here." He pulled the tape recorder out of his pocket.

"Are we still talking about the man who may or may not exist, his mother's lover who helped her kill his father?"

"Yes. And he's sure that Iris was killed because she was Geneviève's confidante." He kneaded the back of his neck where tension had grabbed hold. "The more we learn, the more sense his theory makes, but I'm not ready to declare his innocence. Did you talk to Tamika?"

"She doesn't remember how she happened to get those old bruises, and short of a lie detector test, we can't do anything about it. She is certain that Devereux was upstairs this morning. The only person who actually saw him before seven-thirty was Matt Truex, a student the family has hired to help Roger get up and dressed. All three staff members saw Truex arrive at six-thirty and go directly to Roger's room. At seven-fifteen Truex brought Roger out to breakfast, where he remained for the next forty-five minutes. This morning like every other morning. I have Truex's contact information, and I'll talk to him, but I don't expect to learn anything we don't already know."

"So, Roger's not the shooter." He'd never really believed it possible. "Anything else?"

"Not much. None of the early morning walkers noticed any other people around, nor did anyone hear the shots. Everyone claims to be terribly upset, but they're loving the excitement."

"You don't like Sunny Gardens," he said. Geneviève hadn't either.

"It reminds me of junior high school." Bea made a face. "Tamika feels bad because she and some of the other staff used to mock Iris behind her back. They say she dressed like a nurse in a sixties sit-com. If she hadn't been talking to me, I think the venue would have been a porn film."

"Does she feel bad because she's lying about those old bruises? "

"Not that I can tell. And I've yet to find anyone, staff or resident, who liked Geneviève. Our two victims formed their own little clique, and no one at Sunny Gardens knew or cared much about either one except..."

"Except the person who cared enough to kill them."

21

"My daughter witnessed a murder, and you did nothing to keep her safe?"

Bill Burton stood next to the chair he'd been offered, clenching and unclenching his fists. Mike remained standing with him. Mrs. Burton sat across the table, Bea beside her.

"As soon as I learned Iris was telling people she'd seen the killer, I began making plans for her protection. It was already too late. I'm sorry." He took personal responsibility. Grieving parents deserved more than a bureaucratic *we*.

"Before you could make your plans or before you knew?"

"Before I knew." It was the truth, but it wasn't going to satisfy Iris's father whose outrage demanded a target more substantial than a shadowy unknown killer. "Mr. Burton, we'll do everything in our power to bring your daughter's killer to justice."

The clichéd response was far kinder than telling this man that his daughter had placed herself in peril. Iris had wanted fame, and in death, she'd gained it. Her murder led the local news. Every TV station ran and reran clips from her interview, shadowy and mysterious but recognizable. Iris had signed her own death warrant, and he hoped her parents never found out.

"Did she suffer?" Carol Burton said.

"No. Death was immediate. The killer was behind her, and there were no signs of a struggle. I doubt she knew what happened or saw who it was." *And I hope you can find comfort in that.*

Mike had seen his first dead man in Vietnam. It was the first of many, comrades and enemies. The lucky ones looked more surprised than anguished. Regardless, that last expression on the faces of men who'd been his friends remained etched in memory, forever obscuring how they'd looked when they were alive. It was something no parent should have to see.

Iris's father must know this too. He had insisted that he alone would identify his daughter. Only one parent would have to stand in the cold room and watch the sheet being drawn back from their daughter's damaged face. Only her father would see the bullet holes. He would identify and claim their child's body. Mike would accompany Mr. Burton to the morgue while Bea stayed with Mrs. Burton.

Bill Burton walked to the door. "Let's go."

Iris's mother watched her husband depart then walked over to the window. "It should be raining." She gazed at the clear blue sky. "That's what I was thinking the whole way driving down here. If this were Shakespeare, the cloud-darkened sky would be shedding hard tears; the wind would be howling with grief. Nature recognizes tragedy in Shakespeare."

"We consider your daughter's death a tragedy," Bea said.

"Is there any chance you've made a mistake? That it's not Iris."

"No. I'm sorry, but no."

"Shakespeare built several plays around mistaken identity; they were comedies, not tragedies." The bereaved mother turned away from the window. "Have you read Shakespeare?"

"Not since high school," Bea said. She'd majored in criminal justice at Orleans Community College and then LSU. It was a curriculum with little room for the liberal arts.

"I'm a high school English teacher. Juniors study Shakespeare, and each year the class puts on one of his plays. Iris's junior year, it was Hamlet. She was Ophelia. I didn't want to give my own daughter the female lead, but the other students insisted. They said the best actress shouldn't be eliminated just because her mother was the teacher."

"Iris told me she'd started acting in grammar school."

"I wish you could have seen her. She wore a long white dress and I wove real flowers into her hair."

"She must have been lovely."

"Of course, Ophelia dies. Although it's not clear if her death was an accident or suicide, Iris wanted it to be an accident, and that's how she played it. She refused to accept the idea of a heroine, even one who had gone mad, *choosing* to die."

If picturing her daughter as a tragic heroine helped Iris's mother cope with the unthinkable, Bea would do her best to go along. "I remember reading Hamlet but I wasn't really confident that I understood everything."

"Do any of us? Still, the better students are captured by the drama. There's sex and violence, insanity and revenge." Carol Burton turned back to the window and the offending blue sky.

"I spent a some time with Iris," Bea said. "Not much, but I felt as if I was getting to know her. I'd like to know more, what she was like, who her friends were."

"She was nineteen but still very much a child with a child's view of the world. Innocent in the truest sense of the word."

"She told me that you two were very close."

"Iris was my only child. I held her near even when we were apart." She hugged herself as if warding off the cold—or the cold knowledge that she'd never hug her daughter again. "It's not even Friday the thirteenth is it?"

"No." It was the fourth, not close. "Would you like to sit down?"

"Thank you." Moving slowly, like a woman decades older, Carol Burton returned to the chair.

"Did Iris ever mention Geneviève Burke?" Bea picked up her pencil.

"She called Sunday night—she called every Sunday night—and told us Geneviève had been murdered. She was extremely upset. We were too. Bill and I tried to talk her into moving back home, but—" A sob kept her from finishing the sentence. She recovered her poise and continued, "The last couple weeks, all Iris talked about was Geneviève. Geneviève this, Geneviève that. She said Geneviève was her mentor. I think she meant role model."

"Did Iris ever talk about Geneviève's past, her marriages, old love affairs?"

"She told me her first husband was at Sunny Gardens, too, in a different area, because he has Alzheimer's." Iris's mother frowned. "Some story that didn't make much sense about him trying to break into Geneviève's apartment. Iris thought that under the craziness, he still loved her and wanted to be with her. You don't think he…"

"No, we don't," Bea said. "Geneviève married twice. Did Iris pass on anything about the second marriage?"

"She was thrilled to learn that Geneviève's son from her second marriage was the glamorous Tony Burke, and then disappointed when Geneviève refused to introduce them. She told Iris that Layton—that's what his mother called him—was the kind of man who'd mess up a young woman's life without a second thought. Of course that only made Iris more determined to meet him." A smile flickered then died. "They never met. She would have told me."

"Did Iris ever mention anything else about Geneviève's ex-husbands. Or old lovers?"

"I thought you wanted to talk about Iris. Your questions are about Geneviève."

"It appears that this all began with Geneviève," Bea said. "But I do want to know about Iris. Was there a boyfriend? A best friend? Someone she might have confided in?"

"Only Geneviève." Carol Burton wiped a tear from her cheek. "Now I'm doing it."

"Do you know of anyone who was angry with Iris or resented her?" She would go through the motions, although this line of questioning was more consolation than investigation.

"No one. Iris wanted fame and fortune, travel to distant cities, and the company of glamorous people, but hers wasn't a walk-all-over-other-people kind of ambition. She was one of the most popular girls in the high school. Everyone liked her."

"The people we've talked to said Iris always had a smile and a pleasant word."

"Bill wants vengeance, like Hamlet did. He feels guilty. We both do."

"Nothing that happened is his fault, or yours."

"Iris dropped out of college after one semester. She moved to New Orleans to pursue a career in show business. Bill and I wanted her to finish school, but she was determined, and we agreed to pay her rent for a year. Last month, the year was up, and we cut her off. That's why she took the job at Sunny Gardens." A tear ran down her cheek. "It wasn't the money; we could afford it. We loved her and wanted what was best for her."

"I'm sure Iris knew that."

"I don't care about vengeance. Whether or not you find the killer, my daughter is gone. Moving to New Orleans was supposed to be the first step toward a wonderful and exciting life, but all she got was one crummy job waiting tables in a night club and another one handing out pills in a retirement home."

"She mentioned going to auditions, taking acting and dancing classes that she really enjoyed." Bea searched for words that might offer some comfort.

"I saw the television interview. We get New Orleans stations on cable. Iris called and told me to watch but not tell her father. She knew he wouldn't approve. She said Geneviève would and that her stepping forward could help find the killer. But it's what helped the killer find her, isn't it?" As she spoke Carol Burton folded in on herself, unable to bear the burden of her knowledge.

"There's a sofa in the ladies room—and a blanket. Would you like to lie down for a few minutes? I'll sit with you until your husband gets back." They'd have to be back soon. Mike had an eleven-thirty appointment with Kyle Winslow.

22

Tony called Judy Boaz and ran into a buzz saw.

"We talked for almost an hour," she said, "and you never told me Geneviève had been murdered."

"I told you she was dead."

"That's not the same thing. I felt like an idiot when I read about it in the paper."

"No it's not the same thing; it's much worse. Put yourself in my shoes, Judy. Imagine how hard it is to tell someone your mother was murdered."

"You asked me who her boyfriends were, but you never mentioned anything about her being reunited with her long lost love."

"That story is… Never mind." He leveled with her, to a point. "I'm trying to find the man who murdered my mother. I hoped you could tell me who he was."

"Geneviève was killed last weekend. You asked about things that happened ages ago."

"The motive for her murder goes way back." *Way back to when she killed my father, the man you claim was your lover, and I don't believe you.*

"I still don't see why you didn't tell me."

Tony, who despised whiners, wanted to tell Judy to suck it up and move on, but he needed her cooperation. He lowered his voice. "There are many things I didn't tell you. For your own protection." If she didn't like the truth, he'd give her a good story. Winding her up would be payback for the cracks she'd made about his father, implying that he was a lousy husband and a drunk. What kind of husband could anyone be to Geneviève? She'd drive a saint to drink.

"My protection? What are you talking about? I haven't seen Geneviève since before Jim died. I hardly knew her, and she never bothered speaking to me."

"The land deal you told me about. That's why she was killed."

"Years and years later? Who still cares?"

"That deal was just one stepping stone in a trail of corruption that continues to this day." He kept his voice low as if he was afraid of being overheard. "Influential people are involved. Geneviève was going to testify against them. That's why she's dead."

Judy gasped. "Why didn't you tell me?"

"I wasn't sure there was a connection, but now I am." He paused for dramatic effect. "Don't worry, Judy, you'll be safe as long as you don't mention this conversation to anyone. I'll keep your identity secret."

"Oh my God."

After another allusion to shadowy conspiracies involving ruthless and powerful interests, he said, "Have you remembered any details that will help identify that land deal? Like when Geneviève sold the property or which highway was going through? Was it an Interstate?"

After several minutes of hemming and hawing about this being really embarrassing, she told him. "It was after I got married. Your dad and I used to meet up now and then. You know, for old times." She sighed loudly. "Bill never found out. I still feel bad about it, but I just couldn't tell Jim no." She giggled.

"So it would be 1967 or '68?"

"More like '69, right before Jim died."

"Nineteen sixty nine?" He echoed. *Was this it?*

"Jim's paintings had started selling, and he had money. Like I told you, he usually blew it on good times, you know, celebrating a sale, but this time he wanted to invest. He'd found out Geneviève was making a bundle because of the highway, and it drove him nuts that she wouldn't let him in on it. If she'd just told him where that road was going, he could have bought land in its path, too. I remember, after he died, thinking that it didn't matter anymore."

"Did he say any more, like where he thought it might be going?"

"It's not like we spent a lot of time together—and when we did, well we didn't spend a lot of time talking."

Tony couldn't stand any more. "You've been very helpful," he said. "If you think of anything else, call Claire and she'll contact me."

"Okay, but when are we going out? You said you'd take me out for dinner." She was back to whining, and her voice grated like fingernails on a blackboard.

"For your own safety, we shouldn't be seen together until this is all over." *Until hell freezes over.*

Claire was at her desk, wrapping up boring but necessary paperwork when Tony called, jubilant because he'd gotten more information from Judy Boaz. What was she doing for dinner? They could compare notes over a good meal. She hesitated. She'd been looking forward to a light supper, a movie on the VCR, and an early bedtime. She didn't want to go out, but ...

"Why don't you come over to my house? I'll roast a chicken."

"I'll bring the wine. What time?"

"Seven or a little before."

At five of seven, the doorbell rang. Tony handed her a long white florist box.

"You didn't need to bring flowers," she said, "but thank you."

"I wanted to." He smiled at her. "Aren't you going to open it?"

"Yellow roses." She lifted the flowers from their wrapping. "They're beautiful. Thank you."

He followed her into the kitchen, set his tote bag on the counter and produced a second box from under his jacket. "Something to put them in."

Claire held the vase up and light shone through the cobalt glass. "It's lovely, Tony, but this is too much."

"Yellow and blue to match your living room. You like houses, so I got something to go with your house."

She arranged the roses in the vase and set them on the coffee table. "They're perfect."

"Now, where's the big guy?" He pulled a little stuffed mouse from his pocket. "This is for him."

Claire called his name, and Dorian sauntered out of the bedroom, maintaining his feline dignity by ignoring her. He wasn't responding to her summons; the timing was pure coincidence. He spotted Tony, and his tail twitched into the upright position, disdain.

Tony sat back on his heels and put the toy on the floor. He twisted the tail, wiggling the mouse a little closer to the cat. Dorian maintained his aloof posture, but his amber eyes followed the movement. "Catnip, big guy. You know you want it." Tony twisted the tail again.

Dorian pounced. The toy skittered across the floor, cat in hot pursuit. He batted it into the kitchen and disappeared after it.

"I just seduced your cat." Tony stood up, a pleased grin on his face.

"Yes you did." Claire chuckled at the sounds of Dorian careening around the kitchen.

"Have you talked to the police today?" he said, his smile gone.

She shook her head.

"Me neither, not that it makes much difference. They don't believe a word I say."

"It's hard to know what they're thinking," was the best she could offer. Yesterday afternoon, she'd watched Mike question Tony about Iris Burton. By the time he left, she was so angry that she never wanted to see him again. Tony read her mind.

"My alibi for Iris Burton's murder is only slightly better than that for my mother's. I was asleep, and I'm sleeping alone these days."

"They reran part of her interview on the news. She told the reporter that she'd seen a man lurking near your mother's apartment right before she was killed."

"No wonder he went after her. Did she describe him?"

"A well-dressed older man."

"Geneviève's old lover. Someday the cops will believe me." He let out a long breath. "I told you I talked to Judy Boaz again."

"You said you'd learned more."

"The land sale was in 1969, not long before Dad was killed. According to Judy, he found out about the deal and wanted a piece of the action, but Geneviève wasn't talking. If he poked around and learned too much, that could be the motive."

"Are you going to tell the police?"

"Eventually, but not when all I have is one old woman's memory. The story will carry more weight if we can identify the land and get copies of the deeds."

"The key is the highway. Which highway was being built in 1969 or soon after?" The police had more resources. They could find out faster, but she understood Tony's reluctance.

He opened the wine and poured two glasses while she put dinner on the table. "I can't remember the last time someone made me a home-cooked meal. Let's talk about more pleasant things while we eat: the food, books, movies, music—you decide. No business talk during dinner and nothing about anything involving the police."

They'd finished eating and were clearing the table when Tony said, "Okay, we can talk business now. I've come over to your way of thinking about the studio. Knock it down."

"How could I forget?" She clapped her hands. "I did talk to the police today. Bea called this afternoon to say they weren't through there yet. She apologized and said she'd do her best to hurry things along."

"No matter where the conversation starts, it ends up at the police. We might as well stop fighting it."

"I can't stop thinking about Iris. She was only nineteen, barely out of high school. Of course it's terrible when anyone is killed. But someone so young." She shuddered. "I think the killer lives at Sunny Gardens. He recognized her on TV. He knew when she came to work."

"You don't believe it was Geneviève's accomplice?" His tone was sharp.

"That's not what I said, Tony, not at all. Her accomplice would be an old man by now and wealthy from his shady land deals. Old and wealthy, like the people who live at Sunny Gardens."

He looked thoughtful. "If you're right, I set myself up." He waved her protest aside. "No, no, I think you're right. He either saw or heard about our argument. He figured out what it was about or she told him. It doesn't matter. Either way, he knew I'd be suspect number one when Geneviève was strangled."

Claire put a plate in the dishwasher. Tony's latest theory was better than thinking his mother had asked someone to kill him. "Not that many people live at Sunny Gardens. Most are women, and we're looking for a man. If we got a list of their names, we could run them by Judy and see if anything jogs her memory."

"No one at Sunny Gardens will help. I'm persona non grata there. The management wants her apartment cleared out by the end of the month, and they suggested I hire someone to do it. They don't want me on the premises for the two minutes it would take to throw her belongings into a garbage bag."

"I can do it, but not tomorrow. I'm going up to the farm to ride, and then staying to have a drink with Kyle."

"The horse thief? I don't think it's a good idea for you to go up there by yourself."

"I was there by myself before." She held his gaze. "I can take care of myself."

"I know you can, Claire, but do you want to?"

There were so many different levels, so many possible answers to his question, that she didn't know where to start, so she circled back around to the beginning. "I can go over to Sunny Gardens any time Sunday. You probably need to set it up. Tell them I'm a friend of the family."

"Would you really do that for me?"

"Of course. What do you want me to do with her things? Box them up?"

"Throw them away."

She protested and after a brief discussion they agreed she would donate any usable clothes to charity and package up any jewelry or valuables for him to give to Geneviève's lawyer. The rest would go in the trash.

Before Tony left, he put his hands on her shoulders. His ocean colored eyes searched hers, and for a moment, she thought he was going to kiss her. Instead, he thanked her for dinner and warned her to be careful with Kyle.

"Tell him I know you're up there. If you don't return safe and sound, I'll come after him."

23

Claire and Kyle rode while a gangly teenager named Robby took care of the tack and walked the horses to cool them down. They moved from one horse to the next without taking a break, which left no time to talk, no chance to ask Kyle about Fast Eddie. By five o'clock, only Tia Maria and Memphis were left. Robby had them saddled and waiting in front of the barn.

"We're about done, Robby. Take care of these two." Kyle gestured to the horses he and Claire had just dismounted, "Then go on home." He turned to Claire. "No more ring. We'll ride over to the ridge. Let them run."

"Sounds good." Claire rubbed Tia Maria's velvety nose. "She's my favorite." The horse reached over and, gently nibbling Claire's shirt, pulled her closer.

"Look at you, cheek to cheek." Kyle patted the horse's neck.

"She's such a sweetheart—and beautiful—I'm surprised she's not been sold."

"Someone's interested, but I wanted to give you first refusal."

"I'd love to, but I have nowhere to keep her and no time for a horse." Claire smiled at an old memory. "When I was a child, I asked for my own horse every birthday and every Christmas."

"You don't have to make up your mind today." He swung into the saddle and waited for her to mount. "We'll walk to the pasture then canter up the ridge. We'll all enjoy getting out of the ring."

The sun was almost down by the time they'd finished putting up the horses. Claire watched Kyle from the corner of her eye as they walked from the barn to his house, a log cabin nestled at the edge of the woods. A smile played at the corners of his mouth. He knew she expected an explanation for Fast Eddie's disappearance. What was funny about that?

"There's beer, soft drinks, and iced tea in the refrigerator," he said. "Glasses are in the cabinet to the left of the sink. Help yourself and take your drink on out to the porch. I want to get dinner going."

She fixed herself a glass of iced tea and curled up in a corner of the settee. Cooking noises, a knife chopping and a spoon scraping, came from the kitchen. A light wind rustled the trees, and a horse nickered in the barn. She should be nervous about the impending conversation, but she felt too comfortable. Tony was concerned about her being here alone, but she didn't feel threatened.

"You can see better without the lights." Kyle flipped the switch and small birds became visible against the sky. They swooped and dove in graceful arcs, pursuing night insects. He placed a plate of cheese and crackers on the coffee table. "You're probably hungry after all that exercise. I'm almost finished in the kitchen. Meanwhile, how about some music?"

He disappeared inside. Moments later the twanging guitar sound of country music floated from somewhere behind her. The easy rhythm and lyrics about lonesome fit the time and place. Across the fields, long clouds caught the last rays of sun and laid gold streaks on the darkening sky.

Such a beautiful place—what will happen to it now?

Kyle returned and pulled up a chair. "I hear you're planning a trip to Tennessee." He rarely cracked a smile, but now he was grinning ear to ear. "You should see the look on your face."

"You surprised me."

"You underestimated me. Just like I underestimated you."

"So you admit that Fast Eddie is missing?"

"Just because you don't know where he is doesn't mean he's missing."

"He's supposed to be here and he isn't," she countered. "As you apparently know, I'm going to look through the registry. I'll find him."

"You'll find the records, but you won't find the horse. Not without my help."

"The people in Tennessee will help me. Their business is keeping track of registered walking horses."

"Their business is helping their members make money." He spoke as if to a child. "We're talking about an industry: owners, breeders, trainers, exhibitors, equipment makers, vets. It takes money to produce a champion. If the owner's lucky, the champion earns it back plus some. A champion stallion is a gold mine."

"I know that."

"Do you know that you're going up to meet with the people your friend Geneviève thought were in league with the devil?"

"And you're saying that they're not going to help me."

"They'll help you find information about the horse. It won't do you any good because he'll be long gone by the time you find him. If you persist, which seems to be in your character, you'll keep him from being shown, which will lower his value at stud, and that's where the money is." He cut several slices of cheese and put them on crackers. "Help yourself. Food won't be ready for another hour. We have plenty of time to talk."

"I'm listening."

"The horse Geneviève called Fast Eddie is named Garland's Magic Man. His dam is Garland of Roses. Rose has a good pedigree and nice conformation, but not the spirit to be a champion. A trainer—we'll call him Hal—bought Rose for his daughters to ride. The girls talked their parents into breeding her, and Hal negotiated a good deal on the stud fee for a middling stallion named Midnight Magician. The colt turned out better than either parent, better than anyone dreamed. Magic won his first blue ribbon at two months."

"Geneviève told me he'd won more than one ribbon."

"He has, and you can find them listed in the association records. Would you like to hear the rest of the story?"

"Yes." He knew she would.

"Hal could have sold Magic for a pretty profit, but his girls loved that colt, and Hal, who is a decent man and a pretty good trainer, thought he had a champion. There'd be more money down the road."

Claire nodded. Taciturn Kyle had turned long-winded, and she was just going to have to endure it.

"Magic won a few more small shows, and he placed in the big ones, but he wasn't living up to his early promise. Fact was, he'd grown fast and needed time to catch up to himself, but someone got impatient, and they sored him. Do you know what that means?"

"Putting irritants on their legs to make them step higher. Geneviève told me about it." She let her tone convey her revulsion. "I thought Hal was a decent man."

"No one said it was Hal. Magic, who is a smart horse, doesn't like grown women. That tells me Hal's wife did it." Kyle's lips compressed in anger, and a moment passed before he continued. "She did a bad job, and Magic came up lame. By now, Hal's in a bad position. They've invested a lot of money in this horse, more than they could really afford, and it looks like they might have to put him down.

"Hal called a vet from over in Kentucky—no one local because if word gets out, no reputable owner will hire him. The vet, I guess he was disgusted with what he saw, and he knew about Geneviève's crusade. He called her and they hatched their plot."

"To rescue the horse. Good for them."

"To rescue the horse cheap. Geneviève and the vet agreed that he'd tell Hal odds were Magic would never go back in the show ring, never be good for anything but pleasure riding, like Rose, and it would cost a bundle to fix him up. Just doing that would take money Hal didn't have and didn't know where to find."

"Geneviève had her faults, but she cared about horses. If she paid to fix that horse, then she put her money where her mouth was." Claire defended the woman who could no longer defend herself.

Kyle had been rotating his beer bottle on its coaster, staring at it while he talked, but now he looked straight at her. "But it wasn't true, and it wasn't only about horses. It was about besting someone. Geneviève Burke was an evil and malicious woman. She knew Hal had no money, so she made it about money. It cost to treat Magic, but not half as much as she and the vet told Hal, and he's ready to go back to the circuit."

Claire met Kyle's gaze. His bitter explanation echoed Tony's warning that his mother had an instinct for the jugular. Tony couldn't change the fact that Geneviève was his mother, but Kyle was an employee.

"If that's how you feel, why'd you work for her? Why didn't you quit?"

"I was trying to undo the mess my idiot sister made and help my nieces get their horse back."

Claire sipped of her iced tea, stalling for time while she gathered her thoughts. Kyle's story had the ring of truth, but... "Did Geneviève know who you were when she hired you?"

"From the get-go. Hal told me what had happened and asked what I thought. I tracked the horse down and tried to buy him back, offered Geneviève twice what she'd paid, and told her I could guarantee he wouldn't ever be mistreated again. I knew she couldn't work with Magic. He hated women; she couldn't get near him. She said she couldn't sell him the way he was, but I could try to retrain him long as I did it here at her farm. If I failed, she'd keep him as a companion for her other horses. If I succeeded, she'd sell him to me. I believed her."

He sat knees apart, forearms resting on his thighs, staring down at his hands. Claire couldn't see his face but his voice dripped with disgust.

"It took me a while to figure out I was being played for a fool, but I did, and I quit. I was inside packing my gear to go home when Geneviève decided to show me that she didn't need my help with Magic. She mounted him, and he threw her. She ended up in the hospital.

"I stayed on because someone had to take care of the horses, but I can't stay forever. My fiancée and I have a horse farm west of Ocala. At least we're working on it. She's carrying the full load while I'm here."

"Geneviève died, and you took Magic," Claire said. In a way, she didn't blame him.

"Wrong. She gave him to me."

"Why would she do that?"

"I called Saturday night, like every night, to let her know how things were going. She gave me some cock and bull story about thinking things over and realizing what a great job I was doing. Then she offered me Magic in exchange for fetching an old trunk from a storage building behind her house in New Orleans."

With Kyle's words, the pieces fell into place, and the picture was ugly. Claire turned away. She didn't want Kyle to see the sick look on her face. There was no honoring Geneviève by tracking down Fast Eddie, because he'd never been stolen. She'd traded him for help in covering up a far worse crime.

"Surprised?" Kyle said.

"I knew about the trunk, but I didn't know she'd asked you to get it."

"I'm not an idiot. I knew there was something fishy, but I said okay. Minute I hung up, I called Hal and told him to get down here and pick up the horse. I wasn't giving Geneviève a chance to back out of this deal. Then I drove down to New Orleans and found the house, but the chest wasn't there.

"I found a pay phone and tried to call Geneviève. She wasn't answering." He shrugged. "I turned around and drove back up here."

"You need to tell the police."

"Already have. I talked to Captain Robinson yesterday and signed a statement today. Seems it wasn't her house. One of the neighbors saw my truck, wondered what I was up to, and took down my license plate."

Claire said a silent thank you to Mike for his discretion. "My company is working on that house. It belongs to Geneviève's son."

"When I heard she'd been murdered, I didn't know what to do," he admitted. "Then you made a fuss about Magic. The police wanted to talk to me." A smile flickered. "It felt good to get it off my chest."

"What happens to Magic now?"

"Long as you don't go after him, he stays at Hal's. My lawyer says I have a claim even if I don't have it in writing. He'll help me sort it out."

"I'm not going to Tennessee." She put her hand on his arm. "Thanks for saving me the trip." She was certain Tony would let Kyle keep the horse. This part of the story would have a happy ending.

"Now that we've got this out of the way, you're welcome to stay for dinner. I made plenty."

"No, thank you. I have to go." She stood up. "But I'd like a rain check."

"It's yours. I'll be here a bit longer. The lawyer asked me to stay on until the horses are all sold, and he's paying me well." Another grin split his face. "If I'm not careful, I'm going to have enough money to get married."

Kyle walked her to her car. The clouds had thickened, and the moon was gone. An owl called from the woods. Its mournful question, *who whoo who whooo,* made Claire feel worse about her suspicions. Whoever killed Geneviève, it wasn't Kyle. He was a nice guy and not a horse thief. She owed him an apology.

"If I caused you trouble, I'm sorry."

"No problem. Elaine called Hal who called me. I promised to straighten things out with you, and I have. It wasn't trouble. I enjoyed the company." He cocked his head. "Listen."

"The owl? I heard him."

"No, traffic on the highway. It sounds like the surf. You only hear it at night when the wind comes from the south. Doesn't happen often, but when it does, it reminds me of Florida. Our farm is near the gulf and when the wind blows right you can hear the water. I miss it."

Beneath the night sounds of frogs and insects, there was a soft murmur that did indeed sound like distant surf. "Time for me to be part of that traffic," Claire said. She and Felicia Miata had a long hour ride back to New Orleans.

24

Ten days had passed, and two women had been murdered, but Sunny Gardens looked just as it had when Claire first visited. The same woman sat at the concierge desk, once again talking to a group of women. The same card players sat at the same tables, and the same woman was reading a magazine, Amanda something. It looked the same but it really wasn't.

When she walked in, everyone looked up. Last time, no one did. Unsmiling, they watched her wait until the concierge was free. The women who'd been talking to the concierge lingered, listening when she introduced herself. She lowered her voice.

"I'm here to clear out Mrs. Burke's apartment."

"We've been expecting you. Please sign in at the register by the door." This time, the woman didn't attempt a smile. Her expression and tone were cool, barely polite. She pressed a button. "Wait by the door. Security will be with you momentarily."

Claire did as directed, and a few minutes later a stocky, middle-aged man wearing a navy blue uniform and a sour expression approached. The nametag on his chest said Calvin.

"I'm here to escort you." He led the way down the hall, keys jingling with every officious step. He unlocked the door, stepped inside, and flipped on the overhead light.

What had been Geneviève's apartment reminded Claire of a suite motel—impersonal, functional, and nowhere you'd want to spend more than one or two nights. She would have hated living here too. The air smelled stale.

"How about leaving the door ajar and opening the windows?"

"The windows don't open. Security," he said.

Fine particles covered the horizontal surfaces, white on the wood end and coffee tables and dark on the light countertop separating a little kitchen from the front room.

Calvin followed her glance. "The police dusted the apartment for fingerprints." He puffed up his chest as if imparting that information increased his importance. "The furniture belongs to the apartment."

Claire took in the big TV, the sofa covered in the same overblown print as those in the parlor, and the matching chairs too small to offer comfortable seating—she believed him.

"Housekeeping will clean the apartment after you remove the personal belongings of the deceased."

"Fine." She opened the package of heavy-duty plastic garbage bags she'd brought with her.

There was a knock on the open door, and Detective Beatrice Washington walked in. "Hey Claire, I heard you were here. It's nice of you to help Tony out."

"Hi, Bea." She had a terrible thought. "Has something else happened?"

"No, no, nothing new. I'm still interviewing witnesses."

"On a Sunday afternoon?" Claire rolled her eyes. "Doesn't Mike give you any time off?"

"Actually, Mike's a great boss, but we're both swamped. He's back at the office, working as we speak. You know he followed up with that horse trainer."

"And he did it without mentioning my name. Please thank him for me."

"I will. You've heard the story?"

"Uh huh."

"Tony's suspicions look right on target."

Claire nodded. It was the second time Bea had mentioned Tony, but she wasn't going to discuss him with the dour Calvin listening.

"I have thirty minutes until my next interview," Bea said. "Let me give you a hand. Is all the food headed for the trash can?"

"Yes, but I was going to leave that for housekeeping. I'm just after Geneviève's personal belongings."

"We should do the kitchen, and carefully. You won't believe where

old ladies hide their valuables. The job will go quickly with two people."
Bea looked at Calvin who was leaning against the wall, inspecting his
fingernails. "Three people. You can help carry out the trash."

They cleared out the kitchen without finding any hidden treasures,
although Bea insisted on checking every box, even the ice cube trays.
Calvin, obviously disgruntled by his assignment but not prepared to
disobey a direct order from a policewoman, carried the full trash bags out
to the dumpsters.

They moved on to the bedroom. It was as sterile as the living
room—no framed photos or personal items. The closet held few clothes.
Geneviève hadn't planned on staying for long, and without being told,
Claire knew that Tony's mother had believed in quality over quantity.

She picked up a cashmere cardigan and caught a waft of perfume.
She had witnessed Geneviève's cruelty, been told that she was a bad
employer, a terrible mother, and possibly responsible for her husband's
death; but the scent of the dead woman's perfume evoked the same
sadness she'd felt in Jim Burke's studio, the same sense of life cut short,
of emptiness where a person had been.

"Are you okay?" Bea said. "You're looking a little pale."

"I'm fine. I'll put things for Goodwill on the bed."

"I'll fold and bag."

Claire threw the underwear in a garbage bag and put everything else
on the bed. Goodwill would be happy to get these nice clothes.

A chamois bag in the bedside table held a heavy gold necklace, a
gold and pearl brooch, and two pairs of earrings. She put the bag in her
purse. "I'll give these to Tony."

"When are you going to see him?"

Claire turned, her hands on her hips. "Not you, too."

"No, not me, too." Bea laughed. "Don't be mad at Mike. He put his
foot in his mouth, all the way up to the knee, but he's worried about you.
And with good cause. There's a murderer at large."

"It's not Tony."

"I don't think so either, but until we've solved this case." Bea raised
her hands in a gesture of supplication. "If you know anything that might
help us, telling me would be helping Tony."

Claire glanced at the security guard, and Bea got the message.

"Hey Calvin," she said. "How about you going to the kitchen and
bringing us back two glasses of milk and some cookies or a couple
pieces of cake, something to keep body and soul together. We're working

hard here."

As soon as Calvin was safely out of hearing range, Claire said, "I think the killer lives here."

"Any particular reason you think so?"

"He recognized Iris and reacted so quickly."

"Anything else?" Bea persisted.

Claire thought before answering. Telling Bea about the photos, looking for the people in them, and learning about the land sale would add credence to Tony's theory about his mother's death. He had agreed they should tell the police, but not until they were ready to listen. Bea was ready to listen.

"There is something else." Claire relayed what Judy Boaz had told Tony about Geneviève's sugar daddy and the shady land deal and how the timing coincided with Jim Burke's death.

"Do you have any idea who this man is or any idea what highway was involved?"

"All we have is the time frame, the summer of 1969. We're trying to learn more."

"I hope that's not the real reason you're here." Claire frowned and Bea put up her hand. "Don't get ticked off. But please don't put yourself in danger. Look at what happened to Iris."

"The paper said she was only nineteen." Claire shivered. "She wasn't much more than a child."

"Those were her mother's exact words."

They worked in silence until Calvin returned with milk and cookies. "Thanks," Bea helped herself to a cookie and passed the plate. "Have one, they're good."

"No thank you, I'm not hungry."

Bea told Calvin to stand outside the door and make sure no one came in. Then she said, "I have to run, Claire, but before I go, there are two things. First, you have my promise that we'll follow up on what you told me. Sometimes a money trail is just what you need."

"Good."

"Second, we'd like to see those pictures."

"Tony took the ones that included his father; I have the others and a list of the names. I'll make you copies, but let me run it by him first, okay?"

"Sure," Bea said. "I understand that you're in a delicate position, and I appreciate your confiding in me. We really are on the same side."

"I know, and I know you're just doing your job."

"So is my boss. Please give him another chance. He likes you a lot."

"Mike is a nice guy, but he has no right to tell me what to do or who to see." This declaration of independence reminded her of Tony's objections to yesterday's visit with Kyle. He'd been out of line, too. "Men." She rolled her eyes.

"Exactly," Bea said, and they both laughed.

"Thank you for your help. Four hands really did speed things along. And I'm glad we had a chance to talk."

"Call me if you think of anything else." Bea waved a goodbye.

Claire balanced the bags for Goodwill on the walker and followed her out. "I'm finished, here," she told Calvin. "There's another bag for the trash inside. Thank you."

Half a dozen people stood in the hall, eyeing the open apartment. Some looked hostile; others merely curious. How long had they been there? Claire ignored them, and they watched in silence as she walked past.

She was at the front door when she saw a familiar couple coming up the sidewalk, Geneviève's ex-husband and his niece, Laura somebody.

Their eyes met, and Laura recoiled. Yes, Claire wanted to say. You did see me with Geneviève, but we weren't friends. I'm sorry for whatever harm she did your uncle, but I had no part in it. I'm here trying to help Tony. That's all. "

"Miss Marshall," the concierge called, "don't leave without signing out."

"Please do it for me. My hands are full."

Laura pulled Roger closer, as if she knew the bags Claire carried contained Geneviève's belongings and wanted to avoid contamination. Roger began whimpering. Claire kept going. She never wanted to see Sunny Gardens again. Thank heaven she'd convinced Tony not to come with her. Clearing out Geneviève's apartment had been harder than she'd expected; it would have been worse for him. Plus, he didn't like Bea.

Too restless to go home, Claire found a parking space on the edge of the French Quarter and started walking. Outside Café le Monde, she paused to watch what could be the world's fattest pigeons waddle from one bit of litter to another, checking for discarded bits of food and occasionally squabbling over a choice morsel. Each pigeon looked more self-satisfied than the next. Claire tried to imagine being that pleased with herself.

She climbed the steps to the park atop the levee and the bench that was like an old friend. Too many times to count, she'd sat up here and sorted through her thoughts, looking for solutions, or if that was too much to ask, a way to cope. The little park was an oasis of peace, largely ignored by the tourists who kept the Quarter humming all hours of the day and night. This afternoon, a soft gray sky added to the serenity. Beneath it, the Mississippi flowed a darker gray.

Heavy-laden barges floated downstream with ponderous dignity, heading for the Gulf where they would offload their cargo onto enormous ships bound for who knew where. Claire looked past them at things not there. She thought about Tony, trying to recapture something long gone by fixing up his childhood home. Instead, he'd found his father's skeleton and become a murder suspect. Kyle's story supported Tony's suspicions. The police should leave him alone now, but he still had to deal with his father's murder—and his mother's.

She thought about Kyle, a good man drawn into a bad situation when he tried to untangle a mess of his sister's making. Geneviève's death had put him in limbo. Until the horses were gone, he would mark time, dreaming of Florida, his fiancée, and the horse farm they were building. She hoped an east wind was bringing him the distant surf sound of the highway.

After Tom died, real surf had helped her find peace. She'd spent hours walking along the beach, counting the waves on Lake Michigan. Their sound and motion had soothed her; their persistence brought solace. Waves had been hitting the shore for thousands of years and would continue for thousands more. She and her sorrows were insignificant in their context.

The sound of cars and trucks might sound like waves to Kyle, but it wasn't the same. The highway was transitory, ephemeral compared to waves. Someday a newer and bigger road would replace it.

"The highway." She spoke aloud, starting a sparrow that had been scouting the sidewalk by her feet. A highway ran alongside Geneviève's farm, not an Interstate but not an old country two-lane either. She used her mobile phone to call Tony.

"I've been thinking about you," he said. "How did it go?"

"It's done. There's some jewelry I want to give you, but that's not why I'm calling. When did your mother buy the horse farm?"

Silence.

"Tony, are you there?"

"I'm thinking. I don't remember her not owning it."

"Was the highway always there?"

"No, we used to have go through Greensburg. The highway went in a year or two after Dad died." A long pause. "Right in front of my nose. How'd you figure it out?"

"It was right in front of my nose, too. I've been there twice."

"If the mystery land was part of the farm, we're back to square one." Tony sounded glum. "Judy made it sound as if Geneviève bought and sold the land bang-bang, but she'd owned that farm as long as I can remember."

"There'll be deed records at the parish seat."

"Greensburg is the parish seat, and I'm driving up there tomorrow morning to meet with Geneviève's lawyer. She left me the farm, but with stipulations that he wants to discuss."

"You could check the deeds when you're there. Once you know the piece of property, searching the title is a piece of cake."

"Why don't you come on over, give me the jewelry, and I'll give you a much-deserved glass of wine. Then you can teach me how to find land records."

"The lawyer will know where to look. Tell him that you want to check for land sales involving the farm and contiguous acreage. It's a perfectly reasonable thing to do if you're considering selling the property." She couldn't imagine him keeping it. She was surprised that Geneviève had left the farm to him. But if not Tony, who else? They'd been the sum total of each other's family.

"We can talk about it when you get here. I'm putting a bottle on ice right now."

Why not? She had nothing else to do, and she wanted to get rid of the jewelry. "Okay, but it will be a good half hour. I have to walk back to my car."

"Welcome." Tony greeted her at the door. "It's not much, and it's not home, but there's no plaster dust." He put his arm around her shoulders and led her into a spacious living room. Floor to ceiling windows provided a spectacular view of the French Quarter and, beyond it, the Mississippi. She walked over to a window.

"See that little green spot?" She pointed. "That's where I was, watching the boats, when I thought about the highway."

"I like to watch the boats, especially at night. Their lights reflect on the water when it's clear and look eerie when it's not."

She turned, planning to say something about pretty lights, but the words flew away. Tony had followed her to the window, and when she turned, he put his arms around her. Instinctively, she raised her face to his. Their lips touched, and she realized that she'd been waiting for this kiss. Still, the intensity of her response astonished her. She pulled back, hoping Tony hadn't felt her heart pounding. She knew better than to fall for Tony Burke. He was a womanizer, not to mention a client. She wasn't his type. He was just playing.

"I talked to Kyle last night." Her voice was husky.

"Should I be worried about Kyle?"

"No. He didn't steal the horse. Geneviève traded him Fast Eddie for his help hiding the skeleton. But it was too late, you'd already found it."

"Kyle told you that?" Surprise loosened his embrace, but he didn't release her.

"He called her every day. I knew that but I'd forgotten. When he reported in Saturday afternoon, she told him your house was hers and asked him to fetch an old trunk from an outbuilding. She never said what was in it."

"Has anyone told the police?"

"Kyle did."

"They'll have to believe me now," he said. "But I was asking about you and Kyle."

"There is no me and Kyle."

"That's good." He brushed her hair back from her face and kissed her again.

Her brain knew better, but her body didn't care. She'd felt his touch before, on her arm, her shoulders, an occasional quick hug, but now his hands caressed and lingered. Something deep inside melted.

"Do you want me to stop?" he said.

"No."

25

Heavy clouds sat low over the highway, trees bent in the wind, and an occasional raindrop splattered against the windshield, but Tony's car was an island of warmth and comfort. Claire shifted in her seat. Yesterday afternoon, she had fallen—no, admit it, she'd jumped—into bed with this man. Even now, when she glanced over at him, her breath quickened. She couldn't look at his hands on the wheel without remembering their touch, couldn't see his lips without hers parting.

Tony caught her eye. "A penny for your thoughts."

She felt the color rising in her cheeks.

"Me, too, sweetheart." He winked. "It's all I can do to keep my hands on the wheel."

"I've never ridden in a Ferrari before."

"I drive them for a living, but this one's a street car, a completely different vehicle. It's still fast, and there's not much traffic. We'll be in Greensburg before you know it."

"Tell me about the farm," she said. "Did you go up there when you were a little boy?"

"A tenant family lived there. We went to see them two or three times a year, collecting rent and checking on the property. After Dad died, they moved on, or Geneviève threw them out. I don't know which. We started going up weekends, holidays, longer during the summer."

"I bet it was fun."

"It was when Meemaw lived with us. She taught me how to find bait and where to fish, how to grow vegetables. She and I built a tree fort.

After she died, things changed. First Dad and then Meemaw." He shrugged. "Losing Meemaw was probably hard on Geneviève, too, but all I knew was that I was twelve years old and on my own. Geneviève had no time for me. I became a very angry kid."

"I was angry after my husband died. I think it's a normal reaction."

"Did you set small buildings on fire?"

"No." Her anger, directed inward and unacknowledged, had manifested itself in panic attacks. "I noticed the charred corner of the studio."

"That stunt earned me a ticket to military school." He brushed his finger across her lips. "I'm telling you all my dark secrets."

She held his hand against her cheek. If Tony had succeeded in burning the studio, the firefighters probably would have found the skeleton. At that point, his father had only been dead for two or three years; people would have made the connection.

"Funny how things work out isn't it?" He took his hand away.

She wanted to comfort him, but he'd pulled back into himself, to a place she couldn't follow. He looked at the road ahead; she looked out her window. Cultivated fields were giving way to forests, stands of pine trees. The sky had darkened, but the rain remained only a promise.

"Perfect weather for a Monday," she said.

"Uh huh." He turned on the car radio. "Find something you like."

She fiddled with the dial and settled on a country music station. The music reminded her of Kyle. "Have you talked to Kyle?" she said. "He'll be relieved to learn there's no questions about him keeping the horse."

"We can stop by the farm on the way back. I'll tell him then."

Thirty miles later a sign welcomed them to Greensburg. Claire had envisioned a charming old town center with a bench-lined square and a statue of a confederate soldier, interesting little shops, and side streets lined with cottages. The reality was no square and half a dozen newish brick ranches interspersed with decrepit barns and sheds.

"This is it?" she said. "A wide spot in the road?"

"In two roads—there's an intersection. And this is the courthouse." He pulled into an unpaved parking area in front of a tan brick building, the only structure taller than one story.

Claire studied the building. The decorative openings that adorned its central section suggested art deco, but the basic structure was garden-variety Edwardian. "I'll bet it was a WPA project," she said. The small white-columned building tucked in the front yard would be the old courthouse.

"You can ask them." He unfastened their seat belts and pulled her into an embrace. "I've been wanting to do this for miles."

She removed the hand that had slipped under her blouse and kissed the palm.

"If I've got the directions right, the lawyer's office is over there." He pointed to a rectangular building, which, if it were longer, might be considered a strip mall. "Next to the sandwich shop. Meet back at the car in an hour?"

"Okay." Checking the deeds wouldn't take an hour, but she could hang out in the sandwich shop. The only other commercial building, an old filling station converted into an auto parts store, held no interest. He helped her out of the car, and they walked in their opposite directions.

A directory in the courthouse lobby said the land office occupied rooms 204 and 205. A heavyset man sat at a desk in room 204. His nameplate identified him as Simms Purcell, Registrar of Deeds. He looked up from his newspaper.

"What can I do for you young lady?"

Claire introduced herself and told him what she wanted to look through the deeds for the property including and abutting the highway interchange.

He heaved himself to his feet—he was a couple inches shorter than she was but as wide as he was tall—and led her to the adjoining room.

"You'll find what you're looking for in here." He pointed to a single shelf of tall dark ledgers.

She must have looked surprised because he explained that there wasn't a lot of buying and selling in the Parish. Nor did they have a bunch of little parcels. He picked out a volume and set it down on a table by the window.

When she opened the book, dust motes flew out and hung in the air. The scent of decay filled her nostrils. *Like Jim Burke's studio.* Claire suppressed a shiver. That smell would be with her for a long time.

Saint Helena was one of the Florida Parishes; these records went back two hundred years. She skimmed through the earliest deeds, turned the pages slowly to avoid stirring up more dust.

"Those deeds tell the story of the Parish." Simms was looking over her shoulder.

"The people and the land," she said.

"This bunch of parishes up here has been part of England, Spain, and France. Now we're part of Louisiana USA, but there are folks will tell you that we are and always will be our own country. We used to be The Republic of West Florida."

Claire smiled and nodded but didn't comment. She waited for Simms to go back to his desk before turning to deeds from the 1960s.

The property she'd always think of as Geneviève's farm had been part of a much larger tract until February 28, 1960. On that date, Pineland Corporation transferred four hundred acres of land to Geneviève Layton Devereux Burke. An attached affidavit said the price was one dollar, not a dollar per acre but four hundred acres for one dollar. Roger Devereux had signed for Pineland. What?

This can't be part of their divorce settlement. They'd divorced years before this. Geneviève was already married to Tony's father.

The next deed, dated May 1967, documented the sale of 250 acres from Geneviève to the Louisiana Department of Transportation. Claire added up the tax stamps and calculated the price at five hundred dollars per acre, a lot more than she'd paid, but a reasonable price.

The plat showed a wide strip of land that followed the path of the current highway. She turned the page and found a July 1968 deed that conveyed 50 acres from Geneviève to Meridian Development Corporation. This land, which surrounded the highway exit, went for four thousand dollars per acre. A much higher price, but still reasonable given its commercial value. She checked the pages before and after but found no other land transfers involving either Geneviève or Pineland Corporation.

The remaining one hundred acres comprised the farm Tony had just inherited. Judy Harmon's story of crooked land dealings looked like nonsense. The only wild card was the very first sale, which was no arm's length transaction. It was possible, but not likely, the highway plans were already in the works back then.

Claire carried the deed book up to the front desk where the registrar had returned to his newspaper. "Excuse me Mr. Purcell, can I get copies of these pages?"

"Call me Simms, honey, everyone else does. It'll cost you a dollar a page because they're outsized. A certified copy is eight dollars."

"I don't need certified." She showed him the relevant pages and handed him a twenty-dollar bill. "Do you have change?"

"My secretary does. She makes all the copies." He picked up the telephone and told someone named Jennifer to come on up, leaving

Claire to wonder if Simms did anything other than read the paper.

While they waited for Jennifer to return, Simms said he'd noticed that she had been looking at deeds relating to the Burke farm. "I guess it going to be up for sale," he said. "Are you thinking about buying it?"

"No. You've heard that Geneviève Burke died."

"I heard she was murdered." He shook his head and his chins wobbled in sorrow. "A terrible thing. I didn't know her except to say hello, but my cousin used to graze his cattle on her land, before the highway went through and cut off his access. He said she was a fair and reasonable person."

"I saw that she sold land for the highway and then for the restaurant and gas station."

"You can bet that land sold for a pretty penny." This thought seemed to cheer Simms. He smacked his lips with satisfaction.

"I wonder why they put the intersection there?"

"It's where the old state road crosses the highway," he said. "Don't know where else they'd put it."

"I bet Pineland wished they still owned that land." She kept probing. "It went for a good price, lots more than they sold it for." It would have to. Pineland had given it away.

"Why are you here asking all these questions if you're not thinking about buying the land?" His eyes narrowed. "What did you say your name was?"

"Claire. I'm a friend of the family."

Simms' frown indicated dissatisfaction with her answer, but before he could ask another question, Jennifer returned with copies of the deeds. Claire thanked her and Simms for their help. She carried the copies down the hall to the tax office. Once again she identified herself as a friend of the Burke family. This time, she added that Geneviève's son had inherited the land and might try to sell it back to Pineland. She asked if they had a representative in town.

"Nope. Their offices are down in New Orleans. We never see them. Pineland's in the timber business. Used to have three or four tenant farms, this being one of them, but there's more money in timber."

"It's a horse farm now, with a nice stable, paddocks, and fenced fields. It would probably be worth more to someone who wants to keep horses, but it can't hurt to talk to Pineland."

"Worse they can do is say no," he agreed. He located the corporate registration form and asked if she wanted a copy.

"No thanks, I just want to see who to talk to and how to reach them." Claire wrote down the contact information for the firm's legal representative and noted the names of the corporate officers.

"It looks like everyone lives in New Orleans," she said.

"Not everyone. I live just a few miles down the road," he joked. "Since we're talking about that property, I suppose you want to see the trust documents, too."

By the time Claire paid for copies of the trust, she'd spent an hour in the courthouse. On her way out, she passed Simms. He was standing in the doorway of the deeds office, rocking back and forth on the balls of his feet.

"I can put you in touch with the right person at Pineland," he said. "They won't pay a lot for that farm, but I don't know who else is going to buy it. This ain't really horse country."

"The grapevine works quickly," Claire said. But it couldn't work that fast. He must have been eavesdropping when she was talking to the man in the tax office.

"If you've got a business card, you can leave it with me, and I'll call you if anyone shows any interest in that property."

"Thank you, but that's a little premature."

"You let me know when they're ready to sell. I can help out." He pressed a piece of paper into her hand. "That's my home number. You call any time before ten at night. If I'm not there, you can leave a message with my wife."

"Thank you." She walked down the stairs rather than waiting for the elevator, anxious to be rid of Simms.

Tony was nowhere to be seen, so Claire leaned against a fender of his car and watched nothing happen in Greensburg. An occasional pick-up truck drove past, and a chainsaw whined in the distance. The breeze carried the scents of manure and pine trees.

Claire pondered the morning's discovery. Knowing what is not the same as knowing why, and she wasn't absolutely sure it was the same family. But who else? And why? That was the real question. The breeze picked up, damp and cool. The rain wouldn't hold off much longer. Where was Tony? It had been well over an hour.

A few minutes later, Tony emerged from the lawyer's office and walked over to join her. She'd expected him to be happy, at least glad to have this meeting behind him, but his expression was stiffly neutral and his eyes a cloudy gray.

"My mother managed to have the last word," he said.

"Do you want to talk about it?"

"Not yet."

"Are you hungry? I've seen several people go into the sandwich shop."

"I've had enough of Greensburg."

"Then let's go." Telling him what she'd learned in the courthouse could wait.

"Right. Let's go see my new farm."

Several miles past the city limits, Claire broke the silence. "So, the farm is yours?" Why, she wondered, had inheriting it put Tony in such a funk?

"Right away, no probate because it was in a trust."

She nodded. Copies of the trust documents sat in her purse.

"I don't know why she bothered with a trust. We weren't rich, and it's not as if the land is worth much. Look around. This is the middle of nowhere." He accelerated, and the car leapt forward. "I was a trust fund kid, and I didn't even know it."

The speedometer needle slid past 100. Tony drove racecars, he could handle this speed, but there were other people around, other vehicles on the road. What if they came up on a tractor going fifteen miles an hour or a school bus going thirty? She braced herself.

"Tony, you're going too fast for me."

He downshifted, and the car slowed. "The lawyer advised me to keep the farm and continue running her horse rescue operation."

"I can't imagine you doing that."

"Neither can I."

"So, are you going to put it on the market?"

"I'm holding off, looking for a loophole." His jaw tightened. "The farm isn't worth much, a thousand an acre tops, but there's another trust. Most of all, there is the principle."

"About?" She waited for an explanation.

"Shortly after Dad died, Geneviève established a second trust. She bought stock in blue-chip companies—presumably with the money from the mysterious land deal—and put it into this second trust, which is now worth over a million."

"A lot more than the farm."

"I'm the beneficiary, but only if I operate the horse farm as a shelter for abused Tennessee Walking Horses for a minimum of ten years. Me." He jabbed his chest with his thumb. "I can't hire people to do it; I have to live there and run it myself."

"And if you don't?"

"Then everything in the second trust goes to some horse charity." He laughed without amusement. "You have to hand it to her. Geneviève is dead, and she's still trying to make me dance to her tune."

"I'm sorry, Tony."

"I'm over it."

She didn't believe him. "Why don't we stop for lunch before visiting the farm?" she said. "There's a restaurant by the highway interchange."

"A little time out?" he said. But when they reached the restaurant, he pulled into the parking lot. "I'll let you off at the door."

"That's okay. It's not raining that hard." She didn't want to leave his side.

He parked at the far end of the lot and insisted on sheltering her under his jacket as they walked back to the restaurant. "This was a good idea," he said, his mood already improving. "I've eaten at Michelin four-star restaurants, but there's nothing like good old southern fried chicken."

They took an open table by the window, and when the waitress appeared, both ordered the fried chicken. Their food came quickly, and they dug in. Two pieces satisfied Claire's hunger. She wiped her fingers and sat back. Tony, who had asked for a large order, was still eating. His mood had definitely improved, and she decided the time was ripe.

"Do you want to hear what I learned this morning?"

"Sorry, sweetheart. I was so ticked off about Geneviève and the long arm of her will that I didn't let you get a word in edgewise."

"Geneviève bought four hundred acres of land in 1960 and put it into a trust. She was the sole trustee and the recipient of all the trust's income. After her death, the land would go to you. In 1967, she sold two hundred and fifty acres for the highway. The next year she sold the fifty acres around this interchange to a developer. This restaurant is on part of that land. So is the gas station across the street. She received a total of three hundred and twenty five thousand dollars from those two sales."

"Shylock told me that she started trust number two in 1968 with just over three hundred thousand," he said. "The mysterious land deal is no longer a mystery."

"No, and both sales look totally legitimate."

"So the whole sugar daddy road thing is a dead end?"

"The road but not the sugar daddy. Don't you want to know how your mother was able to buy four hundred acres in the first place?"

"I'm listening."

"She paid one dollar. That works out to one fourth of a penny per acre."

"Not a bad price. What's his name?"

"Devereux. She bought the land from Pineland Corporation, but the signatory was Roger Devereux."

"You're kidding me."

"She bought the land and created the trust on the same day, February 28 1960." She watched Tony's face for his reaction. "That was how many years after their divorce?"

"Geneviève liked to hint that she had something on Devereux, but if you pressed her she'd shut up."

"Maybe it wasn't blackmail. Maybe they still cared for each other."

"Like the article in the paper?" he said. "You're smarter than that. I never heard her say a kind word about the guy. Trust me, it was a payoff."

"For what?"

"I don't know. I was two weeks old at the time. Did I ever tell you I was born on Valentine's Day?" He picked up another piece of chicken. "If she kept bleeding the family, Devereux really could have killed her. He was right there, living in the same building."

"He's in the secure area for people with dementia. I saw him when I visited her. He seemed out of it, but she said he understood a lot more than people realized."

"Don't believe anything Geneviève told you. She was a liar, and she hated Roger Devereux."

"I don't see how she could create a second trust. Seems to me the money from selling the land should have gone back into the original trust."

"That sounds logical, and it could be the loophole I'm looking for. I'll ask a lawyer, a different lawyer." He stood up. "Let's go back to New Orleans. The rain's not letting up. I'll visit my farm some other time."

"You could call Kyle and tell him about the horse. He really is anxious."

"Are you sure you're not a little sweet on this guy?"

Claire laughed. "Absolutely."

A couple with a little boy walked out of the restaurant ahead of them. They stood for a moment under the overhang, watching raindrops bounce off the parking lot. The little boy raised his arms, and the father picked him up. He carried his son close, sheltering him from the rain, as they all ran to their car. Tony had noticed them too; a flicker of pain crossed his face. He'd expressed indifference about his mother's murder, but twenty-five years after the fact, it was clear that he still mourned his father.

She took his arm. "Ready to run for it?"

26

"Are you doing anything but waiting around for the DNA results? How much time and money have we spent on that crap? And for what?" The bags under Vernon's eyes had grown since yesterday, and he sounded querulous. There'd been rumors he was considering retirement, but the smart money said he'd die with his boots on—probably from apoplexy.

"The Crime Scene Unit confirmed bloodstains on a partially burned canvas found in a wood stove in the studio," Mike said. "They think they've found the murder weapon, a heavy piece of wood used for stretching canvas. I'm sending fragments of both to CODIS. They'll tell us if the blood matches the bones. We'll also send a personal item to verify that the blood belonged to Jim Burke." They should have included a personal item first time round, but Vernon had limited the budget and thus the number of tests.

"Who's paying for all these new tests? I haven't approved another penny. I don't know why I let you talk me into this crap in the first place."

"No extra charge. The people we're working with see this case demonstrating the power of DNA analysis." For paternity suits more than police work, but he wasn't going to share that tidbit.

"More like demonstrating a fuck-up." Vernon groused, but he couldn't really complain about getting free help.

"We'll get the first results Friday at the latest and the others as soon as they can work them in."

"What else?"

"Geneviève Burke knew the bones were there. Less than an hour after her son told her he'd opened the studio, she asked a man who worked for her to retrieve the old chest. We're tracking down people who were Geneviève's friends around the time her husband disappeared."

"You think Tony Burke is right? Geneviève and her lover killed her husband?"

"We haven't found anything that proves him wrong." And it wasn't for lack of trying.

"Can you prove him right? Never mind." Vernon answered his own question. "We're waiting for the DNA results." He pulled a pack of gum from his pocket and took out a fresh piece. "Where are you on the Iris Burton shooting?"

"All we have is her statement. She saw a well-dressed elderly man—"

"Lurking near the victim's apartment." Vernon said. "Everyone with a TV set has that."

"When we have Geneviève Burke's killer, we'll have Iris Burton's killer. I've asked Paul Gilbert for help." He repeated what Paul had told him about the friendship between the two families. "Paul was only a child when Jim Burke disappeared, but he's agreed to ask his parents. And now I'm asking you."

The Super stopped chewing. "What are you asking me?"

He handed Vernon the list. "Do any of these names ring a bell?"

Bea picked him up in front of headquarters. "What did the Super say?"

"Other than wanting an arrest yesterday?" Mike said. "Not much. He didn't like being asked about Geneviève's old liaisons, but he said he'd give the matter some thought. I gave him a list of Sunny Gardens' male residents. I want to give Gilbert a copy, too, let him run it by his parents. Can you take care of that?"

"I'll do it before I leave today." She made a rueful face. "I wouldn't have Vernon's job for a million dollars. Important feathers are being ruffled, not only the Devereux family's but also their friends'. You know some of these old men are afraid their names will surface next, and you know he's hearing about it."

"He was ready to refuse funding for the additional DNA tests, but the lab is doing it for free."

"The lab is working for free? I'm not complaining, but why?"

"When I told Lucy, the lab tech I've been talking to, that one of the things we wished to verify was paternity, she became eloquent on the subject and anxious to work with us."

"I'm sorry, Mike. You've lost me."

"Lucy sees using DNA to establish paternity as a potential goldmine. She volunteered to fast track the analysis at no charge. Her director not only went along, he said they'd do it all for free." Bea continued to look puzzled and he said, "Think how many women would pay to establish a man's paternity and his responsibility for child support. I can see the billboards now. *DNA Testing: Call 1-800 he's the 1.*"

"Ah, and how many men would pay to disprove it," Bea countered. "*Call 1-800 she lies.*"

Both were chuckling when they pulled up in front of Burke's house. Although the rain had stopped, standing water still puddled on the sidewalk, and dark clouds promised more bad weather. A pickup with Authentic Restorations written on the door sat at the curb, but the photographer's car was nowhere to be seen.

"Someone's here. Let's see if it's Claire." Bea hopped out of the car. "Quick before it starts raining again. I don't have an umbrella." She ran up the steps.

Claire was surprised to see Mike and Bea at the front door. Mike wore his customary navy blazer and khaki slacks, and Bea looked elegant in an off-white pantsuit and chunky high heels. Claire, who had been crawling around in the attic when she heard someone knocking, rubbed her dusty hands on the legs of her jeans and hoped she didn't have smudges on her face.

"Hi."

Mike waved toward his partner. "You remember Detective Washington."

"Of course. Good to see you again, Bea."

Bea smiled then looked past her. "Is Tony here, by any chance?"

"No. Have you tried the dealership?" That's where he'd said he was going when he dropped her off.

"We aren't looking for Burke." Mike's manner was brusque. "We're here to gather some items from the studio." He glanced at his watch. "Our photographer is late."

"Can we wait inside, out of the weather?" Bea said.

"Sure, but I think your man just arrived." Claire pointed to a car that was pulling up to the curb. "If you're going to the studio, you might want to walk through the house. The crew has been parking trucks in the side yard, and it's a sea of mud."

"Thanks. We'll take you up on that." Bea said.

Claire watched Mike, Bea, and their photographer follow the now well-worn path to the studio then returned to the attic and the problem of where to put the new ductwork.

She was back downstairs, standing at the makeshift table in the dining room and making notes on the HVAC system plan, when Mike and Bea returned. She put her pencil down.

"Are you finished with the studio?"

"For today," Mike said, "but we don't want you or any of your employees in there yet. The photographer will be another few minutes. He'll put the tape back when he's finished."

"We don't want to go inside. We want to tear it down. And it's been sitting there with your yellow tape all over it for a week now. The delay is starting to cost money." Only the extra expense of keeping a large dumpster on site, but it was more than the money. She was tired of Jim Burke's tomb squatting like a bad omen in the back yard.

"We're doing our best not to inconvenience you," Mike said.

"Inconvenience me?" It was all she could do not to roll her eyes. "Refusing to let me demo the studio isn't an inconvenience; it's a roadblock. What more do you want with that building?"

"Claire, you know we can't discuss an investigation in progress."

She pointed to a plastic bag in his hands. "Does Tony know that you're taking whatever's in there? It's his property."

"It's also a crime scene."

"The photographer should be finished by now." Bea interrupted. "I think he could use a hand carrying all his equipment."

Mike grabbed the excuse and went outside to help.

Claire thanked Bea for heading off an argument. "I'm sure Mike thanks you, too."

"Just doing my job."

"I didn't get a chance to copy the photos yet. I'm sorry. But I did talk to Tony and he's fine with it. I'll get them to you tomorrow or the next day."

"No problem. We've already got someone on the names. So far, Judy Boaz is the only one he's been able to find. From what I hear, she's a real piece of work. At first, she refused to say anything unless we guaranteed her a spot in a witness protection program. She's convinced that Geneviève, and Iris, were killed because they knew too much about some conspiracy." Bea made quote marks in the air. "I don't know where that came from."

Claire knew. Tony had laughed about scaring Judy with tales of dark conspiracies. She hadn't found it funny, and she was sure Bea wouldn't be amused.

"We found her mysterious land deal," she said. "Unfortunately, it looks legitimate. The highway in question runs beside the farm Geneviève has owned for years. I'm sorry I wasted your time." She considered mentioning the first sale, Roger Devereux's gift to Geneviève, and decided no, not until she'd talked to Tony.

"You haven't wasted anyone's time. Part of police work is eliminating false leads. Did you tell Tony what Kyle Winslow had to say?" When she nodded, Bea said, "I hope he appreciates you."

Claire felt herself blushing, the curse of the redhead. Unable to meet Bea's inquiring gaze, she busied herself rearranged the blueprints spread on the dining room table. Tony had been preoccupied on the trip back to town. He'd dropped her off without mentioning seeing her again. For the tenth time in the last hour, she wondered if she'd been a total idiot for thinking their lovemaking meant something to him. The list of women in his life wasn't a short one. What made her think she was special?

"Is the delay on the studio really messing you up?" Bea said.

"It's still at the inconvenience level, but if I can't take it down soon..." Claire raised her hands in an exasperated gesture, grateful for the change of subject.

"I'll do what I can to speed things up."

Mike returned, carrying a tripod and spotlights, followed by a heavily laden photographer. "We're through here. I'll be waiting in the car."

"I'm right behind you," Bea said. "Bye Claire. Keep in touch."

"Bye, and thank you." She let them find their own way out.

27

Claire had finished cleaning up after dinner and was flipping through the channels, looking for something on TV that would take her mind off Tony, when the doorbell rang. It was Tony, looking scruffy. Was this a rerun?

"Can I come in?"

"Of course." He didn't smell of alcohol. "Where's your car?"

"Back at the apartment. I've been walking around in a bit of a fog. I'm not sure how I ended up here."

"I've been thinking about you." She steered him into the living room. "Is everything okay?"

"No, but I'm sober." He sat on the sofa stretched his legs out, and leaned back, pillowing his head in his hands. He'd sat like that when she was tracking down people in the pictures. He'd been relaxed then; tonight felt very different.

"Would you like iced tea or a Coke?"

"I'd like a beer. I haven't given up drinking. I'm just not planning to get drunk."

Claire returned with two beers, handed him one and sat next to him on the sofa. "Do you want to talk about it?"

"Big day today."

"It was."

"Lots of surprises. I never dreamed Geneviève had that much money. When Shylock told me about her trusts, I asked him if he was serious. What you found out about the land explained where the money came from. She must have had something really juicy on Devereux."

"You're sure she was blackmailing him?"

"Geneviève took every advantage she could find or create. She suckered me into paying for her rehab when she could have paid it herself."

"Regardless, it was nice of you." Claire took his hand—it was cold—and held it in hers.

"I still believe she killed my father. The last thing I said to her was that I'd see her hang for it, but I'm angry that someone killed her. I didn't realize that until today. Being up there, talking to Shylock about her estate..." He rubbed his forehead. "When I got back to the dealership, there was a message. The police are ready to release her body."

"She was a difficult woman, but she was still your mother."

"More than difficult, sweetheart. You, on the other hand, are a very nice person." He slid his arm around her and kissed her lightly. "Unlike Geneviève, you're beautiful on the inside as well as the outside."

"You change moods faster than any other man I've known."

"How many other men have you known?" The question came with a smile.

"Just one," she admitted. She and Tom started dating in ninth grade, went to college together, and married right after graduation. "But if there had been fifty other men, you'd still be the one I'm going to remember when I'm a hundred years old."

"When we first met I wondered if you wore colored contacts. Few people have green eyes, and yours are stunning, but your mouth is irresistible. I want your mouth."

Claire lay beside Tony, her head on his chest. They were on her bed, but she didn't remember the trip from the living room. Making love with Tony created a rush so intense it altered her consciousness. She imagined that's how it would feel to fall off a cliff. She didn't want to ever hit the ground.

"What was military school like?" she said.

"It was okay, better than living at home. The boxing coach took an interest in me. He helped me work through a lot of anger, punching the bag."

"You don't look like a boxer." She ran her finger down his straight nose.

"Me and Mohammed Ali, too pretty to take a punch. Remember, 'Float like a butterfly; sting like a bee?'"

"Do you still box?"

"I don't ever want to hit anyone again. I almost killed a man."

"In a match?"

"In a bar." He stared at the ceiling as if the past was being projected onto it. "I married right out of college. It didn't last—nobody's fault—we were too young. Neither of us had a clue."

He'd mentioned a divorce the day she looked at his house. She hadn't thought much about it until yesterday. Lying in his arms, she'd wondered about the circumstances and hoped it was well in the past, that there'd been no children and that his ex-wife was happily remarried with a houseful of kids and living somewhere far, far away.

"I caught her having a drink with an old boyfriend. We'd separated by then, but she was still my wife. I told him to get lost. He said I was out of line, poked me with his umbrella, and told me to get lost. I pulled him out of the booth and hit him as hard as I could. My second punch caught air because he was already down." He exhaled hard. "He was unconscious for two days, two days I spent praying for his recovery."

"It would have been an accident."

"It would have been manslaughter, and it wasn't my first bar fight. My lawyer convinced the cops it was self-defense. I'd been attacked by a man with a weapon, a deadly umbrella."

"If he hit you with an umbrella, he was using it as a weapon."

"That punch was the deathblow for our marriage. Gilbert walked me through the whole mess. First he kept me out of jail, and second he made sure Callie didn't take me to the cleaners."

"Paul Gilbert?"

"You know him?"

"He's helped me out, too. Why don't you ask Paul about the trusts?"

"We can talk about that tomorrow. Tonight, I want to hear about you. Tell me what you were like when you were a little girl. Were you a Girl Scout? Did you sell cookies?"

"Of course." She raised her head and looked him in the eye. "I'm honest, trustworthy, loyal, and anything else you want me to be." She'd be happy to spend the rest of her life on these warm sheets.

The next morning, Claire woke first. She lay quietly luxuriating in the sensation of Tony's body along the length of hers, her breath following the rhythm of his, her pulse and his heart beating together. She propped herself up on one elbow and studied his face. He opened his eyes.

"Did you know morning is the best time to make love?" he said.

"Why morning?"

"I like being able to see what I'm doing."

"Tony." Her cheeks warmed.

"A wanton woman who blushes." He pulled her onto him. "It doesn't get any better than that."

Later, driving him back to his apartment, she asked, "Are you anxious to move into your own house?" He hadn't seemed at all concerned about the delays, but still...

"When it's ready. Meanwhile, the apartment's comfortable." His hand slid up her thigh. "You could spend the weekend and see for yourself."

"You want to cut that out before I run off the road."

He laughed and withdrew his hand. "Okay, but the invitation stands. We could start with dinner Friday night."

Was he saying he didn't want to see her until the weekend? What about tonight and Wednesday night and Thursday night? Stop it, she told herself. You're acting like an infatuated thirteen-year-old.

"I'd like that." She pulled up in front of his building. "Did you ever talk to Kyle? You really should go see the farm. I'm sure it's changed since you were a child."

"I haven't talked to him, and you're right. I should go up there, but I'm tied up through Thursday. We're shooting commercials for the dealership. I could do it Friday morning. Want to come? Fried chicken for lunch."

"I want to, but I have to work. I took off half of yesterday, and I'm already late today. What about Saturday?"

"I have other plans for Saturday." He leaned over and kissed her. "And they involve you. I'll pick you up seven o'clock Friday. Wear a nice dress and pack your toothbrush. Meanwhile would you do me a favor? It shouldn't take a lot of time."

"Sure."

"See if you can get through to Paul Gilbert—he's been avoiding me—and ask him about the trusts. I want to know what my options are."

28

When Claire called Paul Gilbert's office, his secretary said he had no openings on his calendar until the twenty-second. Paul, himself, had called back later that morning. If she didn't mind meeting after business hours, he could see her at five-thirty today. When she arrived, he was alone in the office.

"Thank you for seeing me on such short notice," she said.

"It's my pleasure. Would you like anything to drink? Suzanne made fresh coffee before she left, and I have a selection of teas. Or wine if you prefer. It is after five."

She said no thank you to any drink, and he led her down the hall to a room furnished more like an elegant parlor than a legal office.

"Why don't we sit by the window?" He gestured toward two upholstered chairs with a small table between them. "Before we begin, I want to emphasize that this consultation is *pro bono, pro* my *bono*, because I remain mortified by my role in Frank Palmer's crimes. I am grateful for an opportunity to assist you."

"Paul, you didn't do anything." He, like everyone else, had been taken in by Frank.

"That's exactly the point," he said. "I should have seen, and I didn't. Now, you have questions about a trust?"

"Two trusts. Here's a copy of the first one." She handed him the document. "They're not mine, but you know the people involved—at least one of them."

Paul put on a pair of reading glasses. "An occupational hazard," he said. "Small print ruins your eyesight." When he finished reading, he looked up, frowning. "Where did you get this?"

"The St. Helena Parish Courthouse. That's where the land is."

"I see." He tapped the paper. "What's your question?"

"The trustee sold three hundred of the four hundred acres, but she didn't put the proceeds back into this trust. Instead, she created another trust with similar but more restrictive provisions. I want to know if she had the right to do that."

"What's your interest in this, Claire?"

"The beneficiary asked me to look into it for him. We're friends." Her words earned her a searching look. She felt her cheeks color and hoped Paul didn't notice. "I know you've represented Tony in the past," she said, "but he's changed."

"Before we go any further, I'd like to clarify that I am representing you, not Tony Burke. It's a fine point, given the situation, but an important one." She nodded and he continued. "Now, you say Geneviève created a second trust with the proceeds from the land sale? Are you certain?"

"The amount is essentially the same as the sale proceeds, and she did it shortly after selling the land." She handed him a copy of the second trust. "Her lawyer gave this to Tony. Again, the income goes to Geneviève, and at her death, the assets go to Tony, but she added a stipulation. Tony receives the assets only if he agrees to, personally, continue the horse rescue operation for a minimum of ten years. Otherwise everything goes to a charity that takes care of elderly horses."

Paul leaned back in his chair and steepled his fingers. The corners of his mouth twitched into a smile that became a chuckle.

"You think that's funny?"

"Claire, if I didn't find humor in human behavior, I couldn't stay sane. Are we talking about a significant amount of money?"

"Just over a million dollars."

"That answers my first question," he said. "The stakes are high enough to warrant legal action. But Geneviève may have been within her rights. It appears she provided the assets for the first trust."

"But she didn't. Her first husband, Roger Devereux, funded the first trust. She was a conduit."

Paul rocked forward in his chair and scanned the documents. "I see no mention of Roger Devereux."

"He sold Geneviève the land, all four hundred acres, for one dollar. Here's a copy of the deed. Same date, same lawyer, same witnesses as the original trust." Claire slid her last document across the table. If this didn't convince Paul, he didn't want to be convinced.

"Have you talked to the attorney who prepared these?" He laid the signature pages side by side and aligned their edges.

"He died several years ago. It's been thirty-four years, Paul, the witnesses could all be dead too, but it's obvious what happened."

Paul fiddled with his reading glasses and cleared his throat, obviously uncomfortable with their discussion. Why? He would have been a teenager when the trust was created. He couldn't know the circumstances, plus he'd appeared to be surprised by what she'd learned. Or was it something unrelated? He'd been Tony's lawyer. Was there something Tony hadn't told her?

"What's wrong?" she said.

"I've represented several members of the Devereux family, and in some instances the relationship is ongoing. With your permission, I'll discuss this matter with them. If they object to my involvement, I have a conflict of interest and cannot help you. I will, however, refer you to another attorney."

"A conflict? But why? Isn't it in the Devereux family's interest that the intention of Roger's trust be honored?" She paused. "Or do you think there was something shady about that initial land transfer?" This question was as close as she'd come to sharing Tony's belief that Geneviève had blackmailed Roger Devereux and possibly continued to blackmail the family. She studied Paul's face for clues, but he'd recovered his usual poise, and his expression gave nothing away.

"That's a moot question, Claire, and I'm in no position to venture an opinion. Nor is Roger Devereux." He stared out the window at the darkening sky before turning his attention back to her. "New Orleans is a small town. There are no secrets. I'm aware that Tony has more serious legal concerns than the validity of this trust."

"If you mean Geneviève's murder, he's a suspect because they argued the night before she was killed. There's no evidence against him, and it's a lot more complicated than the argument." She didn't say any more, because Mike had asked her not to discuss the discovery of the bones with anyone.

"The police have taken a DNA sample from Tony. He thinks because they found some evidence on Geneviève. Once they get the results back, they'll know he's innocent." Paul's frown deepened, and she tried to ease the situation. "On these trusts, he just wants to know what his options are. That's all. He's not even sure he wants to pursue it."

"I'm sorry, Claire." Paul handed the documents back to her. "As much as I want to help you, I can't. If you like, I'll refer you to one of my colleagues. That's the best I can do."

"I'll call if I want a reference." *If Tony wants a reference.* "Thank you." She put the papers back in her briefcase and stood to leave.

Paul walked her to the elevator, where she declined his offer to escort her to her car. His willingness to help had diminished when Tony's name came up and vanished the moment he learned the Devereux family was involved. The next time she talked to Tony, she'd ask if he knew why.

Paul watched the elevator door close and the needle mark Claire's descent. Then he returned to the green conference room. Small to the point of intimacy, it was his preferred setting for sensitive conversations. Clients felt comfortable because the location at the end of the hall made it absolutely private, an ambience reinforced by the treetop view of the park across the street. Claire had appeared at ease; he'd been disconcerted by their discussion.

As soon as he read the first document, he'd recognized the situation. He'd set up similar trusts for men who had fathered children they didn't wish to acknowledge but for whom they accepted financial responsibility. That Geneviève would be involved in such a situation was no surprise. But when Claire said Roger Devereux had funded the trust, he'd almost fallen off his chair.

The deeds backed up her supposition. The attorney had been inexcusably careless about leaving a paper trail. Why land and not bearer bonds or some other financial instruments that couldn't be easily traced? He picked up the phone and dialed a familiar number. His father answered.

"I need your help, Dad." It was the second time in two days that he'd made this request.

"If it has to do with Roger and Geneviève, we've already discussed the matter. When their relationship ended is irrelevant. Roger had nothing to do with her death. And you cannot expect either your mother or me to remember events long past that we didn't wish to know about at the time."

"A second woman has been murdered, executed gangland style, presumably because she saw Geneviève's killer. You must have seen that in the news." He gave his father a moment then changed tactics. "I'm still hoping you and mother will recall the names of Geneviève's lovers, but

182

meanwhile, I have a simple yes or no question about something I'm quite sure you remember."

"Which is?" His father's irritation had given way to wariness.

"Is Roger Devereux Tony Burke's father?" Paul waited for an answer. When none was forthcoming, he modified the question. "Who else knows?"

"How did you find out?" His father's question served as an admission.

"Roger set up a trust to provide for his son, but Geneviève pilfered it for her own purposes. A woman for whom I have both respect and affection has become involved with Tony. She's asked me to help him claim his rightful inheritance. If Roger is indeed Tony's father, I have a conflict of interest." He might have one regardless.

"You have both a conflict and a duty, Paul. Tell this woman that you can't help her and, if you truly care for her, tell her to run as fast and as far as she can. Geneviève left nothing but sorrow in her wake. Layton, God help him, grew up as angry and destructive as his mother. As you know, he left New Orleans under a cloud. It broke Roger's heart."

There were at least two sides to every story, but his father was a man with one eye.

"I'm afraid she wouldn't listen," Paul said. The quick smile and the blush that colored Claire's cheeks when she described Tony as a friend suggested a more intimate connection. That was unfortunate but none of his business and, given Tony's *modus operandi*, would undoubtedly end soon. Roger and Geneviève were another matter.

"How long did their relationship persist?" he said.

"Their affair ended decades ago, Layton was still a child. Let it rest, Paul."

"I can't. A homicide detective has asked me to find out if Geneviève's relationship with Roger survived their divorce. Obviously, it did. I can't withhold that information." He assured his father that the police would be discreet, but that wasn't enough. Before they ended the conversation, his father had extracted his promise, albeit hedged, not to tell the police that Roger was Tony's father—not unless they asked.

Paul was painfully aware that the promise he'd given his father could well prove empty. Those directly involved would tell no one. The lawyer who drew up the original trust was dead as was Geneviève, and Roger's memories were blocked by disease, but there were others.

Sooner or later, if she hadn't already, Claire would wonder why Roger had gone to such lengths to provide for Tony. She'd suspect the truth and say something to Tony. The police might already know. Laura had said they'd requested a DNA sample from Roger, and she'd refused permission. Claire said Tony had already provided one.

Paul prided himself upon being a realist. Realistically, it was only a matter of time before the identity of Tony's biological father became known. In the unlikely event that Tony decided to walk away from a million dollars, his mother's murder would still draw attention to all facets of her life. Already, too many people had too many clues to the truth, and if Claire could find the trust documents, so could others.

But why does it matter?

After thirty plus years, who really cared if Roger Devereux and his ex-wife had an affair? Neither adultery nor illegitimacy was the scandal it had been back in 1960, and the trust demonstrated that Roger had taken financial responsibility for his son. As Claire suspected, Geneviève overstepped the bounds of her authority with the stipulations of the second trust. A simple challenge, and Tony would get his million dollars.

All of this could be handled with discretion. Tomorrow, he would tell Mike that Roger and Geneviève's relationship had persisted post-divorce and, with a few carefully worded questions of his own, assess how much the police had learned about this old scandal. Tonight, on the way home, he'd stop by his parents' house and assure his father that the sky was not falling. That left only Laura. He dialed her number.

"I hope I'm not interrupting your dinner."

"We're not eating for another hour," she said. "What can I do for you?"

Paul chose to ignore the cool tone that let him know that he had not been forgiven. He relayed what he'd learned and braced himself for an outraged denial. It didn't come.

"None of that is news," she said. "I've been keeping a close eye on the situation for years. I won't compromise you by sharing the details of how. I suspect at least one law has been broken."

"You never cease to amaze me." His statement was neutral. In truth, he was appalled. He envisioned Laura a spider tending her web of spies and informants. That she'd withheld information from him, while chastising him for disloyalty, rankled.

"Lamont and I are less pessimistic than you are about keeping everything under wraps. It appears Tony wants us to buy the land back. Pineland will offer more than it's worth and pay cash. Tony will go back to Italy, and that will be that."

"It isn't just the farm," he warned. "Are you aware of the second trust? There may be a problem with it."

"I am and there is. Now that you know the situation, you can help us." She spoke briskly, ordering not asking his assistance. "Roger became concerned when Geneviève established a second trust, but she spouted some nonsense, and he agreed to let it be as long as the provisions regarding Tony were identical. She said they were, and he trusted her—God knows why.

"After I became Roger's legal guardian, I obtained copies of all the documents. I saw Geneviève's ridiculous stipulation about her horses and should have taken action then and there, but I didn't expect her to die so soon—short of someone driving a stake through her heart."

Paul remained silent. The new hard-boiled Laura was only a slight improvement over the irrational harridan of their previous conversation.

"I know I've been difficult." Her voice softened. "I appreciate all you do for us, Paul, and should have told you about this sooner. I hope you'll agree to represent us in this matter."

"I'm not sure you need my help."

"Geneviève's lawyer—I don't remember his name, but I can see him, a little weasel of a man—set up that second trust and changed it when she asked him to. I can testify that he knew Roger provided the initial assets and that he and Roger discussed the necessity for identical provisions in the second trust. As Roger's guardian, I can accuse him of malfeasance. He'd be disbarred, wouldn't he?"

"It's a possibility."

"But as you always say, legal action is the last resort. You're a diplomat, Paul. I hope you'll talk to him, convince him that it's in his best interest to let Tony sell the farm back to Pineland and receive the assets from the second trust."

"This is a complicated situation." And he wanted no part of it. If not for the promise to his father, he'd have already told her to find another attorney.

"Only if someone objects," she said. "I'm confident no one will. The bastard gets his inheritance, he has nothing to complain about, and the horses don't have lawyers."

"Laura…"

"I'm sorry, Paul. It's been so hard. I'm trying to hold things together." Her voice quavered. "We have to protect Roger. Please."

"I'll do what I can." He'd talk to the lawyer, but Roger was still embroiled in a homicide investigation, and he couldn't do anything about that.

29

First thing Wednesday morning, Claire met with Anne and Dave Currier. She wanted to do one last walk-through before starting work on their new kitchen and bathrooms. Anne chattered excitedly about how wonderful everything was going to be, and Dave, her usually dour penny-pinching husband, was actually genial.

"Dave and I have been talking," Anne said. "Remember the spa bathroom you showed me? We've decided to go ahead and do it." Dave nodded agreement, and she continued, "We want an extra-long jetted tub, marble instead of tile, and a separate shower with multiple heads."

"Really?" She tried to hide her surprise. She had shown them the more elaborate option because there was plenty of space, and Anne had said she wanted a fancy bathroom. As expected, Dave had immediately squelched the idea, saying there might be room in the house, but there was no room in the budget. They'd moved ahead with plans for a standard tub and shower combination.

"You realize it's going to be a good bit more money," she said. "It's not just the fixtures. We'll have to run more pipe, reinforce the floor." She wished they had mentioned this a little sooner. Changing the plans would require revising the permit.

A cloud crossed Dave's face, but Anne squeezed his arm. "We know. And I hope this won't slow anything down, but it's what we really want."

"I'll need you to sign a change order, Dave."

He had told her more than once that he would pay the contracted amount and not a penny more. She believed him, and she wasn't going to spend one extra penny without his specific written approval. "It will be over five thousand dollars—probably more like seven or eight."

"I want hard costs, not round numbers."

"Of course." She promised to get the information to him as soon as possible. "Unless you have something else, I'd better be going. I want to get your signed change order by close of business today. A delay could cost money."

It was going to be a long day. Synchronizing work on the Burke and Currier projects had been her idea, and it made sense on paper, but implementation was proving difficult. She'd spent hours working with the subs, making sure everyone was on the same schedule, and now this. Any delay would ripple through both projects and destroy her carefully constructed schedule.

She made a mental list of the changes required for the Currier's bathroom, starting with costs from the plumber. The electrical was an additional circuit; she could estimate that. Jack would be able to tell her what extra structural work was required to support the heavier tub. Labor costs for tile and marble work were similar. Thank heaven she'd done drawings for the spa bath option. They were somewhere in the Currier file. Brochures for the fixtures were with them.

Jack and the plumber both should be at Tony's house this morning. Reggie, their HVAC guy, should be there too. He'd cancelled a meeting yesterday afternoon, and she was determined to talk to him ASAP. The central hall would have to include specialized humidity control to protect Jim Burke's paintings.

Calm down. One thing at a time. You can do it.

Jack and Reggie stood nose-to-nose and toe-to-toe in what was going to be Tony's center hall. Claire knew without asking what the argument was about. Reggie was an excellent engineer but if left to his own devices ignored aesthetics—forget historic authenticity

"Reggie wants to drop the hall ceiling and run the extra vents above it," Jack said.

"Can't you run them through the attic and down the linen closet?" That's what she'd worked out, and she'd given Reggie a copy of those plans.

"It's going to cost extra," he said.

"That's okay. Put the numbers together and we can talk about it, but we're going to do it right."

"That's what I told him," Jack said.

"Nothing wrong with double checking," she said. "Where's the plumber? I need his help, and yours, with a change order on the Currier project."

By noon, she was back at the office, preparing the Currier's change order. She faxed the finished document to Dave's office then called to be sure someone had noticed its arrival. It was, she explained to the woman who answered the phone, important that Dave sign and send it back as quickly as possible.

"Dave's at lunch. I'll mention it when he returns."

"He's expecting the fax. If I haven't heard back in an hour, I'll call again."

She locked the office and ran down to the corner deli to get herself a sandwich. When she returned, the signed change order sat in the fax machine. "Thank you, Dave," she murmured and called Jack.

"I have Dave's signature. We're back on track. Have things settled down over there?"

"Burke stopped by, looking for you. Said it was personal, nothing to do with his house." Jack's tone conveyed his disapproval.

"I'm sorry I missed him." She'd been wondering why Tony had no time for her until Friday. The visit made her feel better. "Or maybe not. This has been a crazy morning."

"You've already done a full day's work and then some. Everything's under control, why don't you treat yourself to an afternoon off?"

"I can't. I have to modify the Currier's permit ASAP, and it will go faster in person. That means a trip downtown."

She threw away the remains of her now soggy sandwich and was halfway out the door when the phone rang. Caller ID said David Currier, so she ran back to get it. The call was from Anne.

"You won't believe who's going to call you."

"Who?" Claire played along although she really wanted to ask if this couldn't wait until tomorrow.

"Just a few minutes after you left, Dave had gone to work, and I was standing on the sidewalk, thinking about what I want to do with the landscaping, when Laura Bethea pulled up. Laura and I met last year when I served on a committee she chaired at Saint Agnes. She's an alumna, very active, and our daughter is a student there.

"Laura said she had always admired this house. She asked if Dave and I were the new owners. We started talking about fixing up old houses, and of course, your name came up." Anne paused. "You don't know who she is do you?"

"No," Claire admitted.

"Bethea is her married name. Laura is a Devereux. Surely, you've heard of them. Old New Orleans money." Anne said. "She'd be a wonderful connection for you."

"I do know who she is. Thank you for the referral," Claire said, although she couldn't imagine Laura Devereux Bethea hiring her company, not if this was the same Laura who had seen her with Geneviève. "Dave has signed your change order. I think we can stay on schedule."

"I knew he'd sign, but you were wise to insist," Anne said. "And while I have you on the phone, I want to talk about the landscaping."

"Can we talk tomorrow, meet at the house and you can show me?" Please, I have to get downtown.

Claire grabbed her purse and tried again to leave. This time, she walked out the door, and bumped into a slender woman who was about to walk in. For a long moment, Claire and Roger Devereux's niece stared at each other.

"I'm sorry," Claire said. "I didn't hear you at the door."

"I'm sorry, I was just about to knock. I'm Laura Bethea. Anne Currier recommended you, and I was in the neighborhood."

"Anne told me, and I'd like to talk to you, but I'm afraid you caught me on my way out."

"I want to talk to you about a house I'm considering. Could we go inside for just a minute?"

"This really isn't a good time," Claire said. "What about tomorrow?"

"Not tomorrow." Laura stepped forward, as if she was going to push her way into the office, but stopped when Jack pulled into the driveway.

He climbed out of his truck and hurried toward them. "I'm glad I caught you," he said to Claire. "Reggie is right behind me. He wants to see your original drawings for the Burke project."

"Jack, this is Laura Bethea. Laura, Jack Giordano, my business partner." They exchanged greetings, and Claire said, "Laura wants to talk to us about a project. I was just suggesting tomorrow. Or Friday. Some time next week, just not today."

"I'll leave that to you ladies to arrange." Jack pointed to Reggie's pick-up that had just pulled up to the curb. "Reggie and I have some negotiating to do. Claire, as soon as you finish here, come on in and join us."

"Just for a minute. I have to go downtown." She held her hand out to Laura, who took it reluctantly. "It was nice meeting you. I'd like to talk about your house. Do you have my number?"

"I'll be in touch." Laura backed down the steps, clutching her purse.

Claire watched her depart. Why hadn't Laura acknowledged their earlier encounters? She must have recognized her. Laura Devereux Bethea was a strange woman. Her hand had been cold and damp, her handshake as limp as a dead fish. Claire had heard the expression, and now she knew exactly what it meant.

30

Tony finished his part and told the guy from the advertising agency that he'd be outside if they needed him. He walked around the lot, admiring the shiny automobiles and removing imaginary specks of dust from their polished fenders. The sales force was inside, watching the commercial being shot and drooling over Kerri. Let them have their fun; he'd see her later.

He opened a door and inhaled a new car aroma made even better by the scent of fine leather—no vinyl upholstery here. Back when he was in college, this place sold Chevys and Pontiacs, and he'd worked summers in the service department. That was a long time ago, but he still got a kick out of seeing *Tony Burke Ferrari & BMW* in big letters on the building.

When he bought the dealership, the employees assumed he was lending his name in exchange for a cut of the profits. They knew better now. After observing and interviewing every member of the staff, from the sales manager to the guy who cleaned up the service area, he'd decided to keep the manager and leave the service department as is, but half the sales force needed to be replaced or retrained and quickly. In less than a month he'd be back in Italy, preparing for the upcoming season. And that was cutting it tight. The first race was March 27th.

A Lexus pulled into the entrance, paused, backed-up, and parked on the street. A slender blonde woman got out and walked quickly toward the showroom. She showed no interest in any of the vehicles she passed and twice glanced back over her shoulder as if making sure she wasn't being followed.

People who don't drive their car onto the lot are usually asking directions or looking for a bathroom, nothing to do with buying a car, but neither makes them nervous. What was she up to? Tony stepped out where she could see him.

"Hi. Can I help you?"

"You're Tony Burke."

"And you are?" She looked vaguely familiar, but he couldn't place her, and she was staring at him as if he had three heads. He kept his distance.

"I want to buy my husband a new car, a surprise for Valentine's Day." The blurted statement might explain why she'd left her car on the street but not her strange behavior.

Tony took stock—expensive car, expensive clothes, designer sunglasses—and decided to go along with her. Only five days until Valentine's, so it would have to be something already on the lot, a BMW. They only had two Ferraris in stock, a demo and the one he drove. He gave her a reassuring smile.

"Do you have any particular car in mind?"

"I really don't want anyone I know to see me here. They might mention it to my husband." She glanced back at the street. "Can we go inside?"

"Of course. They're shooting a commercial in the showroom, so we have to go in the side door." He gestured for her to go first. "Walk in front of me, and no one driving past will be able to see you." Not that anyone was likely to look, but…

The customer is always right, even if she's so high strung she twitches.

He ushered her past the crowd watching the shoot and into an empty office. She sat down, a bit calmer now but still clutching her purse to her chest. He handed her a brochure.

"Why don't you look at this while I get a salesman to help you?"

"No, don't do that." Her jitters had returned. "Don't tell anyone else I'm here."

Who would he tell? Now that he'd had a good look at her, Tony was sure he'd seen her before, but he didn't know where, and he didn't know her name. Whoever she was, she was practically psycho about not being seen. He hoped she wasn't psycho period. Last year, a disturbed woman had stalked him, claiming he was the father of her child by osmosis or something. He showed this woman to a chair and sat down at the desk but left the door open.

"It's really Valentine's and birthday combined," she said. "He'll be fifty next month."

"Fifty is a big birthday." He waited for a reaction and got none. "Valentine's Day is my birthday, and no one's ever given me a car." He pointed to the unopened brochure in her hand. "Do you see anything you like?"

"I don't know a lot about cars. I'm shopping around to see what's available."

"Well, let's narrow it down. Do you want a convertible or a sedan?"

"Not a convertible. It's too hot half the year, and the fumes are awful, especially if you get stuck in traffic."

"That's hard to argue with." And the first hint this woman was capable of rational thought.

She pushed her sunglasses on top of her head and began leafing through the brochure.

"If I were turning fifty and someone was giving me a car, I'd want a 540i," he told her. It was his favorite of the new BMWs, not a Ferrari but responsive and fun to drive. He pointed it out and went through the features.

She glanced at the pictures of the car then stared intently at him. Her pupils looked normal size, not dilated or pinprick. She was still clutching her purse as if it held the secret to immortal life.

"It's nice looking," she said.

"It's even better driving. I'll get a salesperson to help you. Let me see if Eleanor is available." He offered the only female on the sales staff in the hope this odd customer would be more comfortable with another woman.

"I told you. I don't want to talk to anyone else." She frowned. "Why can't you take me for a test drive?"

"Only salesmen take customers out. House rules." That it was his house and he made the rules was beside the point. "But I can show you the car. We have several on the lot."

Tony didn't know why he was continuing this farce. Interacting with customers set a bad precedent. He didn't want racing fans cluttering up the lot in the hope of seeing him, and if this woman was for real, something he doubted, the sales force wouldn't appreciate his taking a customer.

"Thank you," she said. "I'd like that."

She followed him outside and, when he opened the car, got in on the driver's side. She seemed to relax as he helped her adjust the seat and showed her the controls, but she kept the purse in her lap rather than set it on the floor or on the seat beside her like a normal woman would.

"I can let you have this car for fifty even." He pointed to the sticker on the window that said $54,900. "Fifty thousand dollars for a fiftieth birthday present. I want to get into the spirit." If she actually bought anything, he'd throw the commission into the pot for the monthly sales bonuses.

"Can you put it in writing? I'm almost sure this is the car I want, but it's the first one I've looked at." She half shrugged, a helpless gesture that struck him as totally out of character. This woman might be nuts, but she knew what she wanted, and she was accustomed to giving orders.

"I'd be happy to," he said. "Let's go back inside."

He talked to her while he filled in a cost sheet. "You're smart to comparison shop. You should also look at Mercedes, Lexus, Jaguar. They make fine sedans, but the 540i is a fine sedan that's fun to drive. Tell you what. I'll let you take it out for a spin."

"Really? I can take it out by myself?"

"I just need to make a copy of your driver's license."

"I don't want to drive it. I was just surprised that you'd let me."

"You strike me as trustworthy." He shrugged. "It's almost too bad this is a surprise. If your husband had the chance to test drive all the cars you're considering, I bet he'd choose this one."

"You're quite the salesman." She smiled for the first time.

"It's easy when you've got a great product." He passed the completed cost sheet across the desk.

"Could you please sign it and write that this price is guaranteed by you? In case I come back and you're not here."

He took the price sheet back, wrote out a guarantee and signed it with a flourish. Then he put it and the brochure into one of the dealerships' envelopes. "Here you go. Signed, sealed and we're ready to deliver as soon as you make up your mind. Today is the ninth. Give us at least a day to prepare the car. Nothing goes out until it's been cleaned and prepped."

"Thank you very much, Tony. I'll be in touch." She took the envelope.

"Give us a call when you make up your mind. If I'm not here, whoever you talk to will honor that price."

He walked her to the door and held out his hand.

After a tiny hesitation, she took it. Her hand was icy cold and damp; her handshake, brief and limp. There was something seriously off about this woman. He still didn't know her name, and she clearly didn't want him to. He watched her hurry back to her car, the envelope still in her hand. She hadn't put it in her purse, and he wouldn't have been surprised to see her throw it away, but she held on to it.

He waited until her car pulled out and merged into traffic before he walked back to the showroom. The shoot was over, and the crew was packing up their equipment. The director waved Tony over to where he was talking to a cameraman.

"We were just raving about Kerri," he said. "I never thought I'd work with someone like her, not doing a commercial for a local dealership. I mean, she's a top model, a real pro and pleasant, none of that prima donna stuff. How'd you talk her into it?"

"We're old friends," Tony said. "Where is she?"

"Changing."

Kerri emerged from the office that had been transformed into a makeshift dressing room, and he asked her if she'd like to go for a ride in the country. He had to talk to a man about a horse.

31

The fax from CODIS came in a little before ten Friday morning. A note on the cover sheet said testing the additional samples wouldn't be done until Monday, but Lucy, the lab tech doing the analysis, thought he'd want these results as soon as they were available. Mike did. He scanned the summary.

Finding number one transformed Tony Burke from semi-prime suspect to innocent man. The four DNA samples came from four different individuals. The skin found under the victim's fingernails wasn't his, nor did it belong to the victim. They had the killer's DNA, and if they ever solved the case, they should be able to get a conviction.

The next finding described relationships among the individuals who had provided the DNA samples. Three were related – including the killer, but the relationships made no sense. A second reading did nothing to dispel the confusion.

Mike tried a diagram. He drew a circle for each DNA sample and labeled the first one GB, the victim. He drew an arrow to the next circle, wrote maternal under the arrow and labeled the circle TB. Funny, Burke's initials were a disease. DNA from the skin scrapings found under the victim's fingernails shared sequences with TB, but none with GB. The killer was related to Tony Burke but not to his mother.

Mike labeled the third circle SKIN, drew an arrow from it to the TB circle and wrote "paternal" beneath that arrow. He wrote JB in the last circle. No arrows, because DNA from the bones found in Jim Burke's studio came from an unrelated individual. Mike crossed out the J, leaving that circle labeled B, for bones. Bones unknown.

He studied his diagram and saw what must have happened. The results from the skin had been switched with the results from the bones. Switch them back, and Jim Burke was Tony's father. The killer was an unrelated individual. That made sense.

Mike didn't want to think about what this would do to the admissibility of DNA evidence if they ever matched the skin scrapings with a suspect. *Damn.* He threw the fax down on the desk. Using DNA had been his idea, and he'd pushed hard. Vernon, who'd been skeptical from the beginning, wasn't going to be gracious about the botched results.

He called Lucy. "We have a little problem." He explained what he thought had happened and asked her to investigate the possibility of a mix-up.

"No way," she said. "It's simply not possible. We have procedures, layers of safeguards. We have to. Our findings are used in legal proceedings. And we know the difference between bone cells and skin cells."

"I'd like to speak to your supervisor." There was no point in arguing with her.

"He's at a meeting out of the office. I'll give him your message when he returns." Click. Lucy was annoyed.

Mike tried to call Bea, but her phone was out again. If he ever found the culprit or culprits behind the sabotage, he or they would be walking a beat. Muttering under his breath, he walked down the hall to Bea's office. She was at her desk, eating the omnipresent cookie and working on a laptop.

"The DNA results are a disaster," he said. "Tony Burke is innocent."

"Wait a minute, let me save this." She hit a key and then pushed the computer aside. "Why is that a disaster? I'm not surprised. Are you? Really?"

"Sorry, Bea. Those were unrelated statements. The lab mixed up the samples; that's the disaster." He handed her the summary and waited while she scanned it.

"Four different individuals." She ran her finger down the page. "Okay. We have the killer's DNA. Two samples are related to Tony. Okay. Geneviève is Tony's mother; the bones belong to his father." She frowned. "A paternal relative... Why don't they just say father?"

"Read it again. They're talking about the skin, not the bones. The skeleton's not related to any of the others." He watched her expression turn incredulous.

"Tony's *father* killed Geneviève?"

"That's what the report says, but I think I know what happened." He laid his diagram on her desk and walked her through it. "I called the lab and talked to Lucy who says no way, but I don't see any other explanation."

"Give me a minute." Bea stood up and started pacing. Her office was small, and her legs long. After four steps she had to turn around. "What if they didn't make a mistake?" She kept pacing.

"Can you sit down? You're driving me nuts."

"I can't think sitting still." She laughed. "I used to drive my teachers nuts, especially my math teacher. She'd give us word problems, and I'd be hopping up and down behind my chair without even knowing that I'd stood up."

"This isn't math." He was watching a Ping-Pong match, and Bea was the ball.

"No, it's logic. Remember the old classic: that man is my brother's father, but I am not his son?" She looked at him expectantly.

He shook his head, grateful that she'd stopped bouncing off the walls but not sure word games were an improvement.

"I'm his daughter," Bea said. "That's the solution, a simple and logical explanation that most people miss." She reached the wall and turned around.

"Very clever, but what does that have to do with finding our killer?"

"You resolve the apparent contradiction by differentiating between facts and expectations." She stopped pacing. "There are two logical explanations for the DNA results as reported."

"Which are?"

"First is that the bones were not Jim Burke." He frowned and she said, "Stay with me. What if Jim Burke killed Mr. Bones? He and Geneviève faked the accident, he took off for parts unknown, she sealed up the studio, and all is well until Tony uncovers the skeleton."

"No one missed Mr. Bones?"

"How many people disappeared during Camille?"

"A lot," he conceded. "But I still don't like it. If no one is looking for Mr. Bones, why did Jim Burke have to disappear? Why put the bones in his studio?" She didn't have an answer, so he said, "What's your other explanation?"

"The bones belong to Jim Burke, who is not Tony's biological father."

"Not nearly as far-fetched." He thought about it. "Not far-fetched at all, given what we've heard about Geneviève's love life."

"Start with Tony's scenario, and make the lover also Tony's father. Son discovers his parents' crime, and threatens to reveal it. Mom wants dad to kill their son. Dad kills her instead, because only she knows who he is." She shrugged. "He could be reluctant to kill his own flesh and blood."

"That plays like a Greek tragedy." And if true, would knock the ground out from under Tony Burke.

"The man Iris saw could have been Tony's father. She said he was tall. Tony's a couple inches over six feet. How I wish…"

"Don't beat yourself up, Bea. It wasn't your fault. Iris put herself in danger, and the killer acted before we could protect her."

"I know, but…"

"The timeframe says he already had a gun. That tells me he was prepared to kill again."

"I don't know. Crime is up, and old people feel vulnerable. Rich old men, they're packing. Old women carry cute little pearl-handled pistols in their purses."

"You're not kidding are you?" Once again, he wondered about the city he'd chosen for his civilian career.

"Why'd you take the job, Mike?"

"Where did that come from?" Could she read his mind?

"Everyone in Homicide knows you came from military justice and have a law degree, but no one can figure out why you took this job. Why not the DA's office? They were hiring. The hours and the pay are better."

He'd asked himself the same question, and the answer was control. As head of the homicide division, he was in a position to make sure a case was solid, something even a mediocre prosecutor couldn't screw up. As a prosecutor, he'd found himself presenting more than a few cases made weak by sloppy investigations and once, to his horror, a capital case based on fabricated evidence.

"I like investigative work," he said, "building the case and doing it right. How about you?"

"I love being a detective. It's a big step up for me." She resumed wearing a path in her carpet. "I bet the skeleton is Jim Burke, and the old boyfriend-slash-Tony's father is still around.

"He might even live at Sunny Gardens. I know Iris said she didn't recognize him, but she hadn't worked there long and didn't necessarily know everyone, even if she thought she did. If we could test all the men's DNA, we might find him."

They both knew that wasn't going to happen.

"We owe Burke an apology." He rubbed his forehead where a headache threatened.

"I'd be happy to deliver it."

"I bet you would. You've got a lot of ground to make up. 'Wings off butterflies', remember?" He stopped joking. "Tell him he's no longer a suspect, but don't mention his father. I'm leaning toward your second explanation, but there's no point jumping the gun. We'll find out where the truth lies Monday when the other results come in. For now, I'll call Lucy, the lab tech, and apologize to her. Then I'll let Claire know that we're almost finished in the studio, and apologize for our last conversation. Apologies all around. Do you want one?"

"No, but I've got another riddle for you." She sat back down at her desk. "This one involves simple addition, and the answer is approximately ten years."

He'd been thinking along the same lines. "What do you get when you add a nine-year-old child and a nine-month pregnancy?"

"If the two murders are related—and we both think they are—the relationship between the victim and our killer lasted at least that long. Someone else has to know about it, probably more than one someone. We should be able to find this man." Bea finished the last of the cookies, wadded up the box and tossed it into the wastebasket. "Two points."

"I'm waiting to hear from Paul Gilbert. He called Wednesday morning and told me that Roger and Geneviève's relationship survived their divorce by an unknown number of years. His parents top my list of people who had to know who else was involved with Geneviève, but they're reluctant to name names. He's working on them."

"Is he really trying to help?"

"Paul is not a bad person, and he realizes that their silence could be shielding a killer."

"What about Claire and Tony? Poking around in Geneviève's past, which they are doing, could stir up a hornet's nest."

"I'll warn Claire when I talk to her."

"Carefully." The phone rang, interrupting Bea's chuckle. She picked up, listened a moment then handed the phone to him. "The lab director from CODIS is returning your call."

Mike took the receiver, time for his first act of contrition. "I owe you and Lucy an apology," he said, "especially Lucy. The confusion was ours. It's entirely possible the skin under the victim's fingernails came from sample number two's father."

"No it's not. Haven't you read the full report?" the director said.

"I read the summary," Mike admitted, "and jumped the gun."

"You certainly did. That DNA came from a female."

32

Claire left her Friday morning meeting with a newly signed contract in her brief case. Authentic Restorations was fully booked through the end of April, which was a major relief after the year's slow start. If she brought in any more work, Jack really would need another crew. She returned to the office and found a message from Mike. The police were through with the studio. She'd give Tony the good news tonight.

Tonight, the word made her smile. *Tonight, when she slept at his apartment.* That thought reminded her that Kyle expected her to come up and ride on Saturday. She called him and told him that she was busy all weekend.

"And I can't buy Tia Maria. Much as I love her, it's just not practical. But promise me you'll find her a good home." Even turning down a horse she'd love to own, Claire couldn't keep the big smile out of her voice.

"That's easy. I'll keep her. She's the perfect horse for Susie, my fiancée who will soon be my wife." Kyle also had a big smile in his voice.

"Congratulations. Have you set a date?"

"Soon as I get back. Let me tell you what's happened. Geneviève's son came up late yesterday afternoon."

"He told me he wanted to talk to you."

"Right. I forgot you knew him."

"My company is restoring his house. That's how I met Geneviève." It was hardly the time to say she might be falling love with Tony Burke.

"The guy lives up to his reputation," Kyle chortled. "He and his girlfriend—one of them anyway, a real looker—got here a little before five. I was down at the barn, feeding the horses."

Kyle kept talking but Claire didn't hear much after "girlfriend."

"Claire, are you there?"

"I'm here. I'm sorry, my mind wandered. I was thinking about Tia Maria," she lied. "I'm glad you're taking her." She was grateful Kyle couldn't see her face.

"Her and every other horse here. Tony asked me to show them around, said things had changed a lot since he was a kid. I gave him the fifty-cent tour and told him how much I appreciated him honoring his mother's word about Magic Man. That's when he asks if I want to buy every horse left on the farm. I tell him there's nothing I'd like better, but I don't have the money.

"That's when he asks if I can come up with one dollar. One dollar." Kyle sounded incredulous. "At first, I thought he was kidding, but he said, 'No, it's poetic justice. This farm began with a dollar; let it end with one.' I didn't know what he was talking about. I still don't, and I don't care."

Claire knew, but she didn't say anything.

"I gave him a dollar out of my wallet, and his girlfriend witnessed the transaction. Tony insisted we make it all legal. He wants the operation totally shut down, all the horses gone before the end of March. That's the only condition."

"How wonderful, Kyle." She forced the words out, hoping he was too wrapped in his own exhilaration to hear the strain in her voice.

"I'm still pinching myself. The last year and a half, I've been taking whatever work I could get, saving money so Susie and I could get our horse farm up and running. We have the land and enough put away to finish the fencing. Now we've got the horses.

"Susie is talking to the fence people, and brother's taking a week off to help me move the horses, starting next weekend. If you want to say good-bye to Tia Maria, you better hurry."

"I'll try." It was all she could manage.

"You know, Geneviève hardly ever mentioned Tony, and when she did, she had nothing good to say, but he's an all right guy. And he has style. His girlfriend was on him like white on rice while he's talking to me, but he acts like nothing's happening. We finish, and they walk down to the barn. After a while, I start wondering if everything's okay, so I go check. They're up in the loft, going at it like a couple of horny teenagers." He laughed. "I made a discreet exit."

Claire was too stunned for tears or even anger. Horny teenagers, Kyle's words made her wince. He might have said that about her and Tony, but she'd imagined a special passion. How could she have been such a fool? Tony was a playboy. She knew that before she met him. Everyone knew. Jack had warned her and warned her, but she didn't listen. What had she been thinking? She said good-bye to Kyle and hung up.

The shower is the best place to cry. Your eyes don't get quite as red or quite as swollen because the water washes everything away. And when you've emptied yourself of sorrow, you get out, towel yourself off, and prepare to face the world. The medicine cabinet is right there with the eye drops, aspirin, and whatever else you need. You can stand at the sink and use the mirror to be sure the makeup you put on is covering all that needs to be covered. Use eyeliner instead of mascara in case a few tears are left. You don't want to end up looking like a raccoon.

She knew the drill. She'd been there in those terrible weeks and months after Tom died, but this was different. She and Tony met when, a month ago? Her life wasn't collapsing around her. She'd been foolish, that's all. She wasn't the first, and she wouldn't be the last. Better to laugh than to cry. If she couldn't laugh yet, she'd get mad. As soon as she stopped crying, she'd get mad. She would not be crying when Tony showed up.

Claire was standing on a chair, refilling the birdfeeder, when she heard tires crunch on the gravel driveway. Tony's Ferrari stopped in front of her carriage house. He climbed out, carrying a long florist's box, and walked up the steps to her porch. His slacks and sports coat contrasted with the jeans and tee shirt she was wearing. She ignored his outstretched hand and stepped down by herself.

"I brought you fresh roses." He looked her up and down. "Did I forget to tell you we were going to a nice restaurant?"

"No." She stayed out of reach.

"If you're running late, I can change the reservation."

His expression had turned wary. He could tell she was upset, and he might suspect why, but he was going to make her say it.

"I talked to Kyle. He said you were up at the farm."

"As you suggested. Remember?"

"I didn't suggest you bring a date." Claire hoped her voice sounded less shrill to Tony than it did to her.

"I wanted company, and you turned me down. You were my first choice." He reached for her, and she dodged his hand.

She'd thought about that in the shower, that and a lot of other things. "You must have known Kyle might mention your visit and that you weren't alone."

"You go out with other people, why shouldn't I?"

She looked at him blankly. What was he talking about?

"That homicide detective. Don't tell me you've never gone out with him."

"There's a difference between having dinner with someone and having sex with someone."

"Come on, Claire. You're making a big deal out of nothing. It was just a roll in the hay. Literally." He raised his hands, palms up. "We were in the stable, and she asked me to show her the hayloft. It was her idea, not mine."

"What difference does that make?"

"I like women, women like me. I enjoy making love." When she said nothing he added, "You enjoy it, too."

His words landed like a slap. She put her hand to her cheek.

"I'm leaving before I say anything I'll regret." Tony laid the florists box on the table and walked back to his car. Before getting in, he said, "I wish you saw things differently, Claire. We could have something special. Being with you isn't like being with anyone else."

How many anyone elses were there? Did he compare, rate, and rank them? He was only the second man in her life; she was playing way out of her league.

"Go, just go." Tears clotted her voice.

Tony's car disappeared around the curve of the driveway. She closed her eyes and felt his arms around her. Her lips parted, as she remembered the pressure of his mouth on hers. *Stop it!* You can't lose what you never had, and Tony had never been hers. Still, she felt as if a piece of her had been torn off.

He had melted the chunk of ice at her core. He'd made her happy and made it possible for her to remember happiness. With Tony, she'd been able to experience passion again and more intensely than she'd thought possible.

She threw the florist's box in the trash and chucked the old roses in after it. Then she poured herself a glass of wine and used the last of it to wash down a sleeping pill, anything to dull the pain of crawling into bed alone.

33

Claire put a plate in the dishwasher. *Tony always insisted on helping with the dishes.* She walked into the living room where Tony had sat and stared at the floor while Mike and Bea questioned him about his mother's murder. He'd reached out to her for comfort; that had been genuine.

Dorian dropped his catnip mouse at her feet. She reached down and twitched the tail—the way Tony had done. An orange paw lashed out, and the toy skittered across the floor, cat in hot pursuit.

Tony chose his gifts well. He'd been triumphant when Dorian succumbed to the lure of catnip. "I just seduced your cat." He'd looked into her eyes and smiled. She'd missed the unspoken "you're next." She should have known that all he wanted was a good time. Good time Tony Burke—isn't that what one of Jack's tabloids had called him?

She looked out the window, and the birdfeeder reminded her of Tony's story about finding a dead bird on the studio windowsill. Wherever she looked, her eyes landed on something that evoked a memory she wanted to forget.

"I need a change of scenery," she told Dorian who crouched in his favorite blue chair, gnawing the mouse. He'd been annoyed when Tony sat there. "You're glad he's gone, but I'm not."

She could call Kyle and tell him she'd changed her weekend plans again, that she could come up and ride, but she couldn't face being in the barn where Tony had made love to another woman. Nor did she want to hear Kyle joking about not scaring the horses or telling her again what a great guy Tony was.

"I'm going shopping."

Dorian opened one amber eye.

"If you're lucky, I'll pass a pet store and buy you a new treat. Then I'm throwing that catnip mouse away."

His ears twitched at "treat."

"Take care of things while I'm gone." She left him to his mouse and walked over to Saint Charles to catch the streetcar.

The Shops of Canal connected an office tower to a luxury hotel, all part of a contemporary development that was the architectural antithesis of the historic houses her company restored. Front galleries and tall windows gave the old houses eyes on the street, but the mall's exterior was a blank wall of beige bricks, softened only slightly by a row of palm trees, that kept the world at bay.

Old houses tended to have dark interiors, but entering the mall's central atrium was walking into the light. Sun poured through the glass ceiling, and tropical plants filled corners and nooks with lush greenery. A glass elevator rose from a pool of water and disappeared through the roof. An unattended grand piano played cheerful ragtime tunes, thanks to the wonder of modern electronics. The mall looked inward at an interior landscape both fantastic and unreal. Claire appreciated its exuberance, and she was happy to leave reality outside.

She wandered around the first floor, window-shopping in upscale stores selling pretty things she neither wanted nor needed but enjoyed looking at. Honoring her promise to Dorian, she rode the escalator up to the second floor where the directory said she'd find a pet store. She was watching kittens play in the window when someone called her name.

"Hey, fancy meeting you here." Detective Bea Washington looked elegant in a tailored pantsuit, a pale olive green this time. "I was going to call you."

Claire forced a return smile. She liked Bea but really didn't want to talk about Tony or his mother's murder or any of the things Bea would want to talk about.

"I'm after new shoes." Bea stuck out a foot and twisted it to show the battered heel. "Being a cop is hard on shoes, especially high heels, but don't tell me to wear something more sensible. I had to wear lace-up oxfords when I walked a beat. When I was promoted, I promised myself never again." She glanced at Claire's sneaker-clad feet. "Sexy shoes are my vice. What's yours?"

Caught by surprise, Claire admitted that she liked silky lingerie.

"The way the fabric slides on my skin." She banished the memory of the negligee she'd bought for this weekend.

"Look around you." Bea waved her hand. "Store after store selling lovely silky things for Valentine's Day, but not one shopping bag in your hand."

"I just got here," she lied. She'd been wandering around the mall for an hour, studiously ignoring the red hearts and cupids. Valentine's Day was also Tony's birthday.

"You're looking a little bedraggled," Bea said. "Let me treat you to an ice cream cone. Stone Cold Creamery has opened up in the food court."

"Sounds good." She pulled herself together. "But it's my treat, a thank you for the help clearing out Geneviève's apartment."

"Are you sure? I want two scoops."

"Get a banana split if you want. I signed another client Friday. I'm rolling in dough."

As they rode the escalator to the third floor, Bea described the exotic flavors the Creamery offered, sea salt caramel, rose petal and lavender, along with the old standards. Claire opted for lavender—rose petals reminded her of Tony—and paid for the cones while Bea claimed a table away from other shoppers.

"When this is all over," Bea said, "I hope we'll become friends."

"I do too, but it's not over yet, is it?"

They ate their ice cream in silence until Bea said no, but things had changed. "Did Mike reach you?"

"Yes." Another warning, not about Tony this time, but still nothing she'd wanted to hear.

"I've been trying to reach Tony since yesterday morning. I have good news for him, but he's not returning my calls. Is he out of town?"

"I don't know where he is." She heard her defensive tone and cringed inwardly. "This ice cream really tastes like lavender smells. It's delicious."

"Especially with the dark chocolate chunks. Will you be seeing him soon?"

"Probably. We're still working on his house." At least she thought they were. She'd been absorbed by her own sense of betrayal and hadn't considered the possibility that he might not want to have any more to do with her.

Bea saved the top scoop that was threatening to fall off her cone. "I should have gotten a dish. It's impossible to talk and eat this at the same time." She walked over to the counter and came back with the remains of her cone in a paper cup. "I had the impression you and Tony were friends—more than friends."

Claire had rerun every moment spent with Tony Burke and hadn't been able to get mad at anyone but herself. He never lied to her, never led her on, and never pretended. He'd told her that he'd wanted to make love to her from the first time he saw her. But making love wasn't the same thing as feeling love. He talked about loving her smile, her kiss, but never about loving her. She'd mistaken desire for love. Most girls learn to tell the difference when they're teenagers, but she'd only dated Tom who had both loved and desired her. Thirty-four years old and she'd finally met the man her mother warned her against.

"Right now, I'm not sure that I even like him," she said.

That response earned her a sympathetic gaze.

"We've tracked down four more people from those old photographs," Bea said. "I think that's all we're going to find. No one has any idea who Geneviève's lovers might have been, but they all say she had more than one. We've also gained some insights into Jim Burke."

"Share them with Tony. He treasures memories of his father."

"The wonderful father Tony remembers never existed."

Claire did a double take. "Why do you say that?"

"Jim Burke and Geneviève Devereux married five months before Tony was born. The marriage was not a happy one, and both had frequent affairs. No one took Jim Burke's disappearance seriously because it wasn't unusual. He'd sell a painting and go on a bender. Until that last time, he always turned up when the money ran out. We went back two years and found six missing person reports plus two drunk and disorderly arrests."

"Are you going to tell Tony?" She'd tried to protect him from Judy Boaz's memories, but she couldn't protect him from the police investigation.

"Claire, he already knows. He was nine years old when Jim Burke made his final disappearance. I remember things that happened when I was eight and nine and younger, don't you?" Bea didn't wait for an answer. "Murder investigations have a way of kicking over rocks. Innocent people get hurt."

Claire shook her head. Innocent wasn't a word she'd use to describe

Tony.

"I'm afraid it's going to get worse. Tony will need a friend."

"Tony has lots of friends who are willing and able to offer comfort." She added a smile, hoping the comment would come across as offhand.

Bea's raised eyebrow said she wasn't fooled. "You had to know his reputation."

Claire had been asking herself if it was betrayal when the other person made no effort to mislead, no attempt to keep his other lovers secret. She hadn't settled on an answer and wanted another woman's opinion. "Is this a friendly conversation, Bea, or is it part interrogation?"

"I want to be friends, but I'm a homicide detective, investigating two murders. My first priority has to be finding the killer."

"What does that have to do with me?"

"Tony's father is a key to the puzzle. You've been helping Tony dig into his past. Something you've learned might help us. Mike said you refused to discuss it with him, but Claire, your silence isn't helping anyone."

"Tony has told you from the beginning that his father's murder is the key. Find Geneviève's accomplice and you'll find the man who killed her."

"None of this is easy." Bea bit her lip and looked away as if searching for the right words. She was dancing around something she didn't want to say.

Claire suspected that she knew what it was. Paul Gilbert had had an equally puzzling reaction when she asked for his help untangling Tony's inheritance. After talking to him, she'd gone home and taken another look at the documents.

Tony was the ultimate beneficiary of a trust created two weeks after his birth by a man who had been married to his mother. The trust effectively provided child support plus an inheritance. For his son? Claire had dismissed that idea as fanciful, more soap opera than real life like the newspaper story, but Bea's discomfort gave it credence.

"You wanted Tony's DNA," she said. "You told him it was to confirm the identity of the bones. Was that the real reason?"

"Part of it," Bea admitted. "We'd found evidence on Geneviève."

"Tony guessed as much. You could have told him the truth. He'd still have given you the sample."

"We couldn't take the chance."

You could have, but you didn't want to. She concentrated on her ice cream. "You just called Tony an innocent person. So, the DNA proved that he didn't kill his mother. Is that the good news?"

"You know I can't tell you."

"I'm going to assume that's it. And the bad news is that Jim Burke wasn't the man Tony remembers. What's the even worse news?"

When Bea didn't respond, she said, "You ask question after question and expect me to answer, but you won't tell me anything. You and Mike must get along very well."

"In fact, we do." Bea raised her hands in a gesture of supplication. "I know you're annoyed, and I'm sorry."

Then stop, Claire wanted to say. *Let it be. Let Tony be. Leave him with his memories even if they are false.* Jim Burke was the parent who cared. Learning he had feet of clay would be hard; learning he really wasn't his father could be devastating. Tony had failed to recognize her feelings. He'd hurt her, and she was angry, but she didn't want his world turned upside down. She wiped non-existent ice cream off the tabletop.

"When I talked to Judy Harmon, she told me Tony was a cute little boy and his Dad was crazy about him."

"We'll know more Monday." Bea wouldn't meet her eyes. "I'll probably want to talk to you again."

"I'm going downtown Monday morning to pull permits for one of our new projects. Once that's done, I'll be in my office for an hour or so, and then either at Tony's house or the Currier's, which is a few blocks away." She gave Bea the Currier's address and gathered her things.

"Before you go," Bea said. "I have another question."

"Not about Tony, please."

"No, it's about assumptions. That man is my father's son but I am not his brother. Who am I?"

"His sister."

"Two seconds to answer a riddle that stumps most people. That's why I want to talk to you again."

34

Mike heard the click of high heels and looked up. Bea stood in the doorway of his office, nibbling on the ever-present cookie.

"Sunday morning, I thought I'd find you here." She held out the package. "Chocolate chip?"

He shook his head no. "Didn't I order you to take the weekend off?"

"I went shoe shopping yesterday and ran into Claire Marshall at the mall. I like her, she's good people."

"I like her too, but I don't have time to chat. I'm swamped, and Vernon's breathing down my neck. The Burke-Burton case isn't the only thing on my desk."

"Claire either knows or suspects that Jim Burke isn't Tony's father."

He waved her to a chair and listened without comment while she related her conversation with Claire. When she finished he said, "Are you sure she wasn't reacting to hints you dropped? Claire is perceptive."

"Very perceptive. She heard everything I said and a good bit I didn't say. She got that riddle—you know, I'm his sister—like that." She snapped her fingers. "Claire and Tony are on the outs, but I suspect it's temporary. She really cares about him."

"Did she tell you that?" The question came faster than he meant it to.

"No, but it was obvious."

"He's an adult, she's an adult." Mike could tell he wasn't convincing Bea. He wasn't convincing himself either. "Did you ask her what they were doing up in Greensburg?"

"No. I didn't want her to know we were following her."

"Following him."

"Okay, him. And you've seen the surveillance reports." Bea stood and started pacing. "Every attractive woman who crosses his path."

Mike couldn't argue. They'd kept an eye on their prime suspect until the DNA results cleared him.

The first week, Burke spent two evenings, but no night, at Claire's house and twice hosted an overnight guest at his apartment, an unidentified blonde described as a perfect ten by the envious surveillance officer. Claire visited his apartment Sunday evening, stayed several hours and left after a good-bye described as affectionate. She rode with him to Greensburg on Monday, and he spent Monday night at her house.

Burke slept alone Tuesday night, but on Wednesday picked up a stunning brunette at the airport and brought her home. They went to the dealership together Thursday, where both participated in a commercial being shot there. Later that afternoon, they drove up to his mother's farm. Once again, she spent the night at his apartment. He'd dropped her at the airport Friday morning. A blonde, a redhead, and a brunette—if Claire weren't the redhead, Mike might have been amused.

"Have you talked to Burke yet?" He watched Bea pace. "It's no wonder you needed new shoes. I'm going to need new carpet if you don't sit down."

"I caught him at home this morning, at nine o'clock, which he seemed to think was early." She sat. "I bet he had company."

"That's not against the law."

"It makes me mad on Claire's behalf, although I'm sure she doesn't want my sympathy." After less than a minute in a chair, Bea was back up and pacing. "I told him he was off the hook. Instead of being glad to hear it, he tore into me. He really got under my skin."

"He gets under my skin every time I talk to him, and I don't think it's an accident."

"You're right. He goaded me." She made another circuit before continuing. "He said we'd only wanted his DNA to match what we'd found on Geneviève or in her apartment."

"There's a grain of truth in that."

"Okay, but he was just getting started. He said that you lied about identifying his father's bones and probably hadn't even bothered to test them. Then he went after me. He said the New Orleans police were too intimidated by the Devereux family to conduct an honest investigation, which is why they'd assigned me to the case. I wouldn't recognize the truth if it rose up and bit me."

"And?" He was afraid he knew what was coming.

"I told him he was wrong on every count. We were pursuing every lead, no one had lied to him about anything, and we'd tested the bones. They weren't his father."

"How did he react?"

"At first, it didn't register. He was too busy telling me we ought to find out what dirt his mother had on Roger Devereux. Then, it sank in. He said something anguished about his father and hung up." She made a face. "I'm sorry, boss."

"We were going to tell him tomorrow."

"After the other DNA results came in. I said the bones weren't his father. He heard me say Jim Burke wasn't his father. That's the most likely explanation, but it's not a sure thing, and I should have kept my big mouth shut."

"Don't beat yourself up. You're a good detective Bea, but you're also human. I hope we all are." As if on cue, Superintendent Henry Vernon, the person most likely to have lost his humanity in the course of his career, walked in. The wad of gum in his mouth portended trouble. He looked from one to the other.

"What did you do to provoke the Devereux family?"

"I've had no contact with any member of the Devereux family since talking to Laura Bethea two weeks ago," Mike said. He looked at Bea.

"I've never had any contact with any of them."

"Someone did," the Super said. "Lamont Bethea, Laura's husband, called the Mayor at home this morning. Woke him up to protest our using this homicide investigation as an excuse to pry into the Devereux family's private business. They can't imagine why and want assurances that it will stop. The mayor asked me for an explanation, and I didn't know what the hell he was talking about." He glared at Mike then Bea. "Are you telling me you don't know either?"

"I have no idea." He looked over at Bea and saw a slight widening of her eyes. He waited, but she remained silent.

The Super shook his head in disgust. "I'm getting too old for this job."

"Have you seen the DNA results?" Mike said. "What they say about Tony Burke's parents?"

"Yeah," Vernon pulled out a fresh piece of gum. "We thought his mother had killed his father, but it turns out his father came back from the grave and killed his mother. I told you DNA analysis wasn't worth shit."

"I'm not ready to give up on it. What if we've just learned that Jim Burke wasn't Tony's biological father? From what we know about his mother, that's not out of the question."

"A shotgun marriage to the wrong man? Hah. I wouldn't put it past her."

"We also know the killer was a woman. The skin under Geneviève's fingernails came from a female relative of Tony's father, not the father, himself."

Vernon stopped chewing.

"So far," he continued, "we've identified two women who are related to men who'd been involved with the victim and were at Sunny Gardens on the morning of the murder. Laura Bethea is one. We figured that out late Friday afternoon and haven't acted on it, but we will want to talk to her again."

Vernon, who'd been standing by the doorway, stepped inside and shut the door behind him. When he spoke, his voice was ominously calm. "Do you have one shred of hard evidence that Roger Devereux is Tony Burke's father?"

"Laura refused to let us take a sample of his DNA. Which proves nothing," he said it before Vernon could. "There's a second woman who fits the profile, and there might be others. I'm still waiting to hear back from Paul Gilbert about his parents' recollections." *And from you* went unsaid, but Vernon's eyes narrowed.

"Who's the other woman?"

"Amanda Pierce," Bea spoke up. "She lives at Sunny Gardens. Her brother Reed had a brief fling with Geneviève back in the fifties. He dropped her, and Geneviève blamed Amanda, never forgave her according to Amanda, who believes the world is a much better place without Geneviève, but says she didn't kill her."

"Reed Pierce, from another of our leading families. Any good news?" Vernon's expression was that of a man walking up the steps to the guillotine.

"We've been able to keep the discovery of human remains in Jim Burke's studio under wraps," Mike said. Media coverage, which skyrocketed after Iris's murder, had died down but would flare up again if news of that grisly find got out.

"I'll look through that list you gave me, but don't expect much. It's been years. If Gilbert gives you any names, let me know. I want to be prepared for my next meeting with the mayor." Vernon walked out.

Bea remained seated, biting her lip and looking worried. She'd been uncharacteristically quiet ever since the Super mentioned upsetting the Devereux family.

"Okay Partner," Mike said, "Let's hear it. How did we stir things up?"

"I don't think it was us. Claire and Tony have been looking for Geneviève's old lovers. You know, trying to prove his accomplice scenario. They might have found something. Tony has a bee in his bonnet about Roger Devereux." She thought a moment. "He said, 'Roger paid Geneviève off, but I'm not for sale'. Whatever that means. But he was shocked by the DNA results. I'm certain of that."

"Talk to Claire again, remind her this is a homicide investigation, and see if she has any more to say. I'll get back in touch with Gilbert and do the same."

"What about Tony?"

"Leave him alone for now. We'll step up the investigation into his mother's finances."

35

Claire attended church infrequently, but this Sunday she sought comfort and prayed for guidance. She said the *Our Father* and thought about fathers. The sermon was about Daniel in the lion's den. She only half-listened; her mind wouldn't leave fathers behind.

Bea said Tony's memories of Jim Burke were fantasies. What would happen if he was forced to face the truth? *When, not if.* He might be over his mother's death, but twenty-five years later, he still mourned the man he believed to have been his father. The topic of his father was so fraught she hadn't dared mention her suspicions about Roger Devereux.

After church she went home and changed into work clothes. Although they were only two weeks in, demo was complete except for the studio. Regardless of how he felt about her, Tony's house was past the point of no return. It wouldn't take much to finish the exterior, which would make it much more marketable if he decided to sell. The inside was another matter. She stopped by the office to get her truck. She'd take inventory this afternoon and discuss options with Jack on Monday morning.

She pulled into the driveway and sat for a moment. One month had passed since she first looked at this house, one month that felt like a lifetime. *I'm not the person I used to be.*

The clang of metal hitting stone came from the backyard: several bangs then a pause, several bangs then a pause. *Now what?* None of her crews worked on Sunday, and the police were supposed to be finished. She climbed out of her truck and went to investigate.

There was someone back by the studio. Tony. He stood with his back to her, attacking one of the cinderblock piers with a mattock. His shirt hung from a nearby tree branch. He'd been at it a while. Despite the cool day, rivulets of sweat ran down his torso. She waited until he paused.

"Hi."

He turned around, surprised to see her, then wary.

His expression brought to mind all the times she'd felt someone's eyes on her and looked up to see Tony. Behind the smiles and jokes, he'd always been watchful. Why hadn't she seen the vulnerable child behind the self-confident man?

"Working on a Sunday?" he said.

"I didn't see your car."

"Igor's in the shop. I'm driving a loaner."

He'd caught the meaning behind her words. She wouldn't be here if she'd known he was. He'd all but said the same to her. Far more than ten feet of weeds separated them, and delivering Bea's message or asking if he'd talked to the police would only make things worse.

"Can I help?" she said.

"Did you drive over in a bulldozer?"

"Just my truck, but there are tools in the back." She glanced at the studio. "It's falling in on itself, toward the center. Knocking down the outside pillars is doing it the hard way."

"Claire, I have two good eyes and a degree in engineering."

"But you don't have anything that will get to those interior pillars." His expression remained stony; she plowed ahead. "I have chain and a come-along in the truck."

Still no response—they were both treading water. "Do you want me to get them for you?" she said.

"I'll help you carry them." He leaned the mattock against a tree. "I borrowed the mattock from the guy next door. Not the ideal tool, but this was spur of the moment. My weekend plans changed at the last minute."

Claire nodded. She could say that her weekend plans had changed too, but she didn't want to go down that path. She didn't trust him, nor did she trust herself.

"I've been thinking about the best way to demo this." She knelt and pointed underneath. "See those three pillars in the middle? They go, and the building goes. I think. We can use that big tree to anchor the come-along."

"You're not still mad at me?" He might have been going to put his hand on her shoulder, but he changed direction and scratched his ear instead.

She shook her head no. Mad wasn't the right word.

"That's good. I'm going to be really vulnerable if I'm running the chain under there."

She had to smile. "Tony, I'm not going to drop a building on you, not even a small one."

"I won't be very far under, and I'm quick. Odds are I'd escape." He winked, the old Tony.

She looked away so he couldn't see the chaotic emotions written on her face.

Working together, they slid the chain behind the outside pillars, looped it back on the other side, and pulled it tight. The chain was wrapped around the three center pillars. If they were dry stack like the outside ones, they'd pull over. If not, it was going to take a bulldozer.

She started to show Tony how to thread the chain into the come-along, and he brushed her away. "I know how to use a hoist." He tapped the come-along. "This is a reflex-lever hoist."

"Be careful. When a pillar goes, the chain could whiplash. Don't let it catch you by surprise."

"I appreciate your concern, sweetheart, but I've used a hoist before."

"To bring down a building? Which reminds me." She fetched two dust masks and two sets of goggles from the truck. "There'll be a lot of dust when it goes."

The first pillar gave way without much resistance, but the studio didn't move. Tony peered underneath. "No change."

"You pulled the pillar down. This is going to work." She hoped.

He replaced his mask and went back to the come-along. The second pillar also gave way easily, but again without affecting the building. The third one resisted. The veins on Tony's forearms stood out as he turned the handle, tightening the chain one link at a time. He paused to wipe the sweat from his forehead. "The entire weight of the building is on this pillar."

"Do you want to take a break?"

"I've almost got it." He pushed the handle again, there was a loud rattle, and the chain went slack. "Fall, baby, fall."

The studio shivered then sang, a chorus of creaking wood, whining nails, and cracking mortar. The front wall leaned inward, tottered, and fell, hitting the floor with a clap like thunder. The opposite wall went next, crashing forward with a violence that made Claire jump. The roof pancaked. Each collapse raised a column of dust, until a billowing cloud covered the rubble. The side walls still stood, looking like phantoms in the thick dust then, as if tipped by an invisible hand, fell away at the same time.

We did it!

She felt exuberant, but what about Tony? He stood beside her, close but barely visible in the dust. What was he thinking? They'd both felt Jim Burke's presence inside his studio. Tony had sensed a spirit anxious for release after years of imprisonment. She'd felt as if someone was calling to her, but once inside, she'd felt darker emotions—anger and the residue of violence, a lingering evil that made her anxious to demolish the building.

"Let's go where we can breathe." She headed back toward the house.

He took her arm and walked beside her, just as he'd done the day they met. When they reached the end of the path, he put his hands on her shoulders, held her at arm's length, and burst out laughing.

"You should see yourself."

"What makes you think you look any better?" She joined his laughter. Except for patches where the goggles and mask had been, he was covered in dirty gray powder, darker where it had mixed with his sweat.

"You can have the first shower. The upstairs bathroom is still intact." When she hesitated he said, "You want to get that stuff off you. Who knows what's in it—asbestos, lead paint, nothing good. Come on in. No funny business, I promise."

"I don't have a change of clothes with me."

"I'll shake them out when you're in the shower. They're just dusty. I was the one sweating." He climbed the back steps and held the door open for her. "Go ahead. You know the way. Yell when you're finished."

Claire turned off the water and stepped out of the shower. She stood in front of the sink and searched for herself in the clouded mirror. *What are you doing, standing here naked and dripping wet? You should have gone home.* She rubbed the glass with a corner of her towel, and Tony's wanton woman stared back at her. She thought about pride and standing her ground, but the woman in the mirror didn't care.

"How's it coming in there?" Tony called through the door.

"I'm sorry to take so long. I had to wash my hair twice. Where are my clothes?"

"Lying on the bed. Can I come in?"

She wrapped herself in a towel and opened the door.

"I don't want to rush you, but this stuff is turning into concrete skin. Beware the mummy." Imitating a movie monster, he staggered stiff-limbed past her to the shower.

"It's okay," she said. "I'm finished."

He looked her over. "There's a hairdryer in the second drawer. Help yourself."

"Thank you."

Tony had shut the door behind him, but there was nothing keeping her in the bathroom. Not really. All she had to do was turn the knob, open the door, and walk out. She found the hairdryer. There were outlets in the bedroom; she could dry her hair there.

Tony's dirty jeans lay on the floor in front of the shower. She could hear the water splashing on his body. She plugged the dryer into the electrical outlet next to the sink. Switched to high, its whirr blotted out the shower sounds. She concentrated on drying her hair, leaning over to let it fall forward, combing it with her fingers and refusing to think about what else she was doing.

The movement in the foggy mirror was Tony standing behind her. She switched the dryer off and turned to face him. They both knew where this was going, but he didn't touch her.

"Are you sure this is what you want, Claire?" His eyes searched hers.

He was standing between her and the door, but if she said she just wanted to get dressed and go home, he'd step aside and let her pass. Or she could tell him the truth, that all she wanted from life was to breathe air that had touched his skin.

"I'm sure." She stepped into his embrace.

Claire lay in Tony's arms, savoring the closeness she knew wouldn't last, wondering if she could live for the moment and forget the rest. Already, she could feel him pulling away.

"Detective Washington called this morning." His hand moved to her chin and turned her face to his. "You knew, didn't you?" His eyes had turned stormy. "Was this consolation, Claire?"

Tears prickled. "This was making love."

"But you did know." He wasn't asking a question.

"I knew she wanted to talk to you. I didn't know she had, and I don't know what she said."

"Don't ever play poker for money."

"I'm not lying."

"You're bluffing."

"What did she say?"

"They tested the bones. Jim Burke wasn't my father." He released her chin. His voice, angry when he challenged her, had lost all emotion.

"I didn't know, but I suspected." She lay beside him and looked at the ceiling and told him about bumping into Bea at the mall and what the detective had said.

"They'll know more Monday?" he echoed. "More about what?"

"I don't know. What if the skeleton wasn't Jim Burke?"

"Geneviève used to tell me that my father was her one true love. Anyone with a brain could see that wasn't Jim Burke, but I never figured it out. During our famous fight, she swore on her mother's grave that she hadn't killed my father. Killing Jim Burke, now that's something else."

"I'm sorry." She searched for more potent words, but it didn't matter. Tony wasn't listening.

"I've been asking myself, what did he know? Was he tricked into marrying a woman who was carrying another man's child, or was he paid to do it?" His voice broke.

She grabbed his shoulders. "Open your eyes and listen to me. So what if Jim Burke was a flawed human being, we're all flawed. We all do things we regret."

"What's your point, Claire?"

"Jim Burke loved you. I saw that picture of him playing with you. You told me that he always had time for you. Judy Boaz told me he was crazy about you. Next to that, none of this mess about DNA tests means anything. Jim Burke was your real father. The other man was just a sperm donor."

"Did you just call Geneviève's one true love a mere sperm donor?" His smile was bitter.

"Forget her; this is about you, you and your father." Claire leaned close. Tony said he could read her face. Let him see the truth in it. "Your father is the man who loved you and took care of you. Jim Burke was your father."

"I love your mouth. I've said it before, but it's true. Your mouth is incredibly sexy, the way your lips move when you talk drives me crazy." His finger traced the curve of her lower lip.

She drew back. "You can't use sex as an escape."

"If you'd cooperate, we both could." She protested, and he became serious. "I heard what you said. Now you listen to me. I don't care who killed Geneviève. I don't care who knocked her up. I don't care who killed that nurse. I'm moving on. Racing season starts soon, and I need a clear head."

"When do you go back to Italy?"

"In a few weeks." She stiffened, and he said, "You knew that, Claire."

"I don't want to think about you leaving."

"Then don't." He pulled her close.

36

Paul Gilbert sat on the terrace overlooking the garden that separated his home from the street. He raised his glass in a toast to the end of the day. Low rays from the setting sun shimmered golden through the deeper gold of the wine, but nagging thoughts marred what should have been a perfect moment.

This evening had brought an extremely disturbing phone call from Mike Robinson. Soon he'd have to betray his promise to his father, a betrayal made more painful because, like most betrayals, it was ultimately pointless. What he'd been told, and what his father believed to be true, was a lie and a hoax.

He brought the glass to his mouth and inhaled deeply, taking in the scent of fruit, a hint of dairy, a suggestion of stony mineral. He slid the fine crystal along his bottom lip, enjoying its cold smoothness and letting his anticipation build. He exhaled a slow deep sigh then finally allowed himself a sip of his favorite white wine.

The average American wine drinker has learned to sneer at Chablis. Before the French succeeded in restricting that appellation to wine from grapes actually grown in Chablis, US vineyards sold vats of mediocre white wine and called it Chablis. Today those wines are called Chardonnay, after the variety of grape, and most people remember Chablis as something they used to drink before there was Chardonnay.

All the more for me. Although, in truth, few could afford the price this ten-year-old Grand Cru commanded. A good Chablis is one of the few whites that improves with age, and 1984 had been an exceptional year. Paul took another sip, letting the wine sit in his mouth for precious seconds before swallowing. If burnished steel had a taste, this would be it. The French called this lingering mineral character *gout de pierre a fusil*, which translates as gunflint. It should be a verb, not a noun, the taste of steel hitting stone. A bullet...

The thick walls surrounding his property muted the street noise, but nothing silenced the noise in his head, Mike Robinson apologizing for calling him at home on a Sunday afternoon, explaining that this was a matter of extreme urgency, and asking if he knew who, other than Jim Burke, might be Tony Burke's father. And if he didn't know, would his parents?

Of course they did, but he'd stalled for time, and Mike had explained further, telling him in strictest confidence that Geneviève had fought for her life. Scraps of the killer's skin had become lodged under her fingernails. DNA analysis revealed that the killer was related to Tony but not to Geneviève. Thus, the identification of Tony's biological father had become crucial.

The police believed the same person had killed the aide, a nineteen-year-old girl. Geneviève's death could have occurred in the heat of the moment, but the aide had been ambushed and executed with two bullets to the back of her head.

Mike's words had evoked terrible images: Geneviève clawing at her killer, a young woman lying in a pool of her own blood. Still, he'd listened in silence and remained silent about Tony's paternity. Silent, although murder was a heinous crime, and it was his responsibility as a member of the bar, as a responsible member of society, to help the police apprehend a murderer. Silent because a decades old gift of land and his father's grudging admission didn't constitute irrefutable proof. That would require analysis of Roger's DNA, something the Devereux family vehemently opposed but would not be able to prevent once he told the police that his father said Roger was Tony's father. He would tell them tomorrow.

"Let me talk to my father once more," he'd said. "I'll call you back after I do."

"Please assure your father that we have eliminated Roger Devereux as a suspect." Mike paused. "But don't mention the DNA analysis to anyone. We don't want to alert the killer."

Paul promised to convey the message, but he hadn't, not yet. He was still digesting the astonishing truth that Mike's parting words had revealed. Roger only thought he was Tony's father. He, Jim Burke, and who knew how many other men had been deceived into accepting responsibility for a child that wasn't theirs.

According to his father, Geneviève had seduced several of Roger's friends. It was her vengeance on a family and a society that never really accepted her and had been quick to shun her on Roger's behalf. Those seductions had been only the beginning. Paul's mouth twitched into a grim smile as he imagined Laura's outrage when she learned, as she inevitably would, of Geneviève's spectacular swindle.

The sun moved lower, lengthening shadows swallowed the flowerbeds, and darkness dimmed the garden's colors but heightened its fragrances. Paul inhaled the earthy sweetness of early heirloom roses. His housekeeper had left a cold supper in the refrigerator, but he was neither hungry nor ready to abandon the terrace. He felt sorry for those who didn't experience pleasure in the world's beauty or in a fine wine, who didn't know the joys of moderation and pursued only carnal pleasures.

Sex had been Geneviève's weapon of choice, and it was the jagged rock upon which most of his clients foundered. Those clients included childhood friends now well into middle age. On the surface their lives sailed on smooth water, but the lawyer who cleaned up messy situations knew better. He saw couples bound to each other by habit, loveless unions where passion was a distant memory, armed truces negotiated for the sake of the children, and the cold wars between two adulterers.

From one generation to the next, there was no end to human folly. Geneviève's child had become a troubled man, following in his mother's promiscuous footsteps. Tony's affair with Claire Marshall would end badly. It was merely a matter of time.

Paul looked inward, expecting satisfaction at the careful structure of his life, and received an unexpected jolt. His eye became sharper and his gaze hardened. He saw himself cataloging his friends' unhappy marriages like a miser counting gold coins, relishing each enumeration, ending Tony and Claire's relationship when it had barely begun.

"No," he spoke aloud. He took no pleasure in the sorrow of others. He helped them cope; he wished them well. He was detached from their drama; he didn't feed off it.

He reached to pour himself another glass of wine, and his hand hit the bottle. It started to tilt. He grabbed for it and missed, knocking his wineglass onto the tile floor. Shards of Baccarat crystal sparkled in a puddle of fine Chablis.

Paul felt a despondency far deeper than this trifling accident deserved. He could buy another glass and pour more wine, but no one could put Humpty Dumpty back together again. Geneviève's revenge had ultimately cost her life, and the repercussions were far from over. Tante Geneviève. He would have saved her if he could, but all he could do now was pick up the pieces.

He called his father and asked him to meet for breakfast tomorrow.

37

The Monday morning staff meeting started late and ran later. The run up to Valentine's Day had produced a weekend rife with domestic violence, including three fatalities. Each new homicide was summarized and added to someone's caseload. Once that was done, lead investigators recapped progress on ongoing cases and outlined next steps. The Burke/Burton case was the most complicated, but Bea's summary was a study in brevity.

Because Vernon had ordered silence regarding specifics of the DNA results, she reported only that it had eliminated their prime suspect and suggested two other possibles, although more might surface. The investigation of the victim's finances remained a work in progress. In response to a skeptical question, she described the two approaches as complementary.

"Neither one is paying off yet," Mike said, "but I think we're close to a breakthrough. Our current focus is the money trail. Once we have a suspect, the DNA will help us get a conviction." He hoped.

The meeting finally adjourned. Mike went back to his office to clear some paperwork then walked across the street to grab an early lunch. He put in his order and spotted Bea at a table by herself.

"May I join you?" She smiled a yes, and he pulled out a chair. "Any progress?"

"That land deal Judy Harmon told us about hasn't panned out—I told you Claire found something she thought looked legitimate—but the sugar daddy aspect might. Geneviève's checking account shows quarterly deposits from a brokerage account, a total of sixty thousand last year.

The bank officer I talked to estimated it would take a million dollars to generate that kind of income."

"When did the payments begin?"

"The bank pulled up records for the last seven years. If we want to go further back, they'll have to dig into their archives. It will take time and cost money. We may need a warrant; they are not volunteering."

The waiter brought their lunches, salad with grilled chicken for him and the bacon cheeseburger platter for Bea. He regarded her plate with envy. He was too old to take up basketball, her favored exercise. He could ratchet up his jogging, start running marathons or go in for triathlons. Triathlons would be better, more variety.

"I'm starved." She dove in.

"Could her lawyer tell you anything about the source?" He watched juice drip from Bea's cheeseburger. Life wasn't fair.

"Never got a chance to ask him." She wiped her fingers on her napkin. "We talked last Wednesday, briefly. I asked about Tony's visit, and he said they'd discussed Geneviève's estate. He'd be happy to go into more detail, but he was on his way out the door and wouldn't be in the office the rest of the week. We scheduled a phone interview for eleven this morning."

Mike chewed on a piece of grilled boneless skinless chicken breast with the taste and texture of cardboard and waited for her to continue.

"Now, he's got nothing to say about anything and won't until the will goes through probate, unless I can show him a subpoena." She dipped a french fry in catsup and regarded it thoughtfully. "Someone shut him up. I called the brokerage firm; someone will call back."

"His change of mind might not matter if we can get a name other than the victim's from the brokerage firm, but I'll start the ball rolling on a subpoena." He pushed the half-eaten salad aside. "I'm meeting Paul Gilbert at four. I talked to him yesterday. Our conversation reminded me of your riddle."

"How's that?"

"I told him that the DNA analysis showed that the killer was related to Tony but not to Geneviève, and I told him that it cleared Roger. He immediately assumed it cleared any Devereux."

"He'll never figure it out," she said.

"Reconvene in my office at five."

Bea walked in with a big grin on her face. She mimed a basketball shot.

"Slam dunk. I know where the money came from. She sat down. "When Tony was born, Roger Devereux gave Geneviève Burke four hundred acres of land, most of it a tenant farm, to put in a trust fund. The income went to her, and when she died, the land went to Tony.

"But listen to this. After a few years, Geneviève kicked out the tenants. No more rental income for the trust; she's leasing pastures to a neighboring cattleman and pocketing the money. A few years later, she sells off most of the land, buys stocks and bonds, and sets up a second trust, this one with terms more to her liking. This trust is the source of her income; the name on the brokerage account is hers."

"I'm not sure it's a slam dunk. Still, nice job tracking the money."

"Nice job by Claire." She handed him a large envelope. "Talk about a silver platter. These are copies of all the documents, a present from her to us. This is what she was doing up in Greensburg. Five will get you ten it's what stirred up the Devereux family." Her expression became indignant. "Geneviève cheated her own son to get money for a bunch of broken-down horses."

Mike pulled the documents from their envelope and scanned them. "She cheated her lovers, too, which makes our job tougher. According to Paul Gilbert, Roger Devereux believed he was Tony's father, but so, apparently, did Jim Burke." He relayed Paul's theory about multiple sources of support for the same child and enjoyed the growing incredulity on Bea's face. "He gave me the names of five other potential fathers."

"I want to invest in Lucy the lab tech's DNA analysis company. We'll make Geneviève Burke our poster girl." Bea started to laugh but stopped. "Tony never had a chance, did he?"

"The lab completed their tests. DNA from the bones matches that found on objects in the studio. The bones are Jim Burke's remains."

"Amanda Pierce said her brother had been involved with Geneviève. I'll talk to her again, ask if he paid Geneviève child support." Bea made quote marks in the air with her fingers, "Everything we've learned takes us back to Laura or Amanda."

"Or someone else," he said. "Some or even all of our five other candidates may have female relatives."

"I hate to say it, but I'm thinking someone else, because of Iris," Bea said. "She wasn't a threat to Laura or Amanda. If she'd seen either one in the hall, so what? A frequent visitor, a resident, both had perfectly legitimate reasons to be there." She threw up her hands then slumped back down in the chair. "The only person Iris talked about was the man by the elevator. There was no one else around—I asked, and so did the TV reporter. The killer was a woman, but the man is the key. There's a link that we're not seeing. Otherwise, why kill Iris?"

Bea's line of reasoning made sense, and something about the man by the elevator had been floating at the edge of Mike's consciousness. He retrieved the transcript of Iris's television interview.

"What are you looking for?" Bea had recognized the document. "Ask me. I know every word by heart."

"I found it." He read it to her. "He scrunched his head between his shoulders and turned away like he was trying to hide. The killer didn't want me to see his face."

"Melodrama." Bea put her hand over her heart and gazed upward, but he saw the pain. She'd taken Iris's murder hard. Experience would teach her not to take a death personally. That, or she'd have to transfer out of homicide.

"Do it," he said. "Show me what she described."

Bea lifted her shoulders, tucked her chin to her chest, and rotated her torso away from him. He watched her and knew they'd identified both the man and the killer.

"That's precisely what Roger Devereux did when we were introduced," he said. "It's how he reacts to strangers."

"But the man Iris saw by the elevators was alone. Everyone I talked to said Roger is too timid to go anywhere alone."

"We already know Laura was with Roger at Sunny Gardens when Geneviève was killed." He pointed at Bea "Iris didn't see Laura because…?"

"Laura was inside Geneviève's apartment. She didn't know anyone had noticed Roger in the hall until Iris went on television and told the world."

"And signed her own death certificate. Laura couldn't risk Iris seeing Roger again—and it was practically inevitable." He tapped his fingers on the desk. "We have a plausible scenario. Pick it apart, Bea. Play the devil's advocate."

"My favorite role." She squared her shoulders. "Opportunity is easy. Laura knew her way around Sunny Gardens, and we know she was there that Sunday morning. But what about motive? Why, after all these years, kill Geneviève, who was careful not to offend the Devereux family. Tony insists she had something on Roger, although he doesn't know what. She implied to both Iris and Claire that she knew things she couldn't say, but she never went any further. What changed?"

"That's easy. Tony was the catalyst. He discovered Jim Burke's remains, accused his mother of murder, and vowed to avenge his father."

"That's Tony's motive," Bea said. "Where is Laura's?"

"Roger Devereux was responsible for Jim Burke's death. He is the lover/accomplice that Tony has been looking for and the sugar daddy Judy Harmon told you about—not to mention Tony's biological father. This is all about Roger, and Laura was extremely protective of her uncle—as well as the family name."

"Jim Burke was murdered fifteen years after Roger and Geneviève divorced, and it was not an amicable divorce. Do you expect me to believe that he remained involved with his ex-wife all that time?"

"More like thirteen years, but that's a good question," Mike agreed. "However, I have confirmation from Paul Gilbert's father, who was Roger's best friend, that the relationship persisted until around the time of Jim Burke's death."

"Will he testify to that?"

"If necessary." Paul had asked him to do everything in his power to avoid that eventuality. "What else?"

"How did Laura find out, and so quickly, that her uncle was threatened with exposure? Numerous people witnessed the mother-son argument, and I've interviewed them all. No one heard what either said. If Laura knew, Geneviève or Tony told her."

"Not Tony. He was drunk and getting drunker." Mike almost laughed at the vision of the elegant Laura Bethea in some bar with an inebriated Tony Burke crying on her shoulder.

"Not Geneviève," Bea said. "She made no phone calls after she learned that Tony had opened the studio, and the only call she received was from the trainer. She spoke to no one at the cocktail party. After the argument, she returned to her apartment and stayed there alone. The staff was keeping a close eye and would have noticed any visitor. Her next contact was Iris, delivering the morning meds. Iris said that Geneviève appeared tired, not fearful."

"Something happened after that." Mike thought a minute, and he had it. "According to one of the waiters, Geneviève went to the dining room a little before eight. What if, on the way back, she ran into Laura and Roger?"

"Are you saying this was pure happenstance?"

"Nothing about our first murder suggests premeditation. The victim was strangled with the scarf she was wearing."

"Okay," Bea said. "They bump into each other. Then what?"

"Geneviève tells Laura that Tony found Jim's remains. He has accused her of murder. She's kept silent all these years, but she's not going to take the blame for a murder Roger committed." Bea nodded agreement and he continued. "Laura tries to reason with her. She leaves Roger standing by the elevator and follows Geneviève into her apartment. The argument becomes heated. "

"Laura loses her temper, grabs Geneviève's scarf, and strangles her." Bea moved the scenario to its conclusion. "Do you want to bring her in for questioning?"

"Not yet." He remembered Laura Bethea's performance when she came to his office. "She's clever. She told me the marriage failed because Roger was homosexual. What better way to throw me off the track?"

"Especially if she knew Roger was Tony's father."

"Paul says she did. "

"Motive and opportunity," Bea said.

"We still need proof."

"We know that Roger was involved in Jim Burke's death, but we'll never in a million years prove it. He, and perhaps Geneviève, got away with murder. We know Laura killed Geneviève and Iris, we have a scenario, but we don't have proof. Will Laura get away with it, too?" The speed of Bea's pacing increased with her agitation.

"Sit down. Please." Mike waited until she had lowered herself into a chair. "The answer to your question is, not if we can help it. Step one is bringing Vernon on board. He's a political animal, but he's still a cop." He hoped he was right. The case against Laura Bethea would remain a mix of fact and conjecture without her DNA or some other proof that hadn't yet surfaced.

"Convincing Superintendent Vernon that we need Laura's DNA and convincing a judge to issue a warrant is going to take time," Bea said. "And then it will take at least a week to get the results. If she thinks we're on her trail, she'll react. She has to be at the end of her rope."

"We're going to be very careful not to alarm her. Paul is informing the family that Roger is no longer a suspect. That should reassure her."

"Let's hope."

"Only Vernon and the two of us will know what we're up to."

"I want to warn Claire. At least tell her that we have a suspect, a person generally considered above suspicion."

"Don't do that, but tell her to avoid situations where she is alone or alone with someone she doesn't know well. Give Burke the same message." He gritted his teeth. He was practically ordering them into each other's arms.

38

Claire walked through the house, checking off the work that had begun and listing what remained. Satisfied that she hadn't missed anything, she went back outside and sat on the steps to wait for Tony who was due any minute.

Felicia Miata sat in the driveway, her bright blue the one cheery note on a gray evening that was growing grayer as an invisible sun set behind heavy clouds. Claire's mood was as somber as the sky. Barely two weeks ago, she'd sat here waiting for the police to come see the human skeleton Tony had found in his toy chest. Since then, two women had been murdered. The killer remained at large and, according to Bea, it wasn't over yet. Of course, it wouldn't be over for the police until they had identified the killer.

But I'm out of it, and so is Tony.

Still, he might have changed his mind about living in this house. If he'd decided to put it on the market, finishing the interior was a given— he'd never find a buyer for a house in mid-renovation—but she thought he should do more. Painting the exterior and freshening up the landscaping would make the house much more saleable, and only the painting would be expensive. From an economic perspective, it all made sense.

What didn't make sense was the additional climate control in the center hall. Its purpose was to protect Jim Burke's painting, a non-issue if Tony was going to sell. Reggie had already begun work on a dehumidifier. The unit was to go in the attic and have its own drainpipe. One vent would run through a closet in the second bedroom and the other, through the linen closet. The carpenters should have blocked out the spaces by now, but the framing could be removed and the old walls repaired without too much trouble.

She was beginning to wonder if Tony had forgotten their meeting when a dark green BMW pulled in behind Felicia.

"Sorry I'm late."

"Where's Igor?"

"He's being prepped for travel. His boat leaves next week." He sat down and put his arm around her. "We have to stop meeting like this."

She fit perfectly into the space between his arm and his chest. Like interlocking pieces in a jigsaw puzzle, they belonged together, but he'd already begun preparations for his return to Italy. If he felt sad about leaving her, he was keeping it to himself. She handed him the list.

"If you decide to sell," she said, "this is what I think should be done before it goes on the market. The systems will be in by the end of next week, and the kitchen is well underway, but you'll get a better price if you also finish the outside work. Curb appeal is worth a lot to your average buyer. You should get your money back plus some."

His arm moved from her shoulders to the step behind her. She raised her face to kiss him, but he'd turned away, and her lips caught a bit of cheek, a bit of ear.

He read the list. "What prompted this?"

"After all that's happened, I didn't know if you'd still want to..." She shrugged, reluctant to mention the center hall gallery or anything to do with Jim Burke.

"You're right. I have been thinking about it."

Claire held her breath.

"I want to go ahead with both the renovation and the retrospective," he answered the real question. "Jim Burke wasn't my biological father, but he claimed me, and I'm going to claim him."

"I'm glad." This kiss found its mark.

"I'm also claiming that second trust. Shylock called to say he'd done in-depth research and now realizes that Geneviève had no right to add the stipulation about keeping the farm. The money is mine."

"I bet a phone call from Paul Gilbert figured in his research," she said. "Paul wanted to help, but he was worried about a conflict of interest. He could have checked with the Devereux family and gotten a go-ahead."

"That's an interesting suggestion." Tony said. "The Devereux family or Pineland Corporation, which might be the same thing, is trying to buy me off."

"Why do you say that?"

"Shylock again. He says Pineland Corporation will pay me half a million for the farm, that's three or four times what it's worth." He laughed without humor. "Geneviève had something on them, and now they think I do."

"What did you say?"

"I told Shylock to tell them no."

"No?"

"Pineland sold the land for one dollar, and now they want to buy one-fourth of it back for half a million. I don't know what this is about, but I'm not for sale."

"And neither is your house. Do you want to look around anyway?"

"I was inside yesterday, remember? You were with me." He winked.

Claire felt her cheeks warm. Of course she remembered. The bed was still there; the sheets, still tangled.

"Today is my birthday, and it's Valentine's Day. I know a nice restaurant."

"Look at me, Tony." She ran her hands down her tee shirt and dirty jeans.

"I'll pick you up at your house at seven. Is an hour and a half enough time?"

"More than enough."

Tony left, and Claire went back inside to turn off the lights.

A white Toyota sedan pulled up and parked across the driveway, blocking it. A woman got out, rummaged in her purse, and pulled out a pair of gloves. She pulled them on and strode up the walk like a soldier marching to battle. Claire, who'd been about to leave, recognized Laura Bethea and stopped, her hand on the front door knob. She didn't want to talk to Laura, not now.

What on earth is she doing here? Did she mean to block me in?

Laura's expression was grim. Claire remembered Bea warning her not to be alone with anyone she didn't know well. She remembered how Laura had tried to catch her alone at the office, how her insistence on going inside and talking had vanished when Jack and Reggie showed up. Laura?

Laura Bethea's uncle was married to Tony's mother, years ago when all of this started. He's probably Tony's father. Laura hated Geneviève.

Claire turned and ran. The door to the attic steps was in the master closet. Laura wouldn't know that.

"Claire, it's Laura Bethea. I was driving past and saw your car."

Claire considered the possibility that she was acting like an idiot. Laura had talked to Anne Currier about hiring her company, Felicia was parked in the driveway, and she was a distinctive car. But how did Laura know what her car looked like, and why had she just walked in without knocking?

"Claire, where are you?" Annoyance sharpened Laura's voice. Her heels tap-tapped on the wood floors as she moved from room to room. The sound of doors opening and shutting revealed that she was searching the first floor. She'd come upstairs next.

Claire tiptoed into the closet and crept up the steps, keeping to the edge to avoid any creak that might give her away. Slowly, she opened the attic door. Reggie had been up here, shoving furniture around to make room for the humidifier. She followed the path he'd cleared, looking for a place to hide in case Laura found the attic.

An old armoire was big enough to hold her. She climbed inside and pulled out her mobile phone, muted the ringer and dialed 911.

"This is Claire Marshall, calling for help. Tell Captain Robinson or Detective Washington that Laura Bethea is at Tony's house, 712 Terpsichore. I'm hiding in the attic."

"Please repeat your name and location," the operator said.

"Claire Marshall. 712 Terpsichore. If you can't reach either of them, send someone else. Hurry. Please."

She heard the front door open and heavy footsteps come into the hall. *The police already? They must have been waiting outside.* She climbed out of the armoire.

"Claire, where are you?" It was Tony. "I forgot to mention—

You," he said. "What are you doing here?"

39

Claire eased over to one of the openings for the dehumidifier vents. She was above the linen closet. Someone had turned the lights on in the downstairs hall. If she craned her neck, she could see Tony's lower legs. He was standing a few feet inside the front door.

"Claire and I have some matters to discuss, but now that you're here, I can kill two birds with one stone." Laura's laugh tinkled like broken glass.

"Have you made up your mind about that car?"

"The car?" She laughed again. "Did you really fall for that? Shame on you Cousin Tony, you're supposed to be intelligent."

"Cousin? Are we long lost cousins?"

"I really should have told you the other day, but I wanted to surprise you."

"I thought you looked familiar. You don't look like Geneviève. I'm guessing your mother was one of Dad's models."

"You know damn well Jim Burke wasn't your father. You're a Devereux, and so am I."

Claire worked herself through the vent opening. Head, one shoulder, and then the other. She pulled the rest of her body through while bracing on the sides to keep from tumbling headfirst into the linen closet. Using the framing as a ladder, she climbed down as quickly as she dared, being careful not to make any noise.

A protruding nail caught the back of her tee shirt and held. Trying to free herself only made it worse. She wriggled out of the shirt and kept going. In a few more feet, she'd be on the closet floor. Tony and Laura were still talking. She reached bottom and peered through the hold in the hall ceiling.

She could see the back of Laura's head and all of Tony. He would be able to see her if he would just take his eyes off Laura. She stared at him, willing him to feel her watching, but he didn't look up. She waved her hands, hoping the motion would catch his eye. He blinked twice. Did he see her?

"I told myself it was all Claire," Laura said. "I tried to get to her before she infected you, but I couldn't catch her alone."

"How about moving our family reunion into the living room?" Tony said. "You can tell me who you are and what this is all about."

"I saw Claire Sunday when she cleared out Geneviève's apartment. The next day, she was in Greensburg, asking questions and copying documents. That's when I knew Geneviève had left one of those 'open after my death' letters." Laura's tone shifted from regretful to contemptuous. "She was determined to hurt Roger even if she had to do it from beyond the grave."

"I don't know anything about a letter," Tony said. "Geneviève left me as little as she thought she could get away with."

"You're talking about the trusts. I fixed that, but you weren't satisfied. Then you turned down Pineland's offer, and I knew it was too late. If you'd just taken the money and kept quiet like your mother did, I wouldn't be here. But you and Claire are greedy. You've left me no choice." She raised her voice. "Claire, come down here or Tony will be sorry you didn't."

"Claire's not here. She must have walked out the back door just as you walked in the front."

"How gallant of you, Tony, but I know better. Her car is in the driveway, and Claire's upstairs. I heard her moving when you called her."

"You probably heard the rain," Tony said. "It's raining hard, but I'll bet you're prepared. You have an umbrella, don't you? You have an umbrella in your purse."

"What are you talking about?"

"Umbrellas. Don't you know what an umbrella is? You must be distracted." Tony pinched the bridge of his nose with his thumb and forefinger. He cut a quick glance at the ceiling and held the other three fingers up. He lowered one finger, then two, then three. On three, Claire dropped through the vent opening, landed on the floor, and rolled toward

Laura.

"Laura! Laura! Laura!" she yelled. *Watch me, Laura; take your eyes off Tony for just a few seconds.*

She banged into the wall and looked up. Laura stood over her. She reached into her purse. Tony grabbed Laura's wrist and the purse dropped away, revealing the gun in her hand. He forced her arm up so the gun pointed at the ceiling.

Screaming curses, Laura clawed at his face with her free hand. He lifted her into the air, and she kicked wildly at his legs and groin.

Tony's punch snapped Laura's head back. He released her wrist, and she crumpled into a heap on the floor. Claire crawled over and took the gun from her limp hand.

"Call an ambulance and the police," he said.

"I called 911 from the attic, but I'll call again."

"I've never hit a woman before." He carried Laura, unconscious but moaning, into the bedroom and lay her on the bed.

"If you hadn't hit her, she would have killed us both." Claire put the gun on the dresser, out of reach.

"She stopped by the dealership a couple days ago, and I think I've seen her somewhere else, but I don't know who she is. My cousin?"

"She's Roger Devereux's niece."

"Do you know what's going on?"

"No, but I think the police do. They learned something from those DNA tests."

"Where are the police?" He looked her up and down. "And where are the rest of your clothes?"

"Climbing down, I caught my shirt on a nail."

He took his off and draped it around her shoulders.

The ambulance arrived first. Minutes later, a police car raced up. Claire led the uniformed officers back to the bedroom where Tony was watching the EMTs work on Laura. One of the policemen gestured for them to move to the far corner of the bedroom.

"Wait over there. Keep your hands where we can see them."

"She's the only one who had a gun. It's on the dresser." Claire started to tremble, only now realizing how frightened she'd been. She became aware of her disheveled appearance, Tony without a shirt, and the rumpled bed. *What were these policemen thinking? Did she care?*

She stepped closer to Tony, and he put a protective arm around her shoulder. One uniformed policeman watched them; the other watched the EMTs strap Laura, now semi-conscious, onto a stretcher.

Mike and Bea came in together. Bea checked to see that she and Tony were okay, while Mike conferred with the EMTs. He assigned one of the uniformed officers to accompany Laura to the hospital.

"As soon as she regains consciousness, tell her she's under arrest for attempted murder."

"Is she going to be all right?" Tony exhaled hard. "Even if she planned to kill… I still don't want…but I couldn't risk…"

"She has a broken jaw and a concussion," an EMT said. "Looks like she took a good hit, but she ought to recover."

"Claire and Tony, I'd like you to wait in another room." Mike said. "You are witnesses not suspects, but I have to ask you not to discuss what just occurred until after we have taken your statements. The officer will sit with you."

After several minutes that felt like hours, Mike and Bea joined them. "The Crime Scene Unit is sending a team," he said. "They'll take pictures and gather evidence. Meanwhile, we'd like you to describe exactly what happened. I'm sure you're tired, but we want to get your version of events while everything is fresh. Bea will talk to Claire, and I'll talk to Tony."

"I can tell you what happened, but I don't get it," Tony said. "Claire says that woman is Roger Devereux's niece. Why did she come after me?"

"We think she was protecting her uncle," Mike said.

"She said he was my father. Maybe he was, but I still don't get it."

"He may have been the accomplice you've been looking for."

"Are you saying that my biological father killed the man who raised me?"

Claire heard the shock in Tony's voice. She put her arm around his waist and held him close.

"I doubt we will ever know the full truth about Jim Burke's death," Mike said. "But I expect no difficulty proving that Laura Bethea killed both your mother and Iris Burton and intended to kill you."

"And Claire." Tony started to describe the confrontation, but Mike held up a hand.

"We'll talk to each of you separately. If at any time either of you decide you'd like to have a lawyer present, say so, and we will wait for you to arrange representation. We are going to do this by the book. If this case goes to court, Mrs. Bethea will be very ably represented.

"We need the truth, no lies, not even little white ones. Any misstatement, no matter how minor or how well intended, reduces the value of your testimony. We know more than you realize."

Claire knew he was looking at her, but she didn't have the energy to meet his gaze. She felt Tony stiffen. He, too, had caught the meaning behind Mike's words.

"Tell the truth." She lifted her chin. "I'm going to."

She marveled at Mike's demeanor. He'd just told her that he knew she and Tony were lovers, and he had done it with zero emotion. He'd knocked the underpinnings out from under Tony without a trace of regret. She wanted to shake him and demand that he act like a human being.

"We'll tape your interviews and get them transcribed tomorrow morning," Mike said. "Tomorrow afternoon, we'll ask you to come in, read over the statements, and sign them. "

She and Bea stayed in the living room, while Mike and Tony went to the kitchen. The Crime Scene Unit team arrived and was directed to the hall and the attic. Part way through the interview, one of the techs appeared carrying her tee shirt. She explained how it had come to be hanging on a nail halfway down the interior wall, and her shirt went into an evidence bag.

When they finished giving their statements, Mike told them they were free to leave if they wished. The police would secure the house.

"I'm ready to go home," Claire said. "But my car's blocked in."

"Leave your car here, sweetheart," Tony said. "Come back to my apartment with me. If you want to go home, I'll drive you there, but first, I'm going to feed you."

"Food? Are you kidding?" She had stopped shaking, but she couldn't imagine eating. She was so tired, if she weren't leaning against Tony, she'd fall over.

He kept his arm around her as they walked down the front steps. "I bought some of the tea you like, and I'll fix you a couple pieces of toast. See if you don't feel better with something in your stomach."

"How do you know what kind of tea I like?"

"I saw what you have in your kitchen, so I bought some for mine." They'd reached his car, and he opened the door to help her in.

"You're very observant."

"I like to observe you." He smiled at her. "It's a two-way street. I've seen you watching me. We understand each other so well, it's almost supernatural. That's why we were able to communicate, and Laura didn't have a clue."

Claire leaned back against the leather headrest. "We must have known each other in a past life."

"We were great lovers like Anthony and Cleopatra."

"I don't believe that one ended very well." She rested her hand on Tony's leg. She wasn't at all sure she understood him, and she doubted that he understood her, but tonight she believed they were going to be okay.

40

"What a beautiful spot." Mike surveyed the gardens, lovely in the low evening light. "Thank you for inviting me here."

"It's my pleasure," Paul said. "But I have to admit selfish reasons. I want our discussion to be relaxed and off the record." He smiled. "I saw you flinch. Don't worry. I'm not asking you to compromise yourself. I merely want to share the truth as I know it and ask your understanding." He lifted a wine bottle. "May I pour you a glass?"

Mike took a sip. The wine tasted of grapes and rust, plus something exquisite and indefinable. He couldn't imagine how much the bottle must have cost. "Can we agree that Laura Bethea is guilty of two murders and two attempted murders? The evidence is overwhelming."

"I'm not concerned about Laura's fate. No." He looked out over the garden. "That's not completely accurate. I do care about her, and I believe she acted to protect Roger. She told me what happened the morning Geneviève died. Would you like to hear it?"

"Of course, but you know I'm obligated to pass relevant information on to the prosecutor."

"What I'm going to tell you will be used by the defense," Paul said. "It was a crime of passion, and I believe she will escape the death penalty."

"On the first homicide charge."

"Perhaps for the second as well, although spending for the rest of her natural life in a home for the criminally insane may be a worse fate. Roger is a different matter. You know, of course, that the story begins with Jim Burke's death."

"Sometimes the truth does not out," Mike said. "Geneviève is dead, and whatever Roger knows is trapped within his dementia. We have no other witnesses."

"You have suspicions," Paul said.

"Suspicions that Roger was responsible for Jim Burke's death, yes, but we have no interest in pursuing the matter. He's clearly not competent to stand trial." Roger Devereux might have gotten away with murder, but no one could envy him his life.

"My father will be relieved to hear that." Paul held his glass up to the light. The setting sun reflected amber in the wine. They sat in companionable silence, sipping the wine, admiring the garden. The sun sank lower in the sky, the shadows lengthened and the fragrances intensified. "Smell the nicotiana," Paul said. "It releases its fragrance when the sun sets. It's a scruffy plant, but the scent justifies its existence."

"You must enjoy spending time here."

"After Laura was arrested, my father told me things he should have mentioned sooner. I feel it's my professional responsibility to share what I've learned, although much of it is hearsay and by now third hand." Paul leaned back and steepled his fingers. "Still, it leads us to Laura's motive."

Mike recognized a gesture used to buy time and he waited.

"I don't know how much Laura told you about Roger and Geneviève's marriage," Paul began.

"She spoke mainly about their divorce."

"Then she told you that Roger was bi-sexual."

"Essentially."

"Did she tell you that he and Geneviève remained lovers long after the divorce?"

"Quite the opposite," Mike said. "But if Roger is Tony Burke's father..." He shrugged.

"According to my father, Roger and Geneviève shared an intense physical attraction that persisted despite her revulsion about his homosexual relationships. He didn't want to end their marriage, but she could not or would not forgive him." Paul sighed. "An intermittent affair persisted until Jim Burke's death."

Mike raised his eyebrows but said nothing.

"No one, at least no one I know of, connected those two events for some twenty years. And even then, the connection was both uncertain and improbable."

"Jim Burke was killed twenty-five years ago, not twenty."

"I know, and before I go any further, are you certain that Jim Burke was murdered. Could his death have been an accident?"

"He was bludgeoned, hit from behind with a heavy piece of wood, more than once. It was no accident."

"I was hoping otherwise."

Mike took another sip of wine. The sun had dropped below the treetops but still painted golden bellies on the clouds. He was willing to wait.

"Roger's descent into dementia became apparent about five years ago. He became emotionally unstable and suffered from crying jags, during which he would confess to anyone who would listen that he had done terrible things. His sins ranged from playing tricks as a child to homosexual activity, from betraying Geneviève's trust to hiding Jim Burke's body." Paul gestured toward the wine bottle. "If we finish this, I have another."

"I'm fine for now, thanks."

"Of course Roger's behavior was an embarrassment, but no one actually believed that he was responsible for Jim's death. Jim had died in an automobile accident, twenty years prior."

"Did you hear any of these confession?"

Paul shook his head. "No, but my father did, on several occasions, and last night he told me about them."

"Had Laura?"

"Numerous times. She was the family member closest to Roger."

"But no one reported it."

"I can't speak for Laura, but my father never dreamed he was hearing a genuine confession. Roger was troubled by numerous imaginary demons. This was just one among many."

"A reasonable interpretation." Mike understood that Paul was straining to put his father's actions in a good light. "I doubt it would be admissible if we ever went to trial, which we are not going to do, but I'd like to know what Roger said."

"It may make you more comfortable with your decision not to prosecute him."

Paul repeated the story of a distraught Geneviève calling Roger and telling him that she'd hit Jim over the head and now he wasn't moving. Roger drove to Geneviève's house and found a dead man. They hatched a plan to hide the body and make it look as if Jim had died in an accident. "This was on the eve of Hurricane Camille. Jim was one of many who disappeared. And so it stood for years, until..."

"Until Tony and Claire opened his studio and found human bones buried under sandbags," Mike said.

"Yes. Famous racecar driver discovers his father's skeleton. How'd you keep that quiet?"

"A Herculean effort."

"Indeed. But you'll present it in Laura's trial?"

"I expect a plea bargain. However, if we do go to trial, yes, because it helps establish motive. We have Claire's testimony—she helped open the chest—and Tony's testimony on videotape, because he's leaving for Italy soon. If we need more, he'll be back in June for a showing of Jim Burke's art. They also found more than a dozen finished paintings in the studio; Geneviève buried both the artist and his work."

"Tante Geneviève angered quickly and didn't forgive easily. Roger told my father that she attacked Jim Burke in a fit of temper because he'd painted an ugly portrait of her. They burned the canvas at her insistence."

"We found remnants of a burned canvas in the studio," Mike said. "Someone had stuffed it into the wood stove."

"So it appears the story is true. At this point, I'm not really surprised." Paul looked away for a moment. "This takes us to Laura's motive. She ran into Geneviève the morning after Tony and Claire discovered the bones."

"We surmised." Mike said.

"According to Laura, Geneviève threatened to say that Roger killed Jim in a jealous fit, that she was the innocent bystander dragged into hiding the body and too afraid of Roger and his powerful family to report her husband's murder. She taunted Laura by saying her story might not be true but there was no way to prove it.

"Laura remembers grabbing Geneviève by her shoulders, pleading, desperate because she'd heard Roger's story and knew he'd been involved. The next thing Laura remembers is Geneviève lying dead on the floor. She covered her face and left."

"And the aide, Iris Burton?" Mike said. "How does Laura justify that?"

"She can't. No one can, although I'm sure her lawyer will try. Could Geneviève's story have been disproved?"

"Perhaps." Mike gazed out at the garden. *Perhaps not.*

"Do you believe that Laura intended to kill Claire and Tony?"

"Yes." He didn't tell Paul that they had found a suicide note, ostensibly written by Tony, in Laura's purse. In it, he confessed to killing both his mother and Iris. That would come out at Laura's trial—if there was one.

"Sometimes it all seems pointless," Paul said. "The first time my father heard Roger's story, he laughed at Geneviève's so-called motive. Soon afterwards, Roger gave him a copy of *A Portrait of Dorian Gray* and said the book had inspired Jim to create the portrait, which was hideous but recognizable. He also said that knowing Geneviève had killed for such a trivial reason destroyed his feelings for her, but Layton was still his son."

"Despite the DNA findings, Tony continues to refer to Jim Burke as his father."

"I know, Claire told me." Paul refilled both glasses. "She's far better than Tony deserves."

"He may appreciate his good fortune. His last words to me were, 'You're not getting her back.'" Mike's smile was rueful. "He imagines more of a relationship than actually existed." It was his turn to hold his glass to the light and study the wine.

"Shall we wish them well?" Paul raised his glass.

"To love." Mike touched his glass to Paul's. The toast was ambiguous but the best he could muster.

If you enjoyed Secrets, Lies & Homicide, please consider leaving a review. And if you'd like to read more about Claire, turn the page to read the first chapter of A House of Her Own, Patricia Dusenbury's third and final Claire Marshall novel,

Patricia Dusenbury

A HOUSE OF HER OWN

CHAPTER 1

Monday March 14, 1994

The prospective jurors who hadn't been chosen straggled back to the waiting room to await the next call. Some opened books, others rattled newspapers, one man studied a crossword puzzle, and a woman resumed knitting. Claire Marshall took out plans for a kitchen renovation that needed one more review before she showed them to the client.

A clerk walked in, cleared her throat, and announced, "You all can go on home. Today's juries are complete. New Orleans thanks you for your time." She added that, because their service had ended before noon, they would not receive a meal voucher.

"Five minutes before noon," crossword puzzle man grumbled, but he like everyone else gathered his belongings and hurried from the room.

Claire's disappointment surprised her. She hadn't wanted to serve. Authentic Restorations was a very small company, and her absence for the days or even weeks a trial might take could cause problems. When her plea of economic hardship cut no ice with the judicial system, she'd resigned herself and cleared her calendar. Now what was she going to do?

If Tony were in town, she could invite him to play hooky, but he was in Italy. If it were nice out, she could go for a long walk, but the day was unseasonably cold and raining, more like January than the middle of March. She exited the elevator at loose ends.

The courthouse lobby bustled with citizens trying to accomplish some legal chore over lunch hour and parish employees heading out for their lunch. People paused at the doors, creating bottlenecks as those coming in lowered their umbrellas and those going out raised theirs. Off to one side, several well-dressed men read official-looking documents. Some had audiences; others talked to themselves. All spoke so softly that only people standing close could hear.

Curious, Claire lingered beside one of the solitary readers. He noticed her—people always notice tall redheads—and nodded before returning to his recitation. She listened for a moment and realized that she'd stumbled upon a foreclosure auction.

The man, whose nametag identified him as affiliated with a local law firm, finished reading the legal description of a property and announced an opening bid from the lender. He looked at her, his only listener. She said nothing. After a moment he said, "Going...Going...Gone," wrote down the time and the bid amount and, without pausing for breath, began reading the next property description.

Someone just lost their home. It should have been more dramatic.

She wandered over to a small group surrounding a different reader. When he announced the opening bid, a woman in his audience offered a dollar more. Without skipping a beat the lawyer repeated her bid and, after a pause, announced. "Going...Going...Gone." He wrote on the documents he held, the woman signed something, and two others in the group witnessed the transaction.

Claire envisioned auctions as lively contests, but no one here seemed to care what happened. She waited until the paperwork was completed then spoke to the winning bidder. "Excuse me, but I'm curious. Just a dollar more, and he let you have it?"

"Are you kidding? The lender doesn't want the property." She grinned. "If it were legal, I'd bid a dollar less, and they'd still sell it to me."

"Don't people ever bid up the price?"

"Occasionally there's competition, but I've never seen unrestrained bidding." She pointed to her printout, on which half a dozen listings were highlighted in yellow. "I'm here to bid on these properties, and I have a limit for each one. If I went over it, I'd be fired."

"So this is your job, investing other people's money."

"That's right."

"Don't the homeowners ever come?" Claire couldn't get past the indifference to families losing their homes.

"Most have given up by the time it's gone this far." A shrug. "If I had to bid on a property with the owner watching, God forbid hoping to save their home, it would hurt my heart." Implicit was that she'd do it, pain or no. "Even with the tax sales, you don't see homeowners. That's what's going on over there." She jutted her chin toward the far corner where seven or eight people surrounded one reader. "You can get a real bargain, but you can also get burned. My investors stick to foreclosures."

Claire looked where directed. "Why are tax sales riskier?"

"Foreclosures come with appraisals; tax sales, not necessarily, and many properties have been vacant for years. You'd better have done your homework. Plus, the owner has thirty days after the sale to pay the back taxes. If he does, get in line. You're just one more person with a lien, and who knows what else is out there."

Claire held out her hand. "Claire Marshall," she said. "I'm a contractor, my company renovates old houses, but this is unfamiliar territory."

"Nicole Dennis," the woman said. "Be glad it's not familiar. I've seen plenty of properties carrying liens from contractors who haven't been paid and will be lucky to get pennies on the dollar." She looked around the crowded lobby. "Are you planning to buy a foreclosure?"

"No, no. I'm just window shopping." She and Jack had discussed buying and restoring properties rather than always working on other peoples' houses. A recent run of high-maintenance clients was making that option attractive, and they'd agreed to keep their eyes open, but that was as far as it had gone. She thanked Nicole for taking time to explain and joined the gathering in the corner.

Sheets stacked on a table listed the properties and the opening bid. Claire picked up a set and skimmed through them. The addresses she recognized were in neighborhoods she'd prefer to avoid. *Wait a minute.* Three-sixty-eight Chestnut Street was in the Lower Garden District, not far from Tony's house, and the minimum bid was under five thousand dollars. What's more, she knew the house. It had stood empty for years, but if she could buy that house for that price or anything near it, no matter how dilapidated it had become, no matter if there was an old mortgage... Dollar signs danced in her head.

Claire wasn't poor, but she wasn't rich either, and the disparity between her finances and Tony's—he could retire tomorrow and live comfortably for the rest of his life—contributed to her sense of disadvantage in their relationship. The money she could make on this house wouldn't put her in his league, but it could give her a little breathing room.

Don't get carried away. The land alone is worth several times what they're asking. You can afford what? Six thousand, seven at most. Someone with deeper pockets will outbid you.

Still, she decided to hang around and see what happened. She had nothing better to do, and whoever bought that house would need a contractor.

The next two properties found no bidders. Three people bid on the one after that, but two dropped out after the first round. Three sixty-eight Chestnut was up. Claire's pulse quickened as the man read the property description and announced the minimum bid, four thousand nine hundred and eighty-seven dollars.

She raised her hand. "Five thousand."

"Five thousand dollars," he repeated.

She held her breath, expecting to hear another bid and steeling herself against the inevitable disappointment, but there was silence.

"Going... Going... Gone, for five thousand dollars." He smiled at her.

Claire signed the papers with shaking hands. This was not like her. She was a rational and cautious businesswoman who did not make snap decisions, but she'd just bought a house, practically on a whim, and after being warned against tax sales. She knew where the house was and what it had looked like six years ago, but nothing more. What if there was a mortgage, a fraudulent refinance for more money than the house was worth? Would creditors come crawling out of the woodwork now that the property had a new owner?

You might have just done something really stupid.

Claire spent the next hour combing through records in the Office of Deeds. Her search surfaced no easements or other encroachments, no mortgage or other liens. Three sixty-eight Chestnut was last sold in 1983, eleven years ago, in a cash sale. Phew! It's better to be lucky than smart, wasn't that one of Jack's favorite sayings? She checked her watch. If he was on schedule, he'd be working through the punch list at their Mimosa Street project.

She drove over, singing along with the radio, smiling and nodding to the other drivers and letting in anyone who wanted to cut in front of her. Three lights in a row turned red in front of her, but she didn't care.

Jack's truck sat at the curb. She pulled in behind him, went inside, and found him lying on the kitchen floor—at least those looked like his legs sticking out from under the sink.

"Hey partner," she said. "What are you doing under there?"

He inched his way out. "A leak in the supply line. What happened to jury duty?"

"I wasn't selected." Her smile broadened. "So I went downstairs and bought us a fixer-upper."

For a moment he looked puzzled, then the light came on. "You bought a foreclosure?"

"Tax sale. Five thousand dollars for a house on Chestnut Street, the Lower Garden District, do you believe it? I was the only bidder. I'm still pinching myself."

"Impossible." Jack frowned. "Opening bid is two-thirds the appraisal. There must be another Chestnut Street."

"There was no appraisal, minimum bid was superior claims plus cost and commission. I know the house. It needs a lot of work, but the potential is there. Big time." She laughed at herself. "I could have paid thirteen dollars less, but I wanted to scare off any other bidders."

"You know the house? You're sure?"

"When Tom and I moved to New Orleans, our realtor suggested we look at it, and I walked around the outside. It was derelict then and too much for us to take on, but I remember thinking what a shame someone was letting such a nice house fall apart." She shook her head in disbelief. "I just bought that house for a fraction of what they were asking six years ago."

"If something's too good to be true..." Jack didn't have to finish the sentence. He was a man of mottos, and this was one of his favorites.

"I had to put ten percent down," she said. "Worst case, someone else really owns the property, they pay the taxes and we lose the deposit. We have thirty days before the rest of the money is due."

"What about outstanding mortgages and who knows how many years of unpaid utility bills? You might have bought a cheap house and a bunch of expensive debts."

"I searched the title back thirty years. It's clean." No need to tell him that she'd done this *after* buying the property. "I found nothing that suggests any problem, but I'll make doubly sure before spending another penny. If it doesn't work out, we lose five hundred dollars and some of my time. Not good, but a learning experience. The upside potential is huge."

"There's got to be a catch, an environmental problem, something."

Claire understood Jack's pessimism. His company had teetered on the brink of bankruptcy before she invested her money and herself in saving it. That experience had left its scars. She understood, but she didn't want to spend any more time listening to him conjure up imaginary problems. Real ones would surface soon enough. She gestured toward the sink.

"Are you through here?"

"I tightened the connection. If that doesn't do it, I'll get the plumber back, but it looks to me like he didn't take time to double-check. Everyone's in a big hurry these days."

Claire, who was practically hopping up and down in her impatience to show Jack the house, waited quietly while he turned the dishwasher on and knelt in front of the open cabinet, watching.

"We're good to go." He stood up and set the machine to drain.

"Then come on, let me show you Authentic Restoration's first in-house project."

Driving over she told Jack about the auctions, and he continued looking for reasons to worry.

"Why no appraisal?" he said. "And no mortgage?"

"The previous owner paid cash."

"Why didn't anyone else bid?"

"Have you been listening to a word I've said? I saw one competitive auction, and it lasted only two rounds. Some properties, nobody bids." She pulled into the driveway. "Here we are." Strictly speaking, they should have parked at the curb, but the house was barely visible behind an overgrown hedge, and no one lived here. No one would care.

She studied the house, trying to see it through Jack's eyes. Two-stories with a first floor gallery and side gables, the original structure was probably about twenty-five hundred square feet. It would have been built in the mid-nineteenth century, barely antebellum. A second-story bump-out drooped precariously from the right side. Behind it, a big magnolia needed pruning. Weeds growing in the gutters and missing roof shingles promised water damage. Peeling paint confirmed it and gave the façade a forlorn appearance, but beneath the mess, this house was intrinsically nice, well-proportioned and well-sited on the lot.

"So," she said, "what do you think?"

He didn't respond.

"The siding looks solid," she said. "Given the age of the house, I bet it's cypress. We'll have to replace most of the trim, but enough of the original is there to serve as a template. This used to be a good-looking house. The neighborhood's okay and getting better. Jack, talk to me."

"I should have known when you said Chestnut Street."

"Known what?"

"The house is haunted. That's why no one else wanted it."

"Haunted?" Surprise made Claire laugh. "Don't be silly. You don't believe in ghosts do you?"

"I do, and so does the rest of New Orleans. We'll never sell this place. We couldn't give it away."

"I have to admit it looks haunted." Claire smiled. "If it is, we'll just remove the ghost along with the other problems." She climbed out and waited for Jack's reluctant exit. "We aren't entitled to enter the property until we've finished paying for it, but..."

"Don't walk under that bump-out." He studied the second story extension through narrowed eyes. "How long 'til you take possession? Thirty days? It could be on the ground by then."

"It looked like that six years ago—or close to it—why would it fall now?"

"Last I heard, the law of gravity hasn't been repealed."

"We can walk around the other side." Claire followed the driveway into the back yard. "Come on."

Most of the houses in this neighborhood had been expanded to the limits of the buildable lot, virtually eliminating the yard, but the only encroachment here was a glassed-in sunroom about twelve feet square. Jack pointed to mud tunnels climbing its foundation. He banged the siding with his fist, and a dozen white bugs dropped out. "Termites." He ground them with his heel. "If they stop holding hands, this addition falls down."

"Save us the trouble of demolishing it."

"Look at your bump-out from the back." He pointed. "See how it's pulling away from the house."

She nodded agreement. "You're right, but it's not original. Whether or not we want to keep it depends on what's inside."

The back door was locked. Claire wiped a clean spot on the glass and peered in. "I can't see much; it's too dark inside. Maybe we can get in the front door."

Jack shook his head. "Curiosity killed the cat."

"Satisfaction brought her back." They went through this routine at least once a week. "Let's at least take a look in those front windows."

She led the way back around to the front of the house and climbed half a dozen steps to the front gallery. The front door was also locked. "Darn."

She heard a sharp noise behind her. Jack's foot had gone through the porch floor. He brushed aside her efforts to help him up and righted himself. "I'm okay, but this floor isn't."

"The front has definitely taken a hit—a fire, a tree, something. I bet there used to be a second floor gallery." She shrugged. "A lot can happen in a hundred and forty years. I'm guessing that's how old the house is."

"The repairs were done on the cheap."

"We'll do it right."

He waved a piece of the splintered wood. "Untreated pine, for Pete's sake, but you're right about the original structure. It's cypress, and ought to be okay."

"Except for the ghost," Claire teased.

"Except for the ghost." Jack wasn't smiling. "I've seen enough. Let's go."

She refrained from pointing out that he hadn't seen a single ghost.

Tony called that evening. He'd left her with assurances that absence made the heart grow fonder. *Maybe, maybe not.* He'd been gone two weeks, and this was only the second time he'd called.

"I was wondering how you were doing." Claire cringed at the whine in her voice. "Sorry, I didn't mean that the way it sounded."

"I've been working long days and going to bed early. By the time you're home from work, I'm asleep." He took an audible breath. Or was that an exasperated sigh? "We're in Brazil week after next, same time zone. I'll call more often. Right now there's a lot to learn, and the curve is steep."

"Why a learning curve?" He'd been racing Ferrari's for five years, test driving them before then. "What's different?"

"Last season we heard a lot of chatter about the equipment becoming more important than the driver, so the owners decided to scale back the technology. No more anti-lock brakes, no more active suspensions, no more traction control. The cars are harder to handle, but no one is slowing down—we can't." A pause. "There will be more accidents."

Before this, Tony had brushed away her concerns about his job, insisting that a Grand Prix race was safer than a Louisiana highway. His change of attitude worried her. "Be careful, please."

"Don't worry, I'm always careful. I'm very attached to my own skin." His tone softened. "But not nearly as attached as I am to yours. I miss my beautiful redhead."

"I miss you too."

"We'll be together in June." He changed the subject to the exhibition of his father's art that would bring him back to New Orleans. "I told the gallery to call you if something came up and they couldn't reach me. The time change makes things difficult." He yawned. "Speaking of which, it's after one, sweetheart. I'm beat."

"Sweet dreams." Claire hung up, frustrated by their five-minute conversation. Maybe Brazil would be easier, but after Brazil was Japan, the other side of the world, then back to Europe until June, when he'd be in Canada and, briefly, in New Orleans before going somewhere else far away. The Grand Prix season ran from May through November, seven long months.

"What did you expect?" asked the nagging little voice that questioned everything to do with Tony. "You've known him for three months. He's practically a stranger."

Claire told the voice to shut up. She thought of all the things she wished she'd said. She should have told him it was okay, more than okay, to call her at work during the day. He had the number for her mobile phone. She could have told him about jury duty, the property auction, and buying that old house; but he'd sounded tired, and she'd chattered enough. She could have told him that she loved him, but she was waiting for him to say it first, and some things are better said in person.

Tony was a client who became a friend and then a lover—too quickly. They should have spent more time getting to know each other, more time talking. She undressed for bed and studied herself in the mirror. The marks left by love had faded from her body. She slipped on her nightgown, a silky wisp Tony had given her, and climbed into bed to lie sleepless and alone on cold sheets.

ABOUT THE AUTHOR

Patricia Dusenbury was one of those children who read under the covers when her parents thought she was asleep. (She still reads into the wee hours but now uses a Kindle.) Despite sleep deprivation, she managed to get through college and a career as an economic analyst/strategic planner. Now retired, she hopes to atone for all those dry reports by writing stories that people read for pleasure.

A Perfect Victim, Patricia's first book, won the 2015 EPIC (Electronic Publishing Industry Coalition) award for best mystery. The sequel, Secrets, Lies & Homicide, was a finalist in the 2016 EPIC competition and a top ten mystery in the Preditors and Editors Readers Poll. A House of Her Own, the third and final Claire Marshall novel was nominated for a Rhone Award. Her work in progress, the first book in a new series, is a Claymore Award Finalist.

Patricia lives in a little apartment on a very steep street in San Francisco. When she isn't writing, she's hanging out with the grandkids or exploring the fabulous city that is her new home.